as the stars

45 Bible Fiction Short Stories

Katrina D. Hamel

This is a work of fiction.
Though based on the Bible and historical events, the author took liberties of imagination.

Scripture quotations taken from the New American Standard Bible® (NASB), Copyright © 1960, 1962, 1963, 1968, 1971, 1972, 1973, 1975, 1977, 1995 by The Lockman Foundation Used by permission. www.Lockman.org

As the Stars: 45 Bible Fiction Short Stories / by Katrina D. Hamel — 1st ed.

Summary: This Bible Fiction Devotional draws on forty-five dramatic retellings of famous Bible stories to inspire readers to enjoy and study their Bibles.

ISBN 978-1-9990338-2-8

"Indeed I will greatly bless you, and I will greatly multiply your seed as the stars of the heavens and as the sand which is on the seashore; and your seed shall possess the gate of their enemies. In your seed all the nations of the world shall be blessed, because you have obeyed My voice."

Genesis 22:17-18

Contents

Introduction

Do you love Bible stories? Then this is the book for you! Maybe you're feeling unsure about Bible stories. Maybe you think they're childish, boring, or full of people who just aren't relatable. This book is for you too.

Bible fiction is a genre that can raise some eyebrows. I had a reader ask me, "Why do we need to have fiction interwoven with the truth?" My answer is: we don't. The Bible can stand fully on its own. It doesn't need our help. Bible fiction is simply a tool, nothing more. Some people find it a helpful way to dive deeper into scripture or refresh a story they usually skim over. It brings out new perspectives they never thought of before or an insight they missed.

It can be easy to assume that Bible men and women had shallow emotions and stiff personalities. With the exception of poetic books like the Psalms, the writing style of the Bible doesn't always show feelings the way we are used to reading them. Yet, the men and women of the scriptures were living, breathing people with the same full range of emotions that we experience. Their culture and understanding of the world were vastly different than our own, but they still felt anxiety, fear, doubt, joy, peace, exhaustion, relief, and rage. It takes a little respectful imagination, but by putting ourselves in the sandals of these Bible heroes, we can pull out a deeper appreciation for the stories that transformed an entire people.

Bible fiction does not try to replace scripture. If used properly, it will turn readers to their Bibles with eagerness. When I finished Lynn Austin's *Restoration Chronicles* late one night, the first thing I did was pull out my Bible and read the books of Ezra and Nehemiah. Details I had previously overlooked jumped out at me. I read the Bible with a better understanding of what the people endured and how their faith in God was tested and affirmed. I was able to imagine myself in the story with them. Bible fiction writers simply seek to bring the Bible alive in very real and tangible way.

WHY SHOULD WE KNOW THESE STORIES?

Everybody loves stories! Stories in all their various forms are woven into our entertainment, our news, our culture, and our social lives. They can make us laugh or bring us to tears. They show us that we have shared experiences and that we're all in this life together.

As a child raised in a believing household, Bible stories were a staple of our bedtime routine. They were my first introduction to the Bible, and though I can't remember sermons from my childhood, I do remember the stories. Stories have a way of connecting life-lessons with us on a deeper and more memorable level than a moral dissertation.

As an adult, sometimes we put aside Bible stories. We feel like they are simply stepping stones to the *real* lessons. We begin to believe they are less important than the how-to and do-not sections of the Bible. And then, in our unconscious separation of story from law, we can forget that the law was made for the people's benefit, not the other way around. It's the gritty moments of life that often show us God's love and our need for Him.

Our Creator knows our love and connection to stories. In His kindness, He inspired the writers of the Bible to write heaps of them! God was like a book editor, selecting and shaping these particular stories that became our Bible. We should look to them for encouragement, for warning, for understanding, and for hope. Stories are where we see the commands of God hit the road. In stories we see that His love for us is not cold and rigid, but compassionate. These stories show God's heart, and how He sees ours.

HOW TO USE THIS BOOK

I'm offering these stories in chronological order, but these are not even close to all the stories in the Bible. These short stories work as "teasers", and it is my prayer that your curiosity will take you back to the scriptures to get the whole story.

Though this is a devotional in the sense that it leads you on a journey to discover more about your faith, it is meant to be entertaining! I want you to find pleasure in reading these short stories. I'm sure that as the people of Israel gathered to retell their history that it was a time of pleasure. I can picture them relaxing around the fire at the end of the day and someone asks for a story. The toddlers would be nodding off in someone's lap. The mother is quietly mending because her work is never finished. The grandfather might tell his favorite story, banging his own staff into the ground as he demands Pharaoh to let God's people go. By retelling and enjoying these stories, you are participating in a tradition that has gone on for thousands of years.

A FEW TIPS TO GET THE MOST OUT OF THIS DEVOTIONAL

* Make your Bible time a pleasurable time!

* A favorite drink and a comfortable spot can help you get in a good frame of mind.

* Begin with prayer.

* Ask God to bless your devotional time and help you understand His word and how to apply it to your life.

- ★ After reading the short story, look up the source Bible passages.

- ★ If you have the time and curiosity, read the paragraphs around them so you can see the bigger picture.

- ★ After that, go ahead and read my comments on the short story. I sometimes share a little bit of relevant Bible history to help understand the context. I offer a few questions to keep the dialogue going, but they are just a launching point.

- ★ Don't be afraid to ask your own questions to the story! You may be surprised at what you discover.

If you find personal devotions challenging, I suggest you buddy up with a spouse, family member, or a friend. You can discuss what you learn face-to-face, on video chat, or email. As a busy mom, email Bible studies are a life-line for me!

Each story section should take you about 10-20 minutes to complete, something that can be fit in while at the park, in the carpool line, while riding the bus, during your lunch break, or before bed. Alright, enough chit-chat, let's get to the stories!

Eve

LIFE AFTER THE FORBIDDEN FRUIT

Her heart pounded in her chest as she hurried through the valley. They couldn't have gotten lost, surely? Her sons were no longer little boys easily distracted by imaginative games and wandering far beyond their knowledge. They were men with responsibilities, and they had never been gone all night before.

Eve hastened over the dewy grass, her muscles fatigued by lack of sleep and food. She cleared her throat and called again, "Cain! Abel! Where are you?"

The only sound was the wind waving in the grass and the chirp of birds. Eve glanced to the side and was relieved to see her husband, Adam. She didn't want to lose sight of him in case he mysteriously disappeared too. A tall, rolling hill blocked her view ahead. Perhaps if she climbed it she could see her sons. She trotted up the slope of yellow blooms humming with bees, ignoring the weary ache in her calves. Sweat beaded on her brow, but she didn't slow. The ache in her heart was stronger than that in her muscles. She had to find her boys.

Painful longing resurfaced, like it did every time she had to struggle through this new life. If only they were back in the garden! Back where they were safe. Regret pulsed through her veins as she finally crested the hill and the valley spread out before her.

She drew a hand up to shade her eyes and squinted. The bright valley was wrapped by a forest of brilliantly green trees and backed by a cerulean sky.

There! There was a figure, sleeping in the grass! Relief made her laugh, and she called back to her husband. "Adam! I found them!" Adam looked up, turned, and hurried towards her. She began to pick her way down the hill. Surely if one of her sons was here, the other wasn't far.

She trotted forward, calling out, "Boys! You had us worried! Why didn't you come home?" An uneasy feeling quivered in her stomach when the sleeping figure did not stir at the sound of her voice. She slowed instinctively as she neared. She recognized that back and those legs, but there was something wrong.

"Abel, wake up!" she called. There was no response. She felt a cold tingle run up her arms despite the warmth of the rising sun. She crossed the remaining distance and saw how awkwardly Abel lay in the bed of grass. She heard Adam's swishing strides behind her as she covered the last few steps and stood over her son and saw his face.

Her own scream filled her ears and echoed around the valley, silencing the birds and buzzing insects. The weight of pain and sorrow dragged her to the earth and she crumpled to the ground. She felt her husband push past her and saw him kneel beside her broken son. Adam's back stiffened with shock. Abel was clearly dead. Dried blood coated his head and ran into his open, glassy eyes.

Her scream ended in tears that shook her whole body. Was this the fate that awaited them all? Was this the true punishment for her disobedience? Oh, it was her fault, it was all her fault! Grief and regret convulsed her body and flooded her eyes until she couldn't see.

"How did this happen?" Adam's anguish broke through her agony, and she dragged her gaze to see tears running down his face. He stared at her as if she could explain. She only shook her head, unable to form words.

Eve reached out to take her son's hand but flinched at the cold touch of stiff skin. A movement flickered in the corner of her eye and she jerked her chin. A figure stood in the trees bordering the valley.

"Cain!" she gasped. Adam wobbled to his feet and took a few steps towards his eldest son. Cain dropped something small and fled from them into the forest. "Come back!" Eve cried out, reaching forward as if to pull him to her. Why was he running? What was happening?

Adam raced across the field after his son, leaving Eve rocking back and forth next to the strange, lifeless body that only yesterday had been warm and full of life. She yearned to go after Cain, but she couldn't leave Abel alone.

Adam disappeared into the thick trees and was gone for a long time. Eve was barely aware of the sun slowly shifting across the sky until it was behind her. Her eyes stayed fixed on the trees. Adam would bring back Cain. They would find out what had happened. Together, they would figure out what to do now.

At last, Adam reappeared at the forest's edge and her heart fluttered, but then sunk again. He was alone. He paused where Cain had been standing, crouched, and picked up something. With painful slowness, he crossed the grassy valley back towards her. She wished he would walk faster, yet she was afraid of what he would say when he arrived. He stopped a few feet away from her, his shoulders stooped with weariness and sorrow.

"Where's Cain?" she whispered, swallowing around the thickness of her parched throat.

"Gone." Adam's voice was as dull as rain on the mud roof of their small hut. "I followed him for hours, but he kept running and running until I lost him in the forest. He didn't want to be found. He doesn't want to come home."

"Why?" she cried out, grief bursting forth afresh.

Adam held out his hand, and she saw a rock a little bigger than a man's fist. He tossed it in the grass and it tumbled to land in front of her. She saw the crusted blood and understood. Cain had done this. She tipped back her head and wailed at the sky, "Why, God, why?"

God was silent, and Eve dropped her face into her palms. She had lost both her sons today.

Adam decided they should bury their son, and they spent the rest of the day covering Abel's body in earth and rocks until there was a mound at the base of the hill surrounded by nodding heads of yellow flowers. Then they went home, Eve feeling as if she was leaving her heart behind in the field.

They approached the house in the dusky twilight, but she stopped in the little yard where the grass was worn away by the feet of her busy family. How could this be home without her boys? Everything was shattered and she couldn't see any way to put it back together.

Adam noticed her hesitation and came to stand beside her. He drew an arm around her waist and they stared at the empty house together. She leaned against him. He alone could understand.

"This is our fault, isn't it? I knew Cain was angry at Abel, but I never thought—" she swallowed painfully. "I should have been a better mother. I should have talked to him. If only we were still in the garden. If only I hadn't …" regret choked off her words. She had hoped her sons would do better. She had given into temptation, but she had hoped her sons would learn from her. Would her descendants be forever doomed to repeat her mistakes?

Adam squeezed her tighter. "I know. I wish I had taken Cain aside and talked to him. But they were grown men," his voice was thick. "Cain knew violence was wrong, and he did it anyway."

"Then what hope is there for us and our children?" Eve wailed, her heart breaking. "If we know the difference between good and evil, and yet choose evil, how can we ever be happy? How can things ever be as they were?"

Adam turned her into his arms, and she burrowed her face in his neck. He stroked her hair and murmured, "Remember the promise."

Eve's throbbing heart reached out and clutched that promise. Yes, one of her seed would crush the evil that she had let loose in the world. There was hope. But how long would she have to wait? And who would suffer in the meantime?

Read this story for yourself in Genesis 3 and 4:1-15

Story Comments

I did not want to write this story. This story made me stare at the realities of sin and the pain it brings. I don't want to look at it. I like sunny stories with hope and laughter. I kept getting up and walking away from my computer mid-sentence, needing to escape.

I can only imagine Eve's suffering. Genesis doesn't say how she felt, but as a mother, I can assume she was heart-broken. She lost two sons in one day, something a parent would never fully recover from. I have no doubt that regret filled her days and nights as she saw the result of sin unleashed on the world. Sometimes we like to point fingers at Eve for eating the forbidden fruit, but I'm sure she regretted it every day of her life.

Eve may have been the first to taste the fruit, but sadly, we all partner with her through our own sin. We are not innocents suffering because of her rebellion. No, each one of us rebels against God in our hearts, in our words, and in our actions. She may have been the first, but we have each reached out and plucked that forbidden fruit and felt the consequences of our sin—damage in our relationships with each other and the earth, and separation from God. (Genesis 3:16-24)

The good news is, God had a plan to bring about restoration. When He had the three perpetrators lined up in front of Him, God cursed the tempter. He promised that the woman's seed would crush the serpent's head. (Genesis 3:15) From the beginning, there was a plan to conquer sin and death once and for all. We see that plan unfold in the life, death, and resurrection of Jesus Christ.

> "But now Christ has been raised from the dead, the first fruits of those who are asleep. For since by a man came death, by a man also came the resurrection of the dead. For as in Adam all die, so also in Christ all will be made alive."
> - 1 Corinthians 15:20-22

There is hope, beautiful hope in these words! Yet, we still live among pain and sorrow. We are caught in the struggle of knowing that we have forgiveness of sins and resurrection in our future, yet we are still living in this world with hardship, sickness, sorrow, and death. Jesus walked through this earth with his eyes wide open. He saw the brokenness. He healed and he comforted, but he also warned his followers that they had a hard journey ahead of them. (Matthew 24:9-13)

I find myself going back to the cross again and again with my hard questions about the struggles of this world. I ask God my questions, and again I find my hope in the Messiah.

QUESTIONS FOR DISCUSSION

★ Why do you think God put the tree in the garden and told them not to eat it?

★ What do you think it was like for Adam and Eve to leave the garden?

★ Do you think Adam and Eve ever played the blame-game with each other?

★ Have you ever heard people preach that when you become a Christian, everything should be easy? Do you think that is biblically accurate?

★ What or who do you turn to when your life is turned upside down?

Noah

LIVING WITH THE PAIN

The wine that flowed into his cup gleamed like fresh blood. His hand trembled slightly at the thought. *Blood. Death.* He took a sip and nearly gagged, but he forced it down. He needed the dullness the wine offered.

Noah took his cup and sat in the doorway of his tent. He looked out over the world and drew a strained breath through the stifling pressure on his chest. The earth was changed. Like a woman recovering from childbirth, it still shuddered with afterpains. The trees had been knocked down in the force of the crashing waves. The soil had been patterned into wavy lines like sand beneath the surface of the sea. The mountain tops had been swept clean—even those who had scrambled to the heights had been lost.

Noah took a long draft of the wine. This was his first batch from his new vineyard. It was now more than a year since he had thrown open the door to the ark and emerged to an unrecognizable world. Despite their long confinement, Noah's family had been hesitant to venture out. The animals, not fearing what they might discover, had been eager to escape the bulky ship. The wild ones had fled to search for burrows and fields and trees in a strangely empty world.

Noah's eyes turned to the empty ark. They had stripped boards from the interior to build new homes. It might have been simpler to live in the ark, but it was not a place of pleasant memories. He only had to close his eyes to remember the pounding of rain upon the roof, the shuddering of beams as the water rose high enough to lift the ark from its berth, and the wails and prayers of his family as they huddled together. The deafening rain had continued to pound on their haven for an entire month. They had longed for the constant drone to stop, but when it finally softened to a mist, the silence had been heavy with finality. Noah had straightened from his work and stared at his wife. Her face had gone pale. There were no words. Everyone they had known, everyone who had not entered the ark, was now dead.

Noah took another mouthful of wine, letting it slip down his throat to heat his belly. Another mouthful and the warmth spread to his fingertips.

He had been afraid of what he would see when he emerged. Would heaps of bodies be scattered throughout the land? Would he see the rotting faces of the townspeople he had known? His family? His neighbors? He groaned, and it rose from the very marrow of his bones.

If only they had turned from their cruel and selfish ways and embraced the truth!

If only they had listened to his warnings instead of laughing in his face!

Tears began to stream down Noah's cheeks, and he tipped his chin and drained the dregs from his cup. He poured another. Bitterness rose in his heart. The fools! Their hardheartedness had condemned the innocent. It had been too long since he had heard the laughter of children. Against his will, his mind churned with images of children screaming as the water snatched them from their mother's arms, their wails turning to bubbles as the waves crashed over their heads. Noah trembled from head to toe and gulped his wine.

A third cup burned its way down his throat. His hometown was gone. The wares his family had brought with them had been crafted by people now dead. His farming tools, the tent they lived under, the very clothes on his back had been purchased from skilled hands that were now only bones, buried in the muck. Tears dripped into his unkempt beard as he brushed a hand down his chest. He remembered buying this very tunic, fingering the fine weave with appreciation. The weaving woman had young ones with her in her booth, a whole brood of dark-eyed children laughing and teasing. Now lost.

Noah groaned. He shook his shaggy head slowly, and the horizon shifted. He felt as if he wavered between waking and sleeping. He ached for a dreamless sleep. He drank another cup, yet the pain would not recede as easily as the floodwaters. There was no one left!

He rose unsteadily to his feet. The garment on his back was now a reminder of what had been lost. His skin crawled at its touch. Reaching back, he grasped the neck of his tunic and pulled it over his head, throwing it into the dirt.

Naked, he collapsed on the floor of the tent. He sobbed and cried aloud, "Why, God, why! Why am I spared when all the world is lost?"

Dizzy, he collapsed on his back and finally found solace in the blackness that overtook him.

He awoke.

He lifted his head and brought a wrinkled hand to his brow with a groan. His tongue felt like leather and his throat burned. As his mind began to clear, he looked down on himself in embarrassment. He was naked, though his tunic had been spread over him like a blanket. Cold air struck his back as he sat up and shrugged the garment over his head.

"Father, you're awake," a voice spoke. Noah looked over. It was Shem. Shem's brow was furrowed as he asked, "Are you all right?"

Noah sighed and went to the large jug of water. He scooped up a cupful and drank it before he answered. "I grieve, my son, for the innocent that were lost."

Shem nodded, understanding in his eyes.

Noah took another cup of water and poured it over his pounding head, letting it trickle between his shoulder blades. He spoke lowly, "Did you find me in my shame? Did you cover me?"

Shem blushed. "Ham found you. Japheth and I covered you." Noah felt his neck flush despite the cooling water. Shem quickly added, "We walked backward. You don't need to feel ashamed."

"But you said Ham found me?"

Before Shem could reply, his brothers ducked into the tent. The women were close behind. Two wore babies on their hips. Noah's wife carried a pot of hearty stew. Her gaze drifted over him with pity and it made his eyes burn. She alone comprehended the pain that branded his heart. With a small, understanding smile, she held out a bowl to him.

Noah shook his head. His stomach roiled at the thought of food, but even worse was the idea that Ham had found him prostrate and drunk with sorrow and had done nothing. No—he had done worse than nothing. He had mocked him for it. Noah's pulse quickened with anger, and it only inflamed his pounding head.

Did Ham take pleasure in another man's suffering? Had he learned nothing from the flood?

"Awake, I see?" Ham smirked at his father. Ignoring his father's swelling rage, Ham reached over and tickled his new baby son under the chin.

Defeat struck Noah like a blow. If Ham hadn't learned, how could he teach his son Canaan to be different? Was the cycle doomed to repeat itself?

"Cursed be Canaan," Noah snapped. Ham's neck swiveled to his father, his eyes widening as Noah continued, his words spilling like bitter wine and staining those around him. "Canaan shall be a servant to his brothers! Blessed be the Lord, the God of Shem, Canaan shall be his servant. May God enlarge Japheth, and let him dwell in the tents of Shem. Canaan shall be his servant."

"Father!" the three sons cried out in one voice, and then Ham's gaze darkened. His wife pulled her baby boy closer to her chest, tears pooling in her large eyes.

Noah, full of hot rage, pressed his palms to his eyes, blocking out the shocked faces of his family. His tongue burned for the tingle of wine. But, no. That would not help him any more than it had this morning. Escaping the stares of his family, he ducked under the tent flap and strode to the edge of his farm. He stared over the hills and the nearby lake with his chest heaving.

Dusk was falling. The frogs and insects were emerging and singing their welcome to the night. The sound was soothing, and it began to siphon his bitterness away. He breathed deep to clear his head, and the air was damp and sweet. He lifted his chin and saw the silhouette of birds flying overhead.

The earth was reviving. The rotting foliage was fertilizing new seeds. Tender saplings shot up through the ruins of their parent trees. Behind him, a baby squalled in the tent and Noah's heart fluttered. It was not a child's joyful laughter, yet it was a sound of life and renewal. He turned and looked at the pens they had made for the sheep, goats, and cattle.

The flocks and herds were expanding.

He closed his eyes and spread his arms open wide, beseeching the Lord to comfort him. He had heard God speak to him before. The Lord told him to build the ark. He had spoken to him again when they emerged after the flood.

Be fruitful and multiply! the Lord had commanded. *Fill the Earth! While the earth remains, seedtime and harvest, cold and heat, summer and winter, and day and night, shall not cease.*

Then God had spread a beautiful rainbow over the sky. Noah had stared at it with his mouth hanging open in wonder, his heart singing with hope for a better world. A world where the people did what was right. A world where every man loved his neighbor and treated him with kindness.

As Noah's face cooled in the dusky air and he felt the world teeming with life again, hope rose in his heart once more. Mankind would do better this time. They would remember the Lord.

Read this story for yourself in Genesis 6-9

STORY COMMENTS

Most people know the story of Noah's Ark, but not everyone knows the difficult and controversial passage that follows. People don't like to picture Noah suffering from something like PTSD or survivor's guilt.

Noah's ark is considered a children's story by many. We latch onto the survival and the rainbow and smile. The ark was a sort of floating zoo, isn't that cute? No! The ark was a lifeboat in the greatest disaster the world had ever known.

We never tell the kids about the part where Noah gets drunk, naked, and curses a family member. Most of us read this story, scratch our heads, and try to understand why this story is included in Genesis. It feels like the sort of story that should be hidden away, not written in scripture for all to see!

As a child, I knew that everyone except Noah's family died, but I shrugged my shoulders at the trauma the survivors experienced. In my childishness, I assumed that because his family survived, Noah would not care that a world of evil people had died. However, Noah had other family members that did not enter the ark. His father was Lamech, and the Bible says that Lamech had sons and daughters besides Noah. Noah lost family. If they didn't care about God, I doubt they were close while Noah was building the ark, but life is more complicated than that. I'd wager he had memories of playing with his siblings as children. I'm sure he spoke to them and tried to convince them of the truth. And what about the innocent children that suffered in the flood? If Noah was righteous, he was also compassionate.

So, did God cast a veil of protection over Noah and his family so they could witness others suffer without feeling pain? It is possible, but definitely not certain. Does God take away our heart-ache when we witness the brokenness of the world?

Did you notice the baby's name was Canaan? This is the origin story of the Canaanites, the ones Israel displaced in the promised land. Some have suggested that this story is included in the scriptures to show why the Israelites had the right to conquer the pagan people of the land of Canaan. Something to note is that Noah's bitter words did not cause Canaan to become a servant, as if Noah could make God do his bidding. Perhaps Noah was saying that because of Ham's hardhearted ways, Canaan and his descendants would suffer from not learning compassion and righteousness.

I have added a fictional backstory to the controversial scriptures that tell about Noah's drunkenness and the curse he cast on one of his own. I see these as symptoms of his emotional trauma. There are many different interpretations of this difficult story, and it would be well worth your time to consider your own thoughts on this scripture.

After all that doom and gloom, there is encouragement at the end of the story. Noah lived a long time after the flood. He would have seen his grandchildren grow. He would have seen his farm flourish. I believe that he would always remember the flood with pain, but he could look around and know that God had a plan for restoration.

QUESTIONS FOR DISCUSSION

★ Why do you think this story is included in the Bible?

★ How do you feel about a traumatized Noah?

★ With the growing awareness around mental health, how do we understand depression, anxiety, PTSD, or other mental distress in people of faith?

★ Do you ever get frustrated with people for falling into the same bad patterns again and again, even after terrible consequences?

★ In Jesus, we have freedom from sin. What are some ways we can keep from falling back into bad habits?

Hagar

UNLOVED, REJECTED, AND CAST OUT

She collapsed to the dust, digging her fingers into the sandy soil. The empty waterskin fell beside her. She could still hear Ishmael's crying. Oh God, she couldn't bear to see her son die!

"God!" she sobbed. "What am I supposed to do? How do I save him? Remember your promises to me! Remember us."

Lying on her face in the ground, her nose filled with the scent of hot earth. Regret sat heavy on her, crushing her with its weight. She should have kept her mouth shut instead of mocking the miracle baby, Isaac. Things had been tense enough between her and Sarah as it was.

It had been Sarah's idea to give Hagar to Abraham. Hagar had been only sixteen—and foolish. She had conceded to the plan with the private hope that carrying the chieftain's child would raise her status. She had been so proud when her middle grew round and full like a ripe fruit. Yet, as her belly swelled, so did the bitterness in her heart. Sarah was the beautiful and beloved wife of Abraham, and Hagar was still only the lowly servant. She was otherwise alone. Sarah wanted a baby.

Hagar wanted to be loved.

Even before the baby was born, the animosity between the two women had grown until Sarah had chased her from the camp, throwing stones at her. Hagar, sobbing and heavy with child, had thought it was the end of her, but an angel had appeared. It was then that God promised her many descendants. He had promised her a son—a wild donkey of a man—but she needed to go back to Sarah and submit.

Ishmael was born with his mother's eyes. Maybe that was why Sarah never could warm to the child that she had arranged.

Hagar had submitted for fourteen long years, until Sarah miraculously conceived in her old age. It had been Sarah's turn to proudly show her ripened figure. It had been Sarah's turn to gloat over her good fortune. And then, when Isaac had been born, Sarah had made it all too clear that Isaac, not Ishmael, would inherit from Abraham. Isaac would be the sole heir.

Hagar had hated every moment.

She was still a young woman, yet she was denied the right to marry again because of her and Abraham's shared son. Hagar would never be pregnant again. She often reflected on the promise given by the angel of God. All her hopes rested on Ishmael, and she clung to them.

Hagar knew she shouldn't have laughed and mocked the baby to the other servants, but oh, how it had hurt to be used and cast aside. Not only her, but her son too! Had he just been a placeholder? Sarah had been furious at Hagar's laughter. The whole camp had heard her loudly complaining to Abraham, insisting that Hagar and her son be sent far away.

The next morning Abraham had led Hagar and Ishmael into the wilderness, his grey head bowed and his shoulders slumped. Hagar had walked with her heart in her throat, knowing what was about to happen but not wanting to believe it.

"You have to go," Abraham had said, handing over a bag of provisions and a waterskin.

"But he's *your* son!" Hagar's voice was shrill.

Abraham had ignored her and pulled Ishmael into a tight hug. Ishmael had been stiff beneath his father's embrace, full of a young man's bitterness at this betrayal.

"So that's it then?" Ishmael had asked, his young chin lifting. "This is what I mean to you?"

"Oh, my son," Abraham's creased eyes had filled with tears. "Be strong and courageous. You will be all right. The Lord told me He will make you into a nation."

That had been days ago. The cast-off mother and son had wandered about aimlessly in the wilderness, uncertain where to go and what to do, grieving the home they had been forced to leave. Then they had run out of water.

Hagar swallowed with difficulty, her tongue thick and sticking to the roof of her mouth. She prayed, "God, where are you?"

"What is the matter?"

She gasped and stiffened. She knew that voice. She had heard it before, fourteen years ago.

"Help my son, please," she begged the angel of God, her face still turned to the dust.

"Do not fear, for the Lord has heard the voice of the lad. Arise, lift him up. Take him by the hand, for I will make a great nation of him."

Hagar lifted her face and saw no one. A wavering glint caught her eye. Water!

She scrambled to her feet and stumbled forward, weeping. She filled the skin, and without stopping to quench her own thirst, ran back to her son.

"Ishmael!" she said, shaking his shoulder. He opened gritty eyes and she poured water over his sunburned face and into his mouth. He gulped the water then sat up weakly.

Only then did Hagar take a drink, the coolness soothing her throat. She drank until she felt bloated with water. She took Ishmael's hand, and he looked at her with sadness in his gaze.

"Don't worry, my son," she said firmly. "God is with us. We're going to be all right."

Read this story for yourself in Genesis 16 and 21:1-21

STORY COMMENTS

One of the wonderful things about the Bible is that it is full of people who are just like us. We see our own struggles in them.

Abraham actually *heard* God talk to him (which is more than most of us can say!), yet his faith wavered again and again. Fear would creep in, and instead of trusting God, he would try to do it himself. Twice we see it when he pretends Sarah is his sister to avoid being killed over her. (Genesis 12:11-20 and Genesis 20)

God promised him a son, but after years of waiting, there was still no baby. Sarah is watching a ticking clock and knows she's out of time. She suggests Abraham uses her servant as a surrogate, and Abraham agrees. As we read the story, we don't hear any mention of Abraham consulting with God about this first.

Then the real trouble starts. I couldn't imagine living with a jealous wife and her proud servant. I'm guessing there were a lot of days when Abraham went for a long walk simply for a moment's peace! He had a son, but at what cost?

Poor Hagar. She must have felt used and abandoned. She isn't called Abraham's wife, and Sarah has full control over her. Her son is destined for greatness, but she doesn't even get the chance to marry and have other children. Is it any wonder that she and Sarah butt heads again and again?

Yet, God works even amidst our screw-ups. Our mistakes cannot undo the plans God has for us. He took care of Hagar and Ishmael even while continuing His plan for Abraham and Sarah. At Sarah's insistence, Abraham sends his son and the boy's mother away, with only the promises of God to give them comfort.

I'm sure Abraham missed Ishmael. He must have looked over to where his son had slept and felt the gnawing pain of loss. I'm sure he looked for his face at the feasts and missed hearing his son talk about his day. There was no way to pick up a phone or send an email. He had nothing to sustain him but God's word that Ishmael would be all right. Abraham tried to do things his own way, and he, Hagar, and Ishmael all suffered for it.

Hagar was only an Egyptian servant girl, full of flaws and badly used, yet God took the time to send His angel to speak with her and give her hope.

QUESTIONS FOR DISCUSSION

★ Have you ever made a wrong turn in life and watched everything spin out of control? What did you do about it?

★ Have you ever seen God work amid disaster to bring about something good?

★ When it comes to big decisions in our lives, how can we know God's will for us?

★ Do you pray before making decisions?

★ How can you remember to ask God before you act?

Abraham

Father of the Faithful

Never had the sunrise looked so bleak. For a painful moment he wished the sun would turn and sink, and never rise again! He rolled from beside his wife and went to the open tent flap, rolling the stiffness from his joints. Resting a wrinkled hand upon the thick cloth, his senses were filled with dew and bird song.

He looked back to his wife. She was a lovely woman, even in her old age. Yet, Sarah had never looked so beautiful to him as she did right now with their five-year-old son curled up against her, his plump lips parted, his dark curls upon her arm.

Abraham raised shaky hands and sent up a prayer. Please God, don't take my son. Remember your promises to me! You promised me that my descendants would be as numerous as the stars in the sky. You told me that all the nations of the world would be blessed through me. I waited so long for Isaac, Lord! Don't take him from me now!

God was silent.

With heavy steps, Abraham roused two of his servants, saddled a donkey, and had wood split for the burnt offering. As he bound the sticks to the donkey, his throat thickened, nearly gagging him. He paused, closing his eyes with his head bowed. This has to be a test, he thought to himself. Surely God will not ask me to do this. He took a deep breath and let that thought settle.

Abraham ducked back into the tent where his wife and Isaac still slumbered. He took a knife and slid it into his belt. He set his gnarled hand upon his son's smooth shoulder and shook him gently. "Come, my son. We are going on a little journey."

Isaac sat up, rubbed the sleep from his eyes, and smiled at his papa. Abraham's heart twisted, and he blinked rapidly. His son was perfect, beautiful, the most precious blessing of everything he had. Sarah woke as Isaac scrambled to his feet, taking his father's hand.

"Where are you going?" she asked, sitting up. Motherly intuition was plain on her face.

"God has asked me to sacrifice on the mountain."

Sarah studied his face, and her brow puckered. After decades of marriage, she knew him so well. "What is going on?"

He turned and walked away, unable to answer her.

Isaac was eager to set off on this special trip with his father. He dashed ahead, the servants hastening after him. Abraham followed at a steadier pace. He dared to glance back at the tent. Sarah was watching them from the doorway, her beautiful face rife with anxiety as she looked at her son.

Don't take her son away! Abraham's heart cried out. She loved Isaac with the force of love increased by countless years of waiting. When her belly had grown, she had laughed aloud, taking Abraham's hand and pressing it to her middle so he could feel the baby leap within her. When she had taken their squalling son to her breast for the first time —her brow damp with perspiration, her body limp with exhaustion— she had laughed again with joy.

As Abraham walked towards the Moriah mountains, he began to recite the promises of God to himself over and over. God had promised him that his line would continue through Isaac. God's promises were eternal, so somehow God would make this right. He clung to that promise as he left the servants with the donkey and prepared to ascend the rocky slope alone with his son. Isaac carried the wood himself.

"Wait here," he told his servants. Holding fast to the word of the Lord, he added, "We will return soon." As they climbed, Isaac grew weary and put his warm little hand in his papa's. Abraham squeezed it tight. He took the wood from his son and recited the promises to himself again.

"Papa, I see the wood and the fire, but where is the burnt offering?"

Abraham answered, "The Lord Himself shall provide the lamb."

Isaac helped his father gather the stones for the altar. They placed the wood. The moment had come.

His heart crying out within him, he took Isaac as God had commanded him to do. His son was so obedient, he didn't cry out or struggle when he was bound, but simply stared at his papa with wide brown eyes. He trusted his father would take care of him. Abraham trusted that God would take care of them both. Abraham scooped him up and laid his little form upon the altar.

He had obeyed God his whole life, and God had blessed him beyond measure. With trembling hands, he took the knife, held it over his son, and held his breath.

Abraham, Abraham! a voice thundered around him.

Abraham's heart leaped with relief. "Here I am."

Do not harm the lad! I know now that you fear God since you have not withheld your son, your only son from Me.

Thank God! Tears burst from his eyes at last, and he cast the knife aside. He scrambled to untie his son, and pulled him to his breast. Isaac's little arms wrapped tightly around his neck.

Abraham lifted his eyes at last and saw a ram with its horns caught in a thicket. Abraham and Isaac sacrificed the ram upon the altar, the thick smoke rising up to heaven.

"The Lord will provide," he said thickly. Isaac looked up at him, and his smile was the most beautiful sight in the world.

Read this story for yourself in Genesis 22 (For the entire story of Abraham, start back in Chapter 11)

STORY COMMENTS

I cried as I wrote this story. I have a son named Isaac, and putting myself in Abraham's place makes tears rain down my cheeks. How could he have faith this great? He is not called the Father of the Faithful for nothing! Abraham trusted that God would keep His word.

He believed that somehow Isaac would be all right. Because of Abraham's obedience, God blessed him and his descendants.

Through Jesus, all who believe are part of the promise given to Abraham,

> "For you are all sons of God through faith in Christ Jesus. For all of you who were baptized into Christ have clothed yourself in Christ … And if you belong to Christ, then you are Abraham's descendants, heirs according to promise."
> - Galatians 3:26-29

Way back, before Isaac was born, Abraham was given a promise that in him all the families of the earth will be blessed. (Genesis 12:3) This is about more than just Abraham's little family, this is a huge promise! Later, Abraham is promised that his descendants would be as numerous as the stars, an uncountable number. (Genesis 15:5)

The author of the gospel of Matthew is very clear that he sees this blessing coming to fruition in Jesus Christ. In the very first verse he writes, "The record of the genealogy of Jesus the Messiah, the son of David, the son of Abraham."

In the story of Eve, we read a promise that her seed would crush the head of the serpent. Then Abraham is promised that through him all the families of the earth would be blessed. As we continue through the Bible, we see this plan moving forward for God to redeem the earth.

This story is often confusing for new believers. Does a loving God ask for child sacrifice?

We see generations after Abraham that God detests the human sacrifice of the pagans, and He punished His people for participating. (Leviticus 20:2-5 and Jeremiah 32:35-36)

Considering what we read later, we know God had no intention for Abraham to harm Isaac. This test does seem harsh, but God had seen the way men turned away from Him and ran after their own desires. Abraham had what he wanted—a son and heir—would he still remain faithful?

Abraham had heard from God that Isaac, specifically, was to continue his line. (Genesis 21:12) Abraham surely remembered this as he took Isaac with him to the mountain. We see his faith even as he uses the plural, "*We* will worship and return to you." (Genesis 22:5)

So what did Abraham expect to happen on that mountaintop? Was he waiting for intervention? Did he think God would raise Isaac back to life again? We're not sure, but he knew God had to have a plan.

QUESTIONS FOR DISCUSSION

* How can we have faith like Abraham? Is it something a person is born with, or can we learn it?

* How do you face difficulties in your life? Do you assume that it is the devil trying to wreck your life, or do you believe God is trying to teach you something or grow your faith?

* Does this picture of God testing Abraham change the way you look at your own personal difficulties?

* Read James 1:2-4 and 12-13. What is the difference between being tested and being tempted?

* Can good Christians suffer hard times? Read Romans 5:3-5 and Matthew 5:10-12.

Joseph

JAILED DREAMER

"Break it up!" he called out, grabbing each of the men by the shoulders and pushing himself between them. "What are you fighting about now?"

Their replies tumbled over one another, each trying to speak louder than the other. Joseph pressed his lips together to smother his frustration, then solved their petty quarrel with a few words. It was always something trifling. A swiped blanket, not enough rations, whose turn it was to empty the waste bucket—every day there was another complaint.

It fell to Joseph to sort it out. The chief jailer had seen how well he handled the others and put him in charge of all the prisoners. Joseph organized the meals and fresh water, made sure the cells were kept clean, and the sick were cared for. It was a lowly position, but at least he had something to keep himself busy.

The jailers praised his abilities, yet Joseph didn't see much to brag about. After all, you can't live among a huge family and not learn something about organizing people. His father, Jacob, had wives, children, servants, livestock, and fields to supervise. It was an honorable life. Such a life might have been Joseph's someday—if his brothers hadn't hated him.

Joseph went to his corner. No one bothered his chosen place. He threw himself down and scrubbed his face with the palms of his hands. The squabbling men reminded him painfully of his brothers. He groaned lowly, assaulted by the memories

Him, sprawled at the bottom of the pit, looking up at their jeering faces.

"Father will punish you for this!" His voice had been petulant as he glared at their sneers. "You can't treat me like this and get away with it!"

But they had. They had done worse.

He had been boiling with rage when they finally heaved him out of the pit. He had rehearsed in his mind everything he would tell their father Jacob, exactly how he would cut his brothers down to size. His imagination had delighted in picturing his father's angry face and the words he would shout at his ten wayward sons, all while he kept Joseph tucked under his arm.

Joseph never had the chance to say any of it. He had not been able to enjoy his father's protectiveness, nor felt his mother stroke the hair at the nape of his neck. He had not even been granted a chance to kiss his parents good-bye.

He had scrambled onto the rocky soil, risen to his full height, and met the flinty eyes of a slave trader who assessed his slight frame like a piece of meat.

Joseph lifted his face and shook off the unpleasant memories like an ox did a fly. Remembering the past only made his time here more unbearable.

He dragged his fingers through his long beard, breathing a deep sigh through his nose. Two years had slipped by while he languished in this prison. He had hoped the cup-bearer would put in a good word for him. Either the man had forgotten Joseph, or Pharaoh did not need a slave who was accused of sleeping with his master's wife. Wrongly accused, he scoffed to himself, though his innocence didn't matter. What was the word of a slave against the word of the captain of the bodyguard? He tipped his head back to hit the stone wall. Why had God given him the dreams if he was going to be sold as a slave by his own brothers?

Why had God raised him to prominence in Potiphar's household just to have a lustful woman cast him into prison?

Why had God helped him interpret the Baker and the Cup-bearer's dreams if he was going to spend the rest of his days rotting in this wretched place?

Did God have a plan for him at all?

What would he give to walk through the fields of his homeland? To draw his hands over the sheep as they entered the corral at day's end, their thick wool oily beneath his fingers. What would he trade to be present at a family feast once more? To hear the storytellers stand up and recite the histories of his Great-grandfather Abraham, and his Grandfather Isaac? He longed to hear about the promises of God, and how God had worked among them. The stories bound his people together and showed them their purpose. What was Joseph's purpose in a jail cell in Egypt? How could he be a part of God's people in a land where they did not know God?

The door swung open, and the jailer thrust his head in. "Joseph, good," the man said—as if Joseph might have been anywhere else. "Pharaoh has summoned you."

Joseph didn't move. "Me? Pharaoh wants me?"

"No, he wants old Mahu," the jailer said, his voice exasperated. Mahu sat up taller, but the jailer rolled his eyes. "He asked for you, Joseph! Quickly now!"

Joseph scrambled to his feet and followed the jailer through the door. It banged shut behind him and he flinched. He felt odd to be on this side of the lock. He was led, unshackled, to the palace and taken to a pool of clean water.

He bathed properly for the first time in over two years. As the water sloshed the dust from his hair, he began to feel as if there was a little flame in his chest, flickering brighter and brighter with hope. Yet, what could Pharaoh want with a slave?

Clothes were laid out for him. Joseph ran his fingers over the soft linen and grinned. It was just a simple outfit, but the new garments looked like a kingly robe to him. He was barely dressed when guards appeared to hustle him down cool hallways. The hasty march ended in a throne room. His eyes widened at the opulence and splendor. He gaped at the alabaster columns, the walls painted in intricate artwork, the polished floors, and the retinues of servants. At the end of the room was Pharaoh himself. As Joseph humbly approached the throne, he saw a deeply troubled man. Dark shadows were beneath his eyes and his lips curled with doubt and bitterness.

Joseph bowed low before the ruler of all Egypt. His mind was tossed like a bird in a storm. For what purpose was he here?

Pharaoh spoke slowly, "I hear you can interpret dreams." Joseph glanced up with surprise and noticed the royal cup-bearer standing near the throne, the man grinning ear-to-ear as Pharaoh continued, "I have had a dream, and none of my wise men could interpret it for me."

Joseph felt the flame within his chest burst into a blaze. He drew a deep breath. "It is not I, but God, who can interpret your dream."

The ruler pursed his lips, considering. Then, as Joseph listened closely, Pharaoh told him his dream.

Read this story for yourself in Genesis 37, 39, and 40

STORY COMMENTS

God did indeed have a purpose for Joseph, yet Joseph did not know what it was, or if his life would ever be more than drudgery and imprisonment. I wonder, at what point did Joseph realize the good that came out of being sold as a slave? He ended up saving not only Egypt but also his family from a seven-year drought. God used him for His purposes, even if Joseph began as a spoiled, favorite son.

We all have our figurative prison times. Times when life has taken an unexpected and perhaps unpleasant turn and we wonder if things will go back to the way they were before. Joseph's prison time wasn't for nothing. It was setting the stage for amazing things! He was honing his abilities. He was likely learning patience, humility, and compassion. Joseph did not sit on his hands while in prison, he kept working for good—something I find very admirable.

QUESTIONS FOR DISCUSSION

★   What is something you've been struggling with?

★ Do you think there is something you could be learning during your difficulties?

★ Is there a way you can use or grow your abilities in this situation?

★ What is a favorite story, verse, or saying that encourages you?

Shiphrah and Puah

MIDWIVES FOR THE LORD

Shiphrah stepped out of the over-heated house and rolled the aches from her shoulders and neck. The dark sky was swiftly fading into a swirl of pinks and oranges. Soon Helios would crack his whip and drive his sun-chariot through the sky. Or so the foolish Egyptians believed.

She heard the door open and felt the heat from the house escape and caress her weary back. A low fire had burned all night to warm the room in preparation for the birth.

Puah shut the door and said wearily, "The mother is sleeping. Let's go home."

Shiphrah stopped the taller woman with an embrace. "He is a fine, healthy boy. We should rejoice that the Lord has given another son to our people."

Puah stiffened. Her reply was bitter. "Tell that to the pharaoh."

Shiphrah sighed. "Pharaoh is just a man, no matter what these people believe. We answer to the Lord."

Puah softened. "I know. It's just … what if someone reports the birth of a boy? What will happen to the child and the parents—or us? I love my job, but everyday I'm putting my own family in jeopardy."

Shiphrah drew a hand over her brow. She caught the scent of the salt she had rubbed over the infant to protect him from infection before she swaddled him a clean linen blanket. She had wanted to be a midwife from the first time she had seen the miracle of birth. She and Puah had delivered countless babies. Every single time an infant was born safely into the world, red-faced and screaming, she had to hold back happy tears. It was a miracle, a blessed miracle, and she was so fortunate to be a part of it.

Puah brushed a hand down Shiphrah's arm. "Don't misunderstand me, my friend. I would protect these babies with my life, it's just—"

"I know," Shiphrah patted her friend's hand. "It's scary, isn't it?" Puah nodded. They each drew a deep breath and turned towards her own home. Shiphrah hurried down the dim, narrow streets where the small houses were pushed close together. People were just beginning to rise and ready themselves for another day of work. Shiphrah yawned, feeling like her jaw was coming unhinged. Why did babies prefer to come in the dead of night?

She arrived at her clay-brick house and ducked under the low doorway of her family home. The furniture was scant. Her people were poor. Puah liked to joke that what they lacked in material possessions, they made up for with children. Shiphrah chuckled as she wove among the sleeping forms of her family and lay on her mat, her eyelids too heavy to keep open.

A bang on the door brought her rudely awake. She sat bolt upright, blinking rapidly. Her bleary mind tried to figure out what was going on. From the warm light pushing through the shutters, she could tell it was almost midday. She looked around. The house was empty. Everyone else had gone to work. Another loud knock on the door jerked her to her feet. Husbands were often anxious as they summoned the midwife, but this one sounded angry.

Before she could make it to the door, it was kicked open. She stumbled back in fear as an armed palace guard ducked into her home.

"Shiphrah the midwife?" he demanded, holding a spear in his fist. She trembled but lifted her chin in a show of bravery. "I am. Are you in need of my services?"

"You've been summoned to the palace. Come with me. Now." He didn't wait for her reply but went back outside.

Shiphrah's stomach clenched, but she had no choice but to scramble into her sandals and tie back her hair with a thick band of cloth. Perhaps one of the palace slaves was in labor? She thought of the baby boy she had delivered safely this morning and shivered. Surely no one had betrayed her? She pressed her lips together and went outside. Two more guards stood in the street, wearing armor despite the baking heat. She swallowed hard. This was definitely not a summons to a birth. Shiphrah's neighbors watched fearfully as she was flanked and marched down the dusty road.

Shiphrah prayed without ceasing as they left the narrow confines of the Hebrew district and made their way down the wide, smooth streets of the wealthier Egyptian city. The closer they advanced to the palace, the more opulent the architecture became. She was hurried past statues of Egyptian gods and columns painted with the scenes of victorious battles. The people she passed wore light linen garments, golden jewelry, thick perfumed wigs, and cosmetics. The Egyptians paused in their shopping and gossip to stare as the disheveled Hebrew slave was marched through their pristine city.

The palace courtyard was full of exotic animals preening or napping in the heat of the day. Wealthy courtiers lounged on benches among lush greenery where the heat was held at bay with white canopies and servants with enormous fans.

She felt a fist grip her heart as she was led through a small side door of the palace itself. She was taken through hallways until they reached a cool, shadowy room with richly ornamented walls and billowing linen curtains. They stopped in the doorway. The air was sweet with incense and a gentle tune was being plucked on a lyre. At the far end of the room was a couch surrounded by servants holding platters of delicacies and wine. A bronze-skinned man lounged on the cushions, looking bored as someone read to him from a scroll. From the regal tilt of his chin and the wide, golden necklace, Shiphrah realized she was in the presence of Pharaoh. She swallowed hard.

She turned nervously at the patter of sandals and felt her stomach drop as she saw her friend. Puah's hair was in wild disarray around her pale face. Apparently, she too had been foisted from her bed. The midwives jumped closer together as one of the guards knocked his spear on the stone floor. The man reading the scroll glanced up. He nodded once, rolling the papyrus. Shiphrah and Puah were pushed forward. Fear rippled through her, and Shiphrah belatedly wished for a moment to use her chamber pot.

They stopped several feet before the couch. The pharaoh didn't look their way, but the midwives bowed low anyway.

The man with the scroll spoke. "Are you Puah and Shiphrah the midwives?"

"Yes, my lord," the women nodded together.

"Word has come to Pharaoh's ear that you are disobeying his order. Were you not commanded to kill every Hebrew boy at birth?"

"We were," Shiphrah said, fear tingling up her spine.

"Then what is this we hear about baby boys born healthy and alive in your district?"

Puah looked at her with wide, fearful eyes. Shiphrah thought fast. She was forced to submit to the Egyptian authorities as a slave, but when it came to matters of morality, God was her only authority. If she told the truth now, she would be killed, and the next midwife might not fear the Lord as she did. She had to protect those babies!

She prepared her lie. "The Hebrew women are not like Egyptian women. They are vigorous and give birth before we can get to them." The man with the scroll bent towards Pharaoh to hear what the ruler would say. Shiphrah reached blindly and gripped Puah's hand. She felt the other woman tremble.

The man stood up straight. "You are dismissed. Remember the commands of Pharaoh. Make a greater effort to be present at the births."

As the relieved midwives hastily began to back out of the room, Shiphrah heard, "Perhaps it is time for more ... open measures." Her heart sank.

The women silently left the room and were escorted back through the palace and out of the courtyards. The guards left them at the edge of the city.

Though fearing what she had overheard, Shiphrah took her first full breath since leaving the house. Puah pulled her into a hug, and they stood together and cried tears of relief.

"Praise the Lord for His mercy," Puah whispered in her ear. "He saved us because we saved those babies, I just know it."

"Yes, He has," Shiphrah said, dashing away her tears before throwing back her head and laughing. "Blessed be the name of the Lord!"

Read this story for yourself in Exodus 1:15-22

STORY COMMENTS

I remembered this story, but I have to admit, I didn't remember the names of these women. Isn't that sad? These women were heroes, saving who knows how many babies from a cruel command from a power-hungry pharaoh. These women are recorded by name in the scriptures because they are worth remembering and emulating!

Despite what the law commanded, Shiphrah and Puah held true to the greater authority, that of the Lord. They were risking their own lives to save helpless babies. Because of the faith of two women, the Bible says,

> "God was good to the midwives, and the people multiplied and became very mighty. Because the midwives feared God, He established households for them."
> - Exodus 1:20-21

Now, this is a guess on my part, but the way this story goes, it sounds like these midwives were supposed to kill the babies secretly, perhaps smothering them immediately after birth while the mother was unaware. It's only after Pharaoh's evil subterfuge fails that we see the command given to "all his people" rather than just the midwives.

Shiphrah and Puah were not able to stop the infanticide that came months or years later when Moses was born, but they did what they could, when they could. We may not be able to save the world, but we can spread love and mercy wherever our hands touch.

QUESTIONS FOR DISCUSSION

★ Is there ever a time when it is okay to lie?

★ How do we balance submitting to authority against obeying God?

★ Read Mark 12:17. How do we give to our country what they require, and give to God what is God's?

Moses

RELUCTANT PROPHET

"Your lunch, Moses!" Zipporah called. Moses turned back sheepishly. His wife was standing at the door of the tent, her eyebrow arched and his satchel in one hand. "This is the third time this week!" she chided as he walked back to her.

"Maybe I'm doing it on purpose," he said with a grin.

She gasped, her eyes widening. "You're not criticizing my cooking, are you? How dare—"

"No, no!" he quickly cut her off, laughing. He swooped forward and caught her in his arms. As she squealed in surprise, he whispered in her ear, "Maybe I'm hoping you'll come and deliver it to a lonely shepherd all alone in the hills."

She swatted him. "Oh? And who will do *my* work while I'm doing yours, hmmm?"

Moses sighed with exaggerated resignation and took his satchel. "Fine, then. I'll see you tonight." He looked past her to where his sons were finishing their breakfast. "Be good for your mama," he warned, but Zipporah rolled her eyes.

"They listen better than you. Now go, before the sheep go to pasture without you!"

He pecked her cheek and she grinned as he left for the day. He went to the stone enclosure where his nephew was guarding the gate.

"Let them out," Moses said with a nod, and the gate swung open. Moses shook the bells on his staff and called out. The sheep knew his voice, and they all trailed after him out of the enclosure to find grazing and fresh water.

Moses led the way into the wilderness dressed in the simple clothes of a Midian shepherd. Before this, he had worn the luxurious clothes of an Egyptian, and long before that, the swaddling of a Hebrew infant. So much change for one man. He knew his Egyptian mother had loved him and saved his life, but no one else knew quite what to do with him. His Egyptian father had ignored him. Moses had never met his Hebrew father. Moses shook his head at the strange turnings his life had taken to finally bring him to a place where he had a wise father-in-law, a wife, sons, and a simple but good life in Midian—a place where he felt like he finally belonged.

Moses led the sheep west until he reached the good grazing at Horeb. Some said that this mountain was the mountain of God. He liked that thought.

A flicker caught his attention. He turned his head and his jaw dropped. A nearby bush had caught fire! The bush was completely engulfed, but no smoke rose into the sky. The branches did not crackle in the flames. The leaves did not shrivel. He felt his heart beat wildly in his chest. What was going on? His curiosity aroused, he stepped closer.

Moses! Moses! a voice called, and he felt the sound move through him like the concussion of a drum.

Moses spun in a circle. He saw no one. Still looking for the source of the voice, he replied, "Here I am."

Do not come any closer! Remove your sandals, for the place on which you stand is holy ground.

Dazed, Moses obeyed as he stared at the burning bush. It seemed like the voice was speaking from within the flames! Yet, how was that possible? The voice seemed to know his thoughts.

I am the God of your father, the God of Abraham, the God of Isaac, and the God of Jacob.

Moses felt the air whoosh out of his lungs. He knew those names! He dropped to the hard ground, hiding his face. The smell of warm earth filled his nostrils as he shielded his head with his hands. Why was the powerful God of his forefathers speaking to him? Had He come to punish him for his sins?

The voice continued, reverberating through him like a strong wind. *I have heard the prayers of My people in Egypt. I have seen their suffering. I have come down to deliver them from the power of the Egyptians and to bring them to a land flowing with milk and honey.*

Relieved at first that God wasn't angry with him, his mind quickly flipped to a new concern. Why was God telling him this?

The voice wasn't finished. *Come now. I will send you to Pharaoh so that you may bring My people, the sons of Israel, out of Egypt.*

Moses tensed on the ground, unable to move. His mind flew in a dozen directions like startled birds, and all of them landed on one thought: God had to have the wrong man! He was just a sojourner and a shepherd—a murderer.

He cried out, "Who am I, that I should go to Pharaoh?"

Surely I will be with you. You don't do this alone. This shall be the sign to you: when you have brought the people out of Egypt, you shall worship God at this mountain.

Moses did not feel comforted. God may go with him, but if God didn't appear in a burning bush to everyone, how would Moses convince them? He wasn't a respected elder or a charismatic leader. He wasn't anybody. And how would he explain the Hebrew God to Pharaoh? Pharaoh only knew the Egyptian gods.

"Who would I say sent me?"

I AM WHO I AM, God's voice echoed forth from the burning bush, and Moses felt his hair ruffled as if in the wind. *You shall tell them I AM has sent you. I have seen their suffering and will rescue you from the affliction of Egypt. They will listen to you and will come with you before Pharaoh. And you will tell Pharaoh that the God of the Hebrews has appeared to you and that you need to take a three-day journey into the wilderness to sacrifice to the Lord.*

Moses licked his lips, fear drying his tongue at the thought of speaking demands to Pharaoh, the most powerful man in the world. He knew perfectly well that there was no way that Pharaoh would agree to let the slaves leave.

The Lord seemed to know that too, for He said, *Pharaoh will not permit it. So I will stretch out my hand and strike Egypt with all My miracles. Then, he will let you go. Indeed, every woman shall ask of her neighbor and will be given gold, silver, and clothing, and you shall put them on your sons and daughters.*

Moses felt sweat break out on his forehead. He was glad his people would be freed from slavery. But why did it have to be him? He had a good life here. In Egypt, he was nobody. Worse, he was a man wanted for murder. If he went back, they might throw him in prison or kill him. He cautiously drew up to his knees, his eyes still fixed on the ground. He clutched the staff in front of him like a shield. "No one will believe me. They'll think I'm lying, or that I had a strange dream."

The voice demanded, *What is in your hand?*

"M-my staff?"

Throw it on the ground!

Moses rose to his feet. He wanted to ask why, but he didn't dare. Instead, he threw the wooden staff to the ground and it transformed at once into a hissing, writhing serpent. He cried out in fear and jumped away.

Stretch out your hand and grasp it by its tail!

With clenched teeth, he reached out his hand. As soon as he had the scaly creature within his grasp, it became his familiar staff once more. He passed the staff from hand to hand in wonderment.

God's voice was calm. *They will know that the Lord, the God of your fathers, has appeared to you.*

Moses nodded, but anxiety still prickled him.

Seeming to know his hesitation, the voice commanded again, *Put your hand into your tunic!* Moses slid his hand into the neck of his tunic. When he pulled it out, he let loose a strangled cry. The skin was white with leprosy! Was this punishment for his reluctance?

Put it in again!

Moses, cringing in disgust, put it back. When he brought it forth, the skin was restored. He puffed out a breath.

If they do not believe these signs, you will take water from the Nile, pour it on the ground, and it shall become blood.

If they do not believe … Moses clutched his staff with both hands, his stomach sour with uncertainty. He had just witnessed two miracles. He knew that God was powerful. But who was he, that God should choose him? Surely there was someone better to speak to Pharaoh and to the elders. The men of Pharaoh's court were highly educated. They were well-practiced in debate and political maneuvering. He had endured their sneers during his youth as they discussed his position in court—not quite Egyptian nobility, not quite a Hebrew. They would chew him up and spit him out.

"Please Lord," he begged. "I am not good with words. I have never been eloquent. I am slow of speech and slow of tongue!"

Moses quailed as God's voice rumbled like thunder. *Who made man's mouth? Who makes him mute, or deaf, or seeing, or blind? Is it not I, the Lord? Now go! I will be your mouth and teach you what to say.*

Moses couldn't help it. He resisted God's desire. He felt like a mouse being asked to move a mountain. He couldn't do this, but how could he refuse the Lord? "Please Lord," he murmured, "send whomever You will."

The Lord spoke in what sounded like frustration, I *know your brother, Aaron the Levite, speaks fluently. Moreover, he is coming to see you, and the sight of you will bring joy to his heart. I shall teach you what you are to do, and you shall tell him, and he shall be your mouth to the people. Now, take the staff which is in your hand, and go!*

Moses, his heart in his throat, turned away from the bush. When he glanced back, the strange flames were gone. He could still hear the Lord's rumbling voice in his head.

He swallowed hard and called to his flock with a wavering voice. They gamboled towards him. His satchel banging on his hip, he hastened for home, his mind reeling at what had just happened.

The first person he would need to convince was his father-in-law. Jethro was wise, surely he would give Moses good counsel.

But what about Zipporah? He groaned. What would she say? His wife was a strong woman. Would she believe that he was commanded to be a spokesman for God—a prophet? His mind stammered over the absurdity. Moses, the man who had spent his life trying to understand who he was, was now declared a prophet. He laughed aloud.

He glanced at his hand and at the staff and sobered. God had said He would go with him. He glanced around, wondering if God was watching him, even now.

He felt like the last person God should have chosen for this task. Yet, God had chosen him. What could he do but obey?

Read this story for yourself in Exodus 3-4:17

STORY COMMENTS

Moses spoke with God and was given explicit direction for his life. We often wish God was so open with us! Yet, Moses digs up every excuse he can to avoid God's command. He performed miracles with his own hands and was still hesitant. I want to shake him and ask, how could you fear after all that?

Yet, was it cowardliness, or a different kind of fear? In Numbers 12:3, it states that Moses was more humble than any man on earth. An impressive trait considering how easy it would have been to let authority go to his head. Yes, we do see Moses flee from the snake in Exodus 4:3, but then we see him reach out and pick up the snake in verse 4, which shows bravery.

As I read Exodus 3 and 4, it doesn't say Moses resisted God because he was cowardly. We hear him ask, "Who am I?" and "What if they don't believe me?" and "I am not eloquent." We know humbleness is an admirable trait, but Moses took it too far and turned it into fear—fear of failure. When God asks us to do something, who are we to say that we aren't good enough? God made us, shouldn't He know what we're capable of?

Maybe the same question could be asked of you and me. I haven't heard God speak to me from a burning bush, but I have heard His voice through the scriptures. I have heard Him tell me to love Him, to love my neighbor, to be a servant, to do what is right, to pray, to make disciples.

Do I respond to Him in faith, or do I pull back in fear?

Have you ever wondered, why me? Am I good enough for this? God does not wait for us to be perfect to use us. Humble Moses becomes a giant of faith. Yes, he messed up. He made big mistakes. He feared. Despite his shortcomings, he was able to be an instrument for the Lord. I find that greatly encouraging.

QUESTIONS FOR DISCUSSION

★ Do you look at Christian influencers in the media or your pastor at the pulpit and think they've got faith you can never aspire to? Is this true?

★ Have you ever felt God nudging you to do or say something, yet you turned back because you were scared you'd mess up?

★ Sometimes we think if we saw a miracle, all our doubt would fly away. Do you think that's accurate, looking at this story of Moses?

★ Moses is called "slow of speech and tongue" which might suggest a noticeable speech impediment. Do you live with a disability? Does it impact your Christian purpose?

★ I am strongest in my faith when I am encouraged by fellow believers. Even Moses needed Aaron. Who encourages you to live out your belief?

Daughters of Zelophehad
Voices of Change

Mahlah paced before the open door of the tent. They needed to decide now, their window of opportunity was closing. She glanced back to her four sisters. They were near in age; daughter born after daughter in their parent's efforts to bring forward a son and heir, but God had other plans. Now the sisters were alone, unmarried, with no brother or father to stand for them.

"We're in the right," Mahlah said with more firmness than she felt. "There is a precedent in the law Moses has given us."

"Levirate marriage," Tirzah said softly, with a nod of her graceful neck. "No man's name shall be blotted out from Israel."

"Exactly," Mahlah said. "So, we're in agreement? We will bring our petition before the people?" Her sisters glanced to each other, silently gauging each other's resolve.

"Yes," Noah said. A dimple showed on her cheek as she smiled. "But let's go quickly before I lose my nerve!"

Mahlah nodded and stepped out into the heat of the day, the others behind her. Together the five sisters moved silently through the camp towards the heart of their people, the tabernacle. All the tents were tidily arranged around the center of worship, everyone grouped according to family. The careful arrangements made setting up camp smoother, and it also made it easier to count the people. As she moved through her kinsmen and their families, Mahlah was keenly aware of a problem that had arisen with the recent, and crucial, census.

She strode past the last tent and paused, letting her sisters fan out beside her until they stood in a united line before the tent of meeting. Thousands of people milled and shifted around the enclosure, sacrificing, praying, and seeking counsel.

"Lord, give me wisdom," Mahlah whispered. "Guide my tongue and my lips, and let my petition be pleasing in your sight." She glanced right and left, and her sisters nodded. In unison, they stepped forward and approached the men who sat at the doorway to the tent of meeting. This was the time set aside for the leaders of the tribes to meet and resolve conflicts, disputes, and to give advice.

Mahlah's mouth dried as she tried to recall everything she needed to say. The minor leaders had the authority to judge smaller matters, but the daughters of Zelophehad had a matter that would affect not only them, but their descendants forever. For this, they needed to speak with men who could decide law—men like Eleazar the priest and Moses their prophet.

People stopped in their tracks as they saw the five young women striding purposefully towards the men gathered at the tent of meeting. Mahlah flushed beneath their gaze but kept her eyes fixed forward. She felt the full weight of authority shift onto her and her sisters. Her fingers fluttered and she gripped her hands before her, drawing a deep breath.

Moses looked at them with surprise, but then nodded as he said, "Peace be on you, daughters. What have you come to speak to us about?"

Mahlah glanced to her sisters, then said, "We are the daughters of Zelophehad. My name is Mahlah, and these are my sisters: Noah, Hoglah, Milcah, and Tirzah. Our father died in the wilderness, yet he was not one of those who joined the rebellion against the Lord led by Korah. No, he died in his own sin, and he had no sons."

Moses nodded once, and Mahlah saw Eleazar draw a hand thoughtfully down his beard. Happy that they seemed inclined to hear her out, Mahlah continued, "Why should the name of our father be withdrawn from among his family simply because he doesn't have a son? Give us—" she gestured to her sisters, "—a portion of land with our uncles."

Mahlah watched as the men glanced at each other in surprise. She tried not to fidget as she heard the people behind her murmuring. She was asking for an inheritance equal to that of a son. It was unprecedented and unheard of. Yet, should her father's line be forgotten as they moved into the promised land at last?

Moses rose to his feet, "I shall need to bring this before the Lord."

Mahlah and her sisters stepped backward and closer together as Moses walked away to pray in the tabernacle. Mahlah's stomach writhed. "Did I say it right?" she whispered.

"You did great," Hoglah patted her arm.

"Yes, you did," Tirzah nodded, her large eyes serious. "You showed that you understand our history and our law."

Mahlah tried to smile at her sisters, but her face felt stiff. Balancing her desire for righteousness with humbleness was a narrow path to walk, with deep crevices on either side. She and her sisters could simply marry into other families and join their inheritance. Yet, memories of her father and a desire to leave him a legacy of honor called her to do otherwise. She and her sisters needed to bring her father's name into the promised land.

It seemed like an eternity passed before Moses came back and took his seat. Mahlah held her breath as he spoke to the sons of Israel. "The Lord has spoken to me. The daughters of Zelophehad are right in their statements. They shall have a hereditary possession among their father's brothers. Their father's inheritance shall be transferred to them." Mahlah let out a whoosh of breath. She had to stifle a laugh of relief as Moses laid out the new laws of inheritance for the people.

Mahlah grabbed Tirzah's arm. "We did it!" she breathed. "The Lord heard us, and He answered!"

Read this story for yourself in Numbers 27:1-8

STORY COMMENTS

The Bible record of these five sisters is really amazing. Here we have five unmarried women (probably young) who, because of their knowledge of their history and law, brought changes to the laws of inheritance.

In an era when women are rarely named in genealogies, these sisters are mentioned specifically in Numbers 26:33. They are mentioned again by name in Numbers 36:1 when they did as Moses requested and married within their tribe to keep their father's inheritance within his own family. The land these sisters ended up occupying was east of the Jordan River, with the sons of Gilead, of the half-tribe of Manasseh, the same tribe that eventually produced the hero Gideon.

The role of women in the church is an issue debated for centuries. We see Paul telling women to be silent in the church as the law says. (1 Corinthians 14:34) Yet, just a few chapters previously, Paul speaks of women praying and prophesying, so he can't mean they don't speak at all. (1 Corinthians 11:5) Acts 21:9 speaks about women prophetesses. Philippians 4:3 and Romans 16 mention many women who worked directly with Paul, the same man who wrote these words to the Corinthians about being silent.

So what's going on here?

Taking 1 Corinthians 14 in context, we see silence is also commanded for other groups of people. (Though not gender specific, which is why this particular command for silence riles us up a bit!) This silence is to promote edification in the church, and so that outsiders did not think they were crazy because of their noisy disorganization!

I would suggest that perhaps in Paul's situation, some of the women were steam-rolling over the authority of the leaders of the churches. Did some bossy-boots drive Paul and the early church crazy?

While it's clear that women had roles they could perform within the body of believers, I think this story also brings yet another element of how women can interact within their church.

I would like to present the daughters of Zelophehad as an example of how women can speak within the group of believers, even in question of how things are run. These women were knowledgeable and well spoken. They were confident, but not rude or bossy.

According to the scriptures, men are to be an authority in the church (1 Timothy 2:12), but that doesn't mean that men unilaterally decide everything. After all, they also submit to the authority of God. If you see something wrong in your church, don't be afraid to say something! Just do it wisely. Like these five sisters, get your facts, know your church history, attend a meeting, and speak boldly to those that God called to lead your church and let them pray and bring it before God.

Seek to honor men within your church. Not because they are better than women, but because they are your brothers in Christ. Different roles do not mean different worth. When trying to decide what roles a woman can play, let's try to stay on the heart of the law. Consider every issue of how a woman should act within a church body through a God-lens. Those who want to serve within the church might want to ask questions like: "Does this honor God? Am I submitting to God's authority and the authority of those He put in charge? Am I being kind, respectful, and polite? Am I seeking my own glory, or God's?"

We often compartmentalize the genders in the Bible, that women did this and men did that, but stories like this one show that women could take a stand for themselves in their desire to live righteous lives before God. The daughters of Zelophehad came before the leaders of their community and clearly asked for what they thought they and their father's legacy deserved—and their request was honored by God and laws were changed!

The daughters of Zelophehad were not afraid to stand for what was right, and perhaps they inspired women like Deborah and Jael, Naomi and Ruth, and first-century women like Priscilla and Lydia.

QUESTIONS FOR DISCUSSION

* Does this story support or go against your current view of women's roles in the church?

* Do you believe there is any difference in roles for men and women in the modern church?

* Is it possible that women needing to submit to the men's authority in the early church was based on their culture, a culture we no longer live in? (The same way women missionaries in a Muslim country cover their hair, out of respect for culture?)

Rahab

SURVIVOR THROUGH FAITH

The sun was rising. Rahab rose from her corner of the cramped room and tiptoed over the many bodies slumbering on the floor. The night had been restless, but her family had tossed and turned their way to sleep at last. The room stunk of unwashed bodies, stale air, and an overfull chamber pot. Rahab wrinkled her nose. She opened her window and flung the filth to the ground far below. Her house was on the city wall, and much too small for the number of people she had crammed inside at the first sign of trouble. She tucked the chamber pot away, and looked over the snoring forms of her parents, her siblings, and their children. They usually lived in a large house near the town center, but she had dragged them here to save their lives.

She turned to the window and leaned her elbows on the wooden frame, drawing a deep breath of the dewy morning air. The sky was tinged pink as the sun raised its drowsy head over the hills. There was hardly a breath of wind. It was going to be a hot one. She felt the now familiar twist in her gut. Was today the day?

For months the city had pondered the tribe of barbarians in the wilderness, a strange, landless people who wandered the barren hills yet somehow managed to survive. Apparently these Hebrews had enough of their dust and brittle grasses, and had turned their eyes on the lush green fields around Jericho, full of grain, vineyards, and groves of olive and date trees.

She readjusted the scarlet rope that hung out the window. It was her lifeline, her family's one chance of hope in the coming attack.

"Let them remember me," she whispered, and the plea turned into a prayer to a God she barely knew. "I helped Your men, God of Israel. Remember Your servant and keep my family safe."

Rahab squinted as beams of light shot over the horizon and touched the foot of the city. They were out there, to the east. This wasn't the first army Jericho had seen, but it was the first one that made them tremble with fear. More than their numbers or skill, it was the stories that made them fearsome. The citizens of Jericho knew how the Hebrew God had parted the Red Sea to lead them out of Egypt. All Jericho whispered about how the Hebrews destroyed Sihon and Og beyond the Jordan.

She listened and heard the soft rumble of feet moving their way. Her mouth dried.

"Are they coming?" a voice whispered, and Rahab jumped. She turned to look at her mother, Tali. Tali's dress was rumpled and she had deep shadows under her wild eyes. Rahab nodded and her mother tensed. Tali's eyes were damp as she murmured, "I dreamed they all marched away in the night."

Rahab turned back to the window. Though the sun was in her eyes, she could see them now, swords catching the dawn. She fiercely gripped the scarlet rope in her hand as she breathed, "Remember."

The army formed a long, snaking line. Seven priests carrying curved ram's horns marched in unison. A mysterious, covered chest was carried on poles by more white-robed priests. The soldiers began to circle the city. They had done the same thing every morning for six days —one circle around the city before retreating to their camp.

The barricaded people inside the walls were on edge. The citizens had food and water to last for months and boasted the thickest and tallest city walls ever built. Jericho had stood against assault time and time again, but this … this was something different.

The priests lifted their horns to their lips, and Rahab's abdominal muscles tensed in preparation. A long, echoing blast rose up. It was one long cry of defiance to the stone walls that kept them out.

The Hebrews marched around the city. Their stamping feet vibrated the floor of the house. The noise woke the rest of the household, who rubbed their gritty eyes, weary and miserable.

"Won't they stop!" her brother protested, putting his hands over his ears. His little daughter started to cry, and her mother hushed her.

Tali brushed a hand over her grand-daughter's hair. "Do not fear, my dear. The walls will keep them out. They can't get in."

Rahab shot her mother a look. "The city will fall, Mama. That is why you are here." Tali pressed her lips together and Rahab's niece buried her face in her mother's chest. They had argued about this every day the whole week. Tali went to sulk by her bed. Rahab resumed watching the soldiers.

When she saw the front of the procession, she waited for them to turn back to their camp. They didn't.

"They're going around again!" Rahab gasped, whirling to look at her family. She jumped at the echoing trumpet blast that struck her between her shoulder blades. Her family clapped hands over their ears and stared at her, waiting for her to do something. She felt their need heavy on her shoulders. This was her plan, after all.

The soldiers finished their second lap and began another one. Rahab rolled her tight neck muscles. Yes, today would be the day. She just knew it. She glanced at her family to reassure herself that they were all there. Her eyebrows drew down in anger. Her mother was kneeling before an idol.

"Are you insane!" Rahab gasped, lunging forward to grab the wooden carving, a goddess ornamented with pure gold.

She shook it in her mother's face, her eyes burning as she yelled at her family, "A greater God than this is with these soldiers. Did the gods of Egypt protect them from the Israelites? Did idols protect those across the Jordan?" She didn't wait for a reply, but leaned out the window to hurl the figurine to join the refuse below. Tali seethed in anger, and her father opened his mouth to chastise Rahab, but the blast of a trumpet silenced them all.

As the morning wore on, the overcrowded house felt like an oven, but Rahab refused to shut the window to block the sunshine. She stubbornly kept to her spot and watched as a river of men encircled her hometown as her family complained and whimpered in turn.

At the end of the seventh lap, the men stopped marching. She sucked in her breath as they faced the city walls. There was a quiet moment that stretched as long as her scarlet rope, then the priests raised the trumpets to their lips and let out a great blast. At the sound, the army shouted in one terrible, deafening roar. Rahab's blood ran cold. The floor beneath her shook as plaster crumbled from the ceiling. Her family wailed.

She leaned out the window and watched a great section of the wall crumble like a children's sand fort. A great plume of dust billowed up to the sky, and she ducked back inside to avoid being choked by it. That's when the screams began.

It felt like time stopped as Rahab huddled in the house with her family. They shoved themselves in the corner furthest from the door, and tried to block out the clash of swords, the yells of fear, and the screams cut short. Rahab sat with her knees drawn up to her chest, her palms over her ears, her eyes screwed shut. Those had been her people. Those wails came from people she knew, her friends and neighbors. It could have been her family.

"Remember me," she whispered over and over again, trying to shut out the noise.

She wasn't sure how much time had passed, but she felt someone shake her shoulder. She didn't respond, afraid to think and feel.

Strong hands grasped her fingers and pulled them off her ears.

"Rahab," a familiar voice said. "It's over." Shakily, she lifted her face. One of the spies she had harbored stood over her. His face and clothes were speckled with blood, but there was no rage in his eyes. He stepped towards the door, gesturing with his head as he said, "Get your things."

Rahab rose on wobbly knees and hastily gathered up her family and their belongings. They stepped out of her house, keeping their eyes averted from the city as they picked their way down the cracked steps and through the collapsed wall. She breathed a sigh of relief once they reached the grassy fields. Soldiers were everywhere, resting or eating. Women were nursing the wounded. The mood was exultant, for Jericho was a mighty prize.

"Thank you for remembering us," Rahab called to the spy ahead of her. She glanced up to the sky. "Thank you," she whispered, grateful tears leaking from her eyes.

Read this story for yourself in Joshua 2 and 6

STORY COMMENTS

No one can doubt Rahab's faith. Centuries after she saved the spies, her family, and her own life, she is mentioned in the book of Hebrews with faith giants like Abraham, Sarah, Moses, and Gideon.

> "By faith Rahab the harlot did not perish along with those who were disobedient, after she had welcomed the spies in peace."
> - Hebrews 11:31

Rahab was the great-great-grandma of the mighty King David. She is one of the few women mentioned in Jesus' genealogy. (Matthew 1:5) She is a true example that it is not our history that defines us, but our faith.

There is, however, one part of the story that I struggle with. I'm sure you've had to grapple with this verse on the destruction of Jericho or others like it:

> "They utterly destroyed everything in the city, both man and woman, young and old, and ox and sheep and donkey, with the edge of the sword."
> - Joshua 6:21

The children? It would be a war crime, in our day. Yet, it seems pretty run of the mill through the conquest of the promised land. We hear a similar refrain time and time again. Perhaps you, like me, often wish that God had given Israel an empty land where all they had to do was move in.

Rahab's faith did more than save herself. Her faith saved possibly dozens of family members. If, through faith, a former unbelieving prostitute was able to save herself and her family from destruction, what would have happened if all of Jericho had done the same?

God is a merciful God. In the story of Jonah, God turns back from destroying sinful Nineveh because they repented and asked for mercy. (Jonah 3:5-10)

Israel did not sneak up on Jericho. The citizens had time to consider, and they knew the stories of God's power. Instead of repenting, they hid behind their walls, trusting in their own strength. For six days, they heard the army circle them, and did they plead for mercy then? No! They trusted in idols and walls of stone.

Jericho could have been like Nineveh. If they had all been like Rahab, perhaps they could have lived—men and women, young and old, and their livestock too.

While I don't have all the answers, it is consoling to know that the citizens of Jericho had forty years to change their ways and believe before their judgment came. I believe God gave them a choice, and *they* turned their back on Him.

QUESTIONS FOR DISCUSSION

★ Read Psalm 9. These are some verses that jumped out at me as I consider the story of Jericho.

"The enemy has come to an end in perpetual ruins,
And You have uprooted the cities;
The very memory of them has perished.
But the Lord abides forever;
He has established His throne for judgment,
And He will judge the world in righteousness . . ."
"For You, O Lord, have not forsaken those who seek
You."
"The nations have sunk down in the pit which they have
made;
In the net which they hid, their own foot has been
caught."

★ If God came today to judge the world, do you think the world could say they weren't warned?

★ Why can't God just ignore sinful people and the things they are doing?

★ How can we share the warning of judgment and the hope found in faith with our unbelieving friends and neighbors?

★ Read 1 Corinthians 6:12-16. If you are the only one in your family who believes, how can you influence and save the rest?

Deborah and Jael

VICTORIOUS WOMEN

Somewhere in the chaos, she had lost her sandal. Running from place to place to encourage the troops, she had been a little distracted. She chuckled at herself, giddy with exhaustion and not quite sure why it was so amusing.

"Are you all right, prophetess?" a soldier looked at her with concern upon his blood-splattered face. He was but one young man among the thousands drawn from the tribes of Naphtali and Zebulun. One of many who had wet their blades with the blood of the Canaanites.

"Yes, of course," she said, but did not decline the proffered wineskin he slung from his shoulder. She took a gulp of the rich warm drink and wiped the back of her hand across her lips. Refreshed, she strode quickly on, her skirt swishing in the grass. Her bare foot would soon be scratched and sore, but she refused to stop. She and the others were following as Barak chased the commander, Sisera, on foot. Behind them was a bloody field, riddled with overturned chariots. Their wheels spun fruitlessly as if trying to escape their ruin.

The pounding of thousands of hooves, the screams of horses, the clash of swords, and the wails of men were still reverberating in Deborah's head. She drew deeply of the clean air, yet her nose was still filled with the tang of blood and stench of gore. She had learned the chaos and horrors of battle for herself.

For twenty years God had given them over to the Canaanites as punishment for their sin, but no more. This was God's land! He had given them victory.

Any pride she could have felt at being the one who directed Barak in battle, she swept purposefully aside. She, a woman, had led the men when Barak refused to trust in God's words. Because of the foolish man's resistance, the Lord had revealed to Deborah that Sisera would sell himself into the hands of a woman.

Her chin lifted slightly and she smiled. Alright, perhaps she felt a little pride.

She quickened her pace when she saw tents spread out before them. She saw Barak at last, his blood-streaked shoulders heaving as he stopped to catch his breath. They had made it to Harosheth-hagoyim, Sisera's home.

The area was eerily quiet. All the men who had lived here, every man of age to draw a sword, were now dead, laying on the battlefield near Mount Tabor.

A woman strode towards Barak from a tent, and Deborah rushed forward, her skin tingling with a strange feeling. She was in time to hear the woman speak.

"I am Jael, the wife of Heber the Kenite," she said. Her eyes flicked nervously. Barak stiffened at her name. Jael's people had made a peace-pledge with Israel's enemies. Could she be trusted? The Kenite woman held a hammer in one hand, and Deborah saw she was trembling slightly. Jael drew a deep breath through her nose. "Come with me. I will show you the man you are seeking."

Barak looked doubtful. His eyes cast around, still searching for the enemy commander. Deborah knew what he was thinking. It wouldn't be a victory until Sisera was dead, and perhaps this woman was trying to divert his attention so the commander could escape.

Barak glanced to the prophetess, and she raised her brows, waiting. He pressed his lips together and huffed a breath through his nose. Deborah wondered, he had followed a woman into battle, would he trust this one too?

Barak nodded curtly. "Show me."

Jael led them to her tent and ducked through the open doorway. Barak stiffly entered the cool shade, and Deborah followed on his heels, feeling the woven mats beneath her bare foot.

Jael's voice shook slightly as she said, "My husband saw your armies amassing for battle on the mountain and informed Sisera himself."

Barak drew a sharp breath, every muscle tensing as he glared at this woman. Jael did not pull back in fear, but gestured further into the tent.

Deborah stepped forward and saw a man curled on his side on the floor. He was covered by a blanket, the remains of a bowl of milk near his head. She recognized him at once as Sisera, the leader of the Canaanite army. Barak raised his sword, but Deborah reached out and put her hand on his shoulder.

"There is no need," she said, and she laughed again, relief mingling with her weariness in strange ways. She looked at the hammer in Jael's hand and this time she noticed the speckle of blood. Sisera had indeed been sold to a woman. Barak looked closer and saw what had made Deborah laugh. A tent peg had been hammered through the commander's temple.

Read this story for yourself in Judges 4 and 5

Story Comments

Deborah is a rare woman in scripture. She is a judge, a person who led the people of Israel before they had kings.

Jael is the wife of a man who was friends with Israel's enemies, yet she took a stand for the Lord.

In the culture and time of this story, a woman was not usually a leader, nor was she normally considered powerful. Yet, God used these women to accomplish His purposes. This seems to be another example of how the Lord often uses something perceived as weak to show His might.

On a historical note, the iron chariot was the "tank" of the day. It could mow through a battle-line and wheel around for another pass, using its speed to cut down enemies while evading their blows. Ten thousand men from the tribes of Naphtali and Zebulun faced a force that would make your knees knock together, yet God's people came out utterly victorious.

Barak had to know it was God's hand that had achieved this amazing victory over a militarily superior force. He even had to admit that it was not he, but a woman, who would get the glory.

QUESTIONS FOR DISCUSSION

★ Can you think of other Bible stories where God used someone thought to be weak to do something mighty?

★ Do you ever feel like you're not strong enough, not wise enough, or not good enough to do God's work?

★ What would you need to believe to step boldly into God's will for your life?

★ Are you trying to live under your own might, or God's?

★ How does trusting in God clash with our self-sufficient culture?

Gideon

FOR GIDEON AND THE LORD

He ducked under the tent flap and strode into the noisy camp. The sword on his hip felt strange. He was just a farmer in a minor family, the youngest of his father's sons, and yet the Lord had called him to be a warrior.

The men nodded to him as he passed. He had blown his trumpet, and thousands of men had flocked to his call. It was time to drive the Midianites back for good. No more would they destroy the crops and livestock of Israel! Israel had turned back to God, and now the Lord would free them.

Purah came dashing up, a gleam in the young servant's eye. "The numbers are in!"

"And?" Gideon asked, hooking his thumbs in his belt.

"Thirty-two thousand, my lord!"

Gideon stared. So many had answered his summons! He clapped a hand on Purah's shoulder. "Good. Come with me."

He strode through the camp, hoping that he had arranged everything properly. This wasn't just his first command, it was his first battle! Men were sharpening blades, checking pikes and spears, and lounging in their tents. Women prepared meals and discreetly folded bandages for the coming battle. The smell of hundreds of cook fires saturated the air, almost drowning out the subtler scent of anxiety. Gideon rolled his neck to ease the tension. The men were not the only ones who were nervous.

He and Purah climbed to the summit. To the north, camped in the valley along the hill of Moreh, spread the Midianite army. Gideon tightened his grip on his sword.

"They greatly outnumber us," Purah said lowly, though it was only his master and him on the hill. "Their army has at least a hundred thousand men, likely more."

Gideon had to agree. He saw thousands of camels as well. These soldiers would be well supplied.

Gideon straightened his shoulders. "They are as numerous as the locusts, and just as eager to devour everything in their path." He put a hand on Purah's shoulder. "Yet, the Lord revealed to me with signs that He is with us. He will deliver us from our enemy."

Purah nodded. Gideon turned his back on the Midianite swarm and surveyed his own troops. He nodded once. Yes, thirty-two thousand would be enough.

It is too many.

Gideon stiffened at the voice of God in his head. "Lord, what do you mean?" Gideon whispered.

There are too many men in your army for me to give Midian into your hands. If your thousands of men go to battle, they will boast that they won by their own strength.

Gideon stood in shock as God revealed to him what to do. He swallowed, his throat dry as chaff. He looked at Purah, who was watching him in confusion.

Gideon said, "Come, I need to speak to the men."

He strode into the center of camp, found a wagon, and clambered aboard. He yelled for attention, and silence rippled outwards from him as the soldiers took notice. Gideon lifted his chin as he called out, "If you are afraid to go to battle, you may go home. Leave Mount Gilead."

Stunned silence was his answer.

Slowly, without looking at their neighbors, men began to gather their gear. Gideon stood like a statue as he watched the trickle of men become a river rushing out of camp and down the southern slope of the hill.

His heart sunk. But, it was what the Lord wanted.

When the river of men dried up, Gideon stepped down. He spoke to Purah, "Talk to the heads of the families. Get a count."

As the sun passed its zenith and tipped towards the west, Purah returned. His face was grim.

"Only ten thousand men remain."

Even as Gideon's hopes withered, he heard the voice of the Lord.

The people are still too many. Bring them down to the water, and I will test them there for you. The one I say stays, stays. The one I send away must go.

Gideon again climbed into the wagon. He had to fight down despair at the sight of the depleted camp. The men fell silent as they saw him, waiting to see what strange edict he would declare now.

"Come down to the stream and drink, all of you." He hopped down and led the way to the nearby spring of water. The men gathered to quench their thirst.

Whoever laps the water in his hand to drink, shall stay. He who kneels to drink water, will go.

Gideon relayed the command to Purah, and the two men watched closely as the men came forward to drink, separating them as God had commanded. In the end, he had only three hundred men. He drew a deep breath and let it puff out.

"This is Your will, Lord?"

I will deliver you from the Midianites with your three hundred men. Send the rest home.

Purah was pale as Gideon sent thousands more men home. By the time dusk fell, the camp was but a shadow of what it once was. Gideon worried his lower lip. He didn't want to doubt the Lord, yet fear was creeping up his neck. God spoke to him again.

Arise and go against the camp, for I have given it to your hands. If you are afraid, take your servant Purah and go down to the camp and hear what they say. Then your hands will be strengthened.

As soon as it was full dark, Gideon and Purah slipped out of camp and into the valley. They approached an outpost on their hands and knees, creeping through the tall grass until they were close enough to hear what the look-outs were saying.

"I had the strangest dream. A loaf of barley bread was tumbling into our camp. When it came to the tent, it struck it down flat."

His friend's voice was high-pitched. "It is nothing less than the sword of Gideon! God has given Midian and all the camp into his hand."

The men fell into an anxious discussion, and Gideon bowed in worship to the Lord. Grinning, he returned to camp, Purah on his heels.

The night air was invigorating as he called the men together under the starlight. He held out his hands as he shouted, "Arise, for the Lord has given the camp of Midian into your hands!"

The men grinned, their eyes and teeth white in the night. Gideon divided them into three groups and outfitted them each with a trumpet, a torch, and a pitcher to hide the flames. He sent them to surround the Midian camp. They all chuckled in approval of his instructions, and their steps whispered through the grass as they moved out.

The camp of Midian was in quiet slumber. When Gideon was sure his men were in position, he raised his trumpet to his lips. As he blew out a great blast, he smashed the pitcher that masked his torch. All around the camp, flames blazed and the crash of broken pottery and peal of trumpets echoed as the men raised a war cry,

"For the Lord and for Gideon!"

A wail of unbridled fear broke out in the valley camp. Gideon watched in amazement as the great Midian army turned on each other, the clash of their swords ringing into the night. Men turned and fled wearing nothing but their inner tunics. Thousands of camels stampeded, knocking tents aside. It was chaos.

The Midian army was scattered, without Gideon's three hundred men striking a single blow. His blood raised, Gideon roared and charged forward in pursuit.

As his legs pumped and he thrust forward his sword, his heart sang.

Victory is the Lord's!

Read this story for yourself in Judges 6 and 7

STORY COMMENTS

Gideon was a nobody. His army was whittled down to three hundred men. His enemy was a hundred and thirty thousand strong. (Judges 8:10) The odds were completely against him, but it didn't matter. God was for him. This is a common theme in the Bible! God does not see strength as we do, and He seems to delight in reminding us of that.

David was also the youngest son, and only a shepherd, yet God made him king.

Joseph was sold as a slave and wrongfully imprisoned, yet God used him to feed his people in a famine.

Esther was an orphaned exile, yet God used her to save her people.

Peter was a fisherman, yet God used him to grow His church.

Do you feel like a nobody? Do you wonder if God can use you? Let the story of Gideon remind you that your ability to work for God is not dependent on your own skill and talents. Cultivate an obedient, humble heart, and maybe God will surprise you with the plan He has for your life.

To encourage and strengthen the early church, Paul wrote the famous verse,

> "...If God is for us, who can be against us?"
> - Romans 8:31

QUESTIONS FOR DISCUSSION

* What battle can you give back to the Lord today?

* What do you think would have happened if Gideon had refused to send the soldiers home?

* Do you feel more or less confident knowing that God is the one in control?

* Can you recall a modern man or woman who stood up against others and brought change?

Delilah

The Woman Who Brought Samson to his Knees

He eats like a wild man, she thought to herself as she lounged on a soft couch of pillows. Samson clutched the roast in both hands, tearing the meat from the bone with his teeth. Juices dripped down his chin and landed on the fine tunic she had bought for him. It was dyed and embroidered and did nothing to disguise the taut muscles that bulged over his chest.

She tipped her head and bit her full lip, her body thrilling at the sight of him. He might be savage, but he was utterly captivating.

She reached out a delicate hand to take the goblet from the table and drank sparingly of the expensive wine. She had to keep her wits about her tonight. She surveyed the Israelite over the rim of her cup. Three times she had tried to draw his secret from him, and three times he had made her out to be a fool.

She sighed, rose gracefully, and adjusted her expensive, scarlet dress. She strolled languidly through the elegantly decorated room to an engraved, wooden chest and opened it. She frowned at what she saw. The coins were nearly spent. She slammed it closed, turned her back to the reminder of looming poverty, and focused her eyes on the barbarian who had shared her bed for months. Eleven hundred pieces of silver were promised to her. All she had to do was bring the strongest man in the world to his knees. Her ruby colored lips curled in anticipation.

She remembered the first time she had seen him swaggering through town. She had heard of his might and how he had killed a thousand men with only the jawbone of a donkey. How he had carried away the city gates and burned the ripened fields. From the stories, it seemed like he hated her people, yet he couldn't seem to stay away from the superior culture of the Philistines. Of course, how could he not be drawn in by their sophistication? Samson was one of those grubby, nomadic people who had emerged from the wilderness with the ridiculous claim that this land had been promised to them by an invisible, unseen god. Busy curating her position in society, Delilah had given the rural, backward Israelites little thought—until chance had thrown Samson in her path.

She shivered with pleasure as she remembered how his eyes had caressed every curve of her figure, burning her with his desire. She had coyly dropped her gaze and turned her back on him. Just as she intended, her rebuff only fueled his lust. A lust she could now exploit.

Gliding sensually across the room, she sat beside Samson, draping herself over him as he licked his fingers clean. She toyed with one of the long braids that hung well past his waist and caressed his cheek. His eyes turned and fell to her exposed cleavage. A new hunger leaped into his eyes.

She let him kiss and hold her, but when she felt his desire burned hottest, she pulled away, turning away from him.

"What's wrong now?" he asked, his tone cajoling.

"You know exactly what is wrong," she said, casting a look over her shoulder in what she knew was a pretty pout. "You say you love me, yet you refuse to share your secrets with me!"

Samson let his head fall back and groaned loudly. "This again? Will you never stop!" She turned her face away from him. He pulled her roughly towards him, and she gave into his caresses for a moment before twisting away again. He tried to seduce her, but she continued the complaining that she had been perfecting for days. Her own ears were weary of hearing her wheedling tone and her constant badgering, surely he must be ready to give in!

"Enough woman!" he cried out at last. He drew her to him, his face mere inches from her own. She could feel his hot breath on her cheeks.

His fiery eyes flicked over her face and rested on her lips. "A razor has never touched my head. It is a solemn oath to God since I was in my mother's womb. If my hair was cut, I would be as weak as any other man."

She could see in his eyes that he told her the truth at last, and her heart leaped. Finally, the money would be hers!

The next evening, everything was prepared. Samson fell asleep with his head upon her lap. She caressed his face, marveling that such a powerful man was in her thrall. She was almost sad that their time together was ending. One glance at her depleted moneybox, and her melancholy fled. She beckoned her manservant to bring the shears.

An hour later, Samson was gone, dragged away by the Philistines. His curses still rung in her ears. She sipped her wine as she considered one of the braids that had fallen on her couch. It was a shame that the fame she had curated as the woman Samson loved would fade. She picked up a braid. Perhaps she needed a memento, something to remind the people that it had been Delilah who had brought the powerful Israelite to his knees.

Months later, Delilah prepared for the sacrificial feast for her god, Dagon. Everybody who was anybody was going. She was dressed in her finest clothes, but instead of jewels, she wore the belt she had made from Samson's hair.

She felt admiring eyes on her as she smoothly worked the room, laughing at jokes, lightly drawing a hand over an arm. She was an expert at casting her eyes demurely to the ground, but then peeking upwards again through her thick lashes. The braziers flickered in the twilight as three thousand of her people reveled in wine and good food. Delilah climbed the steps to the roof where the richest members of society had gathered.

The lord of the city saw her and beckoned her over. She took his proffered hand, and looked prettily around herself as he called to the huge crowd,

"The Israelites claim their god is more powerful than Dagon! Yet, our god has given our enemy Samson into our hands!" Goblets were raised and cheers reverberated around the great, pillared hall. Delilah was thrilled as the eyes of so many powerful men looked her way. The lord of the city continued, "Send for Samson! Let's see this mighty Israelite for ourselves!"

Samson was brought in to the lower level, and the stone building shook with taunts and laughter. Delilah went to the balustrade and looked down upon the ruined man beneath her. He was blinded, dressed in rags, his large hands rough with hard labor. His head was bowed. Was he praying to his weak god? She scoffed at him. She turned away from him and made a joke, jutting out her hip to be sure everyone noticed the belt of Samson's hair.

The floor beneath her feet lurched. Laughter turned to screams as a crack ripped its way across the floor. Delilah nearly lost her balance and was momentarily dismayed as the sloshing wine ruined her new dress—before the floor completely gave way and she plummeted with a shriek.

Read this story for yourself in Judges 13-16

STORY COMMENTS

From a historical standpoint, I was surprised to learn that the Philistines were the advanced society of their day. They had a well-developed culture with art, fashion, fine homes, all sorts of tradespeople, and their blacksmiths made skilled weapons and armor. In the eyes of the world, the Philistines far outstripped the rural Israelites.

Is it any wonder that Israel's people were tempted and swayed by these people? How easy it is to forget the mighty deeds of the true God when the proof of the power of the false god Dagon is right before your eyes: wealth, power, favor, and sophistication.

Samson, who wore the vow to the Lord on his head in his uncut hair, and who had unnatural, God-given strength coursing through his limbs, was not immune to the temptations of a dazzling culture. While he kept the outward symbol of obedience to God, his heart was chasing his own desires. It took him being blinded and enslaved to finally turn to God in prayer. It took Samson's humbled heart to deal the enemies of the Lord a crushing blow—the greatest victory of Samson's life.

QUESTIONS FOR DISCUSSION

★ As you strive to stay true to God in our modern times, do you ever find our culture trips you up?

★ What do you do when you feel tempted to put aside what you know is right in favor of pleasure, power, or conformity?

★ Delilah traded a man's life for money. We might not be so obvious, but in what ways are people today exploited for money or power?

★ As a child, I never felt like Samson really won, because he had to die too. Do you think Samson thought this victory was worth losing his life?

Ruth

FAITHFUL OUTSIDER

The sun beat relentlessly on her back. Far ahead of her, the laborers were swinging their sickles through the ripened field. Behind them, women gathered the barley into sheaves. Last of all, Ruth gathered up the scant remainders—and was grateful.

She straightened her aching back to pull her mantle up to shield her face and felt her dress clinging between her shoulder blades. Blowing a strand of hair out of her eyes, she felt a trickle of sweat run down the side of her face.

While she stretched, she looked around at her mother-in-law's homeland. Would these hills and fields ever feel like home, or would she always be a stranger in Bethlehem? Whether she was at the well or the market, the other women drew back when she approached. She heard everything they said about her.

"Why is she here?"

"If her husband died, why didn't she stay with her own people?"

"What if she brought her idols with her?"

They didn't understand that she had put that life behind her. When Naomi sold all she had to go back to Israel, she had tried to send Ruth home to her parents. The bereaved woman was walking into an uncertain future, and she wouldn't ask the same of her widowed daughters-in-law. Orpah had remained in Moab, but Ruth was determined to stay with Naomi. It had been Naomi who had taught her about the true God.

She had heard of the Israelites before her marriage. Who didn't know about the nation that had thrown down the massive walls of Jericho, turning the most powerful city in Canaan to rubble? They had swept in from the wilderness and broke through the land like a windstorm, sweeping away everyone in their path. And then, the nation of soldiers had put down their swords and turned into tribes of shepherds and farmers. At least, that's how they talked about the Israelites back in Moab. Naomi had shared the truth with her daughters-in-law.

It hadn't been Israel that had conquered Canaan, it had been their God. He had gone before them in the wilderness, sustaining them with bread from heaven and springs of water from solid rock. He had promised their ancestors this very land Ruth stood on now.

She had decided it was better to go to the land of God a poor widow than to have earthly comfort in the shadow of a god of stone.

A shout rang out across the field, interrupting her reverie. The meal was prepared.

Ruth's stomach growled, but she tried to ignore it as the laborers put down their tools and walked to the shady tent. The women chattered companionably. One paused and looked at Ruth, her eyes flitting over her damp brow.

"Come, sit in the shade with us." The other women looked doubtful but didn't protest. Ruth smiled, grateful, and found a spot to sit apart from the others.

A well-dressed man came under the shade. "May the Lord be with you," he said seriously.

It seemed to be a usual saying, for the workers replied with a cheerful refrain, "May the Lord bless you!"

Ruth, listening from her corner, quickly learned the man's name was Boaz and that he owned this field, and others as well. He spoke kindly to each of the workers, clearly a thoughtful and kind employer. Her stomach fluttered when his eyes turned to her. She ducked her head.

Would he ask her to leave?

Instead, he smiled and came right up to her. She noticed flecks of gold in his brown eyes and the barest hint of grey in his beard.

He said, "Do not go and glean in the other fields, but stay here with my maids, it will be safer for you. My men will not trouble you. Anytime you are thirsty, you may come and drink from the water here." He gestured to the tall earthen jugs.

Ruth's eyes widened in surprise. Why was he being so nice to her, a strange woman and a foreigner? As he turned away she blurted, "Why have I found favor in your sight?"

Boaz chuckled, but his voice was gentle. "I've heard about everything you've done for Naomi. May the Lord bless you, for you have chosen to shelter under the wings of the God of Israel."

Ruth's heart was filled, and tears smarted in her eyes. He, of everyone she had met, understood her and saw why she had left her people and her homeland. She kept her gaze fixed firmly on the ground as she murmured her gratitude, trying not to cry in front of the others.

As the food was served, Ruth was handed a dish as well. Blessings on top of blessings, there was so much food that there would be enough to take back to Naomi too!

When she rose to glean, there was three times as much left behind as before. She thought she even saw them drop some grain on purpose for her. She gathered it all, thankfulness making her fingers nimble and her aching back but a minor nuisance. When she had beat out what she had gleaned, she scooped up the barley grains and let them run through her fingers. She laughed with joy. The God of Israel was powerful, yet He had time for a Moabite widow and her bereaved mother-in-law.

Naomi was astonished when she saw how much Ruth had gleaned. "Where did you get so much?" she asked. Ruth told her.

For the first time in months, Naomi smiled.

At the urging of her mother-in-law, Ruth gleaned in Boaz's fields through the barley harvest and then followed the workers to the wheat fields. Every day she returned with generous portions, and Ruth thanked God for Boaz's generous heart. He came to the fields every day to speak with the foreman and his workers, and she always paused to glance over at him. He was good-natured and generous, a considerate employer, and a man of strong faith. Why didn't he have a wife and family?

Spring was waning, and summer would soon be upon them. Ruth turned a slow circle, looking at the field. It was stubble now, showing the evidence of months of work. She nodded once with satisfaction. Her hands were calloused, her face sunburned, but she had stores of food set aside for herself and Naomi. God had provided for this season. She would have to trust that His care would continue.

When Ruth arrived home, Naomi had a thoughtful look on her face. She scarcely noticed the grain her daughter-in-law brought home, but instead eyed Ruth up and down with a speculative gaze.

"What?" Ruth asked, raising a brow.

"Boaz is a close relative of mine," Naomi said.

Ruth nodded slowly, confused. "Yes, you've told me."

Naomi came and set a hand on Ruth's arm. "You've been a daughter to me. The life of a widow is not what I want for you. In our country, when a woman is widowed without a son to care for her, a family member—like Boaz—takes the woman to be his wife, to raise up a child for the husband she lost."

Ruth felt her mouth dry, and she turned away in distress, sifting through her feelings. She felt respect and admiration for Boaz, yet she resisted. She remembered the whispers in the market and bit her lip. How could she make a faithful Israelite a suitable wife?

Noami reached out a hand and turned Ruth's eyes to her own. "I see your reluctance. Is it his age?"

Ruth shook her head.

"Do you dislike him?

Again, she shook her head.

Naomi's face relaxed. "I see what it is, my humble daughter. Ruth, the people here have seen how you have served me. They have seen that you believe in the God of Israel. All of Bethlehem speaks well of you." Ruth ducked her head at the praise. Naomi used a finger to lift her chin. "You will not bring shame on Boaz as his wife. Indeed, I think he would be overjoyed."

Ruth laughed dismissively. "Then why hasn't he asked for me? Surely in his eyes, I am only a poor widow gleaning in his field."

Naomi made a face. "I knew Boaz in my youth. He thinks too little of himself. He probably thinks he is too old for a pretty young woman like you."

Ruth lifted her hands. "Well, then what can we do?"

"Oh, don't worry," Naomi grinned. "I've got it all worked out." Ruth was shocked when she heard Naomi's idea, but did as she was told.

As the sun was setting Ruth went down to the threshing floor. She was freshly bathed, anointed with scented oil, and in her best clothing. Her heart fluttered wildly in her chest like a trapped butterfly.

A large fire was burning, illuminating Boaz and his workers celebrating the end of the harvest. She could hear laughter and jokes, but she stopped a little ways away and waited until night fell and the men lay down.

The stars came out and the air became sweet and cool. Ruth waited until she was sure everyone was asleep. Her entire reputation was on the line. If Boaz misunderstood her, or if he was angered by her boldness and exposed her, then she would never be welcomed in the community.

Her pulse hammered in her ears as she crept forward. Her breath sounded like a raging wind as she tiptoed forward and saw him wrapped in his mantle. His face in the starlight was peaceful, with a smile toying on his lips. If tonight went well, she would have the chance to make that smile reappear again and again. The idea tugged on her heart, and she felt the first stirrings of affection.

She went to his feet and uncovered them. She laid down near them. If someone was to come upon her now, surely they would think she was a harlot. She hoped fervently that Noami knew what she was doing. It was not long before his cool feet awakened Boaz. She heard his breathing change and he shifted and sat up.

"Who are you?" his voice was surprised.

Ruth sat up as well and felt her palms dampen with nervousness. "It is your close relative, Ruth. Spread your covering over me and shelter me."

There was a long moment of silence, where emotion tumbled over emotion until Ruth wanted to run into the night. When Boaz answered her at last, his voice was thick with emotion.

"This is your greatest kindness yet, that you would choose me over the young men. I shall do as you ask, for everyone knows you are a woman of excellence. Yet," he paused, and Ruth's throat constricted. "There is another relation closer than I. I must speak with him first. If he does not wish to redeem you, then I shall." Ruth felt disappointment at the idea that a stranger might claim her, but she could think of nothing to say. "Lay down until morning," Boaz said softly. She curled up on the hard ground, feeling uncertain about the morrow. The stars tracked across the sky long before she fell asleep. If she had been more aware, she would have noticed Boaz shifting in wakefulness as well.

The next morning, Boaz roused her when the sky was just beginning to pale. He gave her a portion of grain and sent her home. She walked the cold road alone, feeling weary and unsure of the success of Naomi's plan. Noami was awake and waiting for her.

"Well?" she asked at once.

Ruth told her.

Naomi laughed. "You will not need to wait long. I am sure the man will not rest until the matter is resolved—today, if he can manage it!"

Ruth poured the wheat in with the rest. She ran her fingers through the earthenware jar, feeling the cool grains sliding between her fingers. All of this bounty was the result of God's providence. Surely she could continue to trust that He would continue caring for her, whether with Boaz or a stranger. Yet, her heart ached with worry.

It was well past midday when she heard a noise outside the door. She lifted her eyes to Naomi, her lips parting as if to speak, but she couldn't utter a word. Naomi went to the open doorway and called out a greeting. Boaz stepped into the little house. He looked flushed, and his eyes were sparkling.

"It is done," he said, and Ruth rose slowly to her feet. What was her fate to be?

"I will prepare the feast, and then come back and take you for my wife."

Ruth felt a smile spreading on her cheeks, and Naomi clasped her hands together and beamed.

The day of the wedding came, and Ruth stood in her bridal array as torchlight flickered all around her.

"May you be like Rachel and like Leah, who built the house of Israel!" the people cried to Ruth.

To Boaz they exclaimed, "May you achieve wealth, and become famous in Bethlehem!"

In due time, Ruth brought forth her firstborn. A son. He was named Obed. Obed was the father of Jesse, and Jesse was the father of David, who became king.

Read this story for yourself in Ruth

Story Comments

Ruth felt like an outsider, like she didn't belong among God's people, even though she believed. The Israelites were warned against intermarriage with foreigners, and marrying men and women who followed idols led the people into scrapes over and over again.

So why is there a whole book dedicated to a Moabite marrying an Israelite?

This believing Moabite became the great-grandma of King David, the great-great-grandma of the wise Solomon, and in the family tree of Jesus Christ. (Read the genealogy in Matthew 1). I think this book is included in scripture to show how Israel was supposed to treat foreign believers. We see Jesus treat believing foreigners with the same acceptance in the gospels.

Moreover, notice the language used to describe what Boaz is doing for Ruth. He is "redeeming" her. You may have heard that same word used to describe what God does for his people. (Luke 21:28, Ephesians 1:7) Do you think this story was placed in the scriptures to show what God wants to do for the entire world?

Questions for Discussion

* Who are the "outsiders" in your church? How can you make them feel welcome?

* Or, are you the outsider? Why?

* How can we copy Ruth's example today when we feel on the outside or not good enough?

* How many different ways did Ruth have to trust in God?

* What are some ways that we can learn to rely on God's providence in our lives?

★ Have you been redeemed by the blood of Jesus? What does that mean to you?

Hannah

PRAYER OF HER HEART

Little Aaron tumbled into Hannah. She let out a whoosh of breath, but then smiled and set the three-year-old upright in her lap.

She leaned to the side to look in his rosy face. "Are you all right, little man?" Aaron smiled and his nose crinkled just like her husband's. He opened his mouth, but before he could say a word, quick hands plucked him out of Hannah's lap.

"Run and play and don't bother her," Peninnah said, directing the busy child towards his older siblings. "She isn't used to little ones like you." Peninnah turned back to Hannah, running a hand down her round middle. Her eyes flashed maliciously as her seemingly innocent words turned to barbs. "So sorry about that."

Hannah's eyes burned, and she quickly rose and walked out of the tent before her rival could see her tears. She refused to give Peninnah the satisfaction of knowing how deep her words had cut. She knew the other woman was only cruel out of jealousy, but that didn't make it any easier to accept—not when Hannah had her own reasons for envy. She looked down at her flat middle and two hot tears slipped down her nose. Fighting would not solve her problems. If Hannah stooped to Peninnah's level, it would only tear the family apart.

She was so caught up in her emotions she didn't hear footsteps approach.

"What's wrong, my love?" a soft voice whispered behind her. She felt large hands run down her forearms and wrap around her. Elkanah drew her back to his chest.

"Nothing," she said, too quickly.

He sighed. "Peninnah is teasing you again, isn't she?"

Hannah sniffed. Did his other wife ever cease? Peninnah had all the children, how could she still begrudge Hannah the position of favorite wife?

Elkanah turned her in his arms and tipped her face up to his. He kissed one damp eye, and then the other. He murmured, "Am I not better to you than ten sons?"

Hannah's lips wobbled. She loved and was loved, yet there was a hole in her chest that throbbed like a broken bone. The wrong thought would send shooting pains through her fractured heart, reminding her that she was childless and had no sons to care for her in her old age. She didn't answer her husband, but buried her face in his neck. She was a joke to Peninnah and a hushed fear to the other women who met at Shiloh as they came to sacrifice to the Lord. Hannah saw her friends come back with new babies, or with bellies swollen with life, and yet every year she was unchanged. Tears ran fresh down her face onto her husband's tunic.

She heard the music start with a sinking feeling. The feast was beginning, and the thousands of men and women spread through the camps around Shiloh would laugh and celebrate another year of blessing.

Elkanah heard too, and he took her arm. "Come, dear wife, let's go join the family." She looked up at his face, so loving and kind. She didn't want to cause him pain, not when he was so good to her. She allowed him to lead her to the dancing fires where the flutes and the tambourines were playing. Everywhere she looked, wine was flowing. The scent of roast meat and spices filled the air.

She pretended to be happy and content, all while feeling Peninnah's mocking gaze and the pitying looks from her friends. Watching the other mothers serving their children, she found she had no appetite to eat.

As the hour grew late, she slipped away unnoticed into the cool starlight on the fringe of the camp. Alone with her thoughts, she drew a shaky breath and wrapped her arms around herself against the chill of the evening. She looked up the hill at the tabernacle. It was enclosed by a cloth wall, but she could see the top of the building. A long time ago, when her people were but nomads in the desert, the Lord had descended on the tabernacle in a cloud and the people had quaked with fear and wonder. It was the sort of place where miracles could happen.

Fighting with her fellow wife or weeping to Elkanah would get her nowhere, but there was One who could help. Gathering her courage, she strode alone up the hill and into the enclosure. She and Elkanah had sacrificed here this morning when the enclosure had been bustling and bright. Now there was a heavy stillness only disturbed by the sounds of the distant feast. She felt alone, and yet somehow seen. The large altar still glowed with a thick bed of coals, and the scant scent of burnt sacrifices hung in the air, mingled with the fragrance of incense.

She swallowed loudly as she stood by herself in the large enclosure, feeling very small and humble. The great tabernacle with its giant columns stood before her, a place so holy that none but the priests could enter. Lamplight flickered from within the massive doors, shining from the golden lamps that never went out. The continuity was comforting. She felt a sense of reverent awe wash over her as she slipped silently over the packed ground to stand before the doorway.

She knelt and felt her emotion break loose. After keeping it bundled up all evening, it surged forward in great sobs.

"God, do you see me?" she prayed. "Do you see my suffering?" She clasped her hands over her heart and whispered a vow, "O Lord of Hosts, if You will look on the affliction of Your maidservant and remember me, and if You will give me a son, then I will give him to the Lord all the days of his life, and a razor shall never touch his head." She slipped back into prayer, swaying forwards and back as her emotion thrummed within her heartbeat.

"How long shall you make yourself drunk?" a sharp voice cut through her prayers. She jerked up her chin in surprise as the voice scolded, "Put your wine away."

Frozen with fear, Hannah stared up into the face of the priest, Eli. He was sitting in the shadow of the doorpost, almost invisible in the dim light. He was a tall man, with streaks of grey winding through his dark hair and beard. As her racing pulse settled, she felt a tug of longing as she looked at him. As a priest, he could go into the tabernacle and burn incense before the Lord. Surely the Lord listened to one like him.

She wiped her tears on her sleeve and scrambled up to stand. "I'm not drunk," she spoke to the ground between them, her throat thick. "I am a woman oppressed in spirit. I have drunk neither wine nor strong drink, but have poured out my soul to the Lord. Do not think of your maidservant as a worthless woman, for I have only spoken out of my great concern and provocation."

There was a long silence, and then Eli spoke in gentle tones, "Go in peace; and may the God of Israel grant your petition that you have asked of Him."

Hannah sucked in her breath and looked up.

Eli gazed sympathetically at her and smiled. Her heart jumped into her throat. If the priest could see the depth of her need, then the Lord he served could see it too. With Eli's blessing, surely God would grant her petition! Warmth flooded her from the top of her head to her toes.

She gasped out, "Let your maidservant find favor in your sight."

She flew from the tabernacle enclosure and back down the hill, her pulse pounding in her ears. The feast was still in full swing. She slipped in among her family and friends, and it was as if she had never left.

She found her place by Elkanah. He glanced her way, and then took a double-take at her happy expression. He grinned wider for a moment before turning back to his conversation. Her stomach growled, and she picked up her neglected plate and ate with pleasure.

The Lord had seen her. He would answer her prayer!

Read this story for yourself in 1 Samuel 1:1-18

STORY COMMENTS

Any woman who has longed for a child finds a sister in Hannah. A lack of children is a true hardship. This was about more than desperately wanting to be a mom, (which was painful enough!) it was security for her future. Her children would care for her in her old age. A woman who gave children to her husband was honored for building up the family's strength, and honor was everything.

She is not the first woman in the Bible to suffer from infertility. Sarah, Rebekah, and Rachel all had to wait to have their first child.

However, the way Hannah handled her situation was unlike the others.

When she was mocked by her fellow wife, she did not lash back. At least, not like Rachel and Leah did with their jealousy and rivalry. There is no mention of Hannah trying to defend her womanly honor with sharp words. I look at her, and I see a beautifully humble spirit. She calls herself a maidservant of the Lord, and then again to Eli. When Eli accuses her falsely, she defends herself, but with gentleness. She has a spirit I wish I could emulate!

Hannah turned to the Lord for her help. Her moment of tearful prayers before God will stir the heart of anyone who puts themselves in her place. Rebekah relied on her husband's prayers to open her womb, and Sarah decided that she needed to do things her own way, but Hannah fell to her knees in prayer.

She knew from whom all blessings come, and was not afraid to give back to God. It boggles my mind how she was able to give this longed-for child to the Lord! (1 Samuel 1:27) Hannah clearly loves her son, and yet she keeps her word and gives him back to the Giver. We know Elkanah agreed to this, but what did he think? How did Peninnah react as she watched her rival leave her firstborn behind to serve God?

We can have a pretty good idea of what God thought. He opened Hannah's womb to have more children (1 Samuel 2:21), and as a result of Hannah's faith in God, her firstborn child grows to be a mighty prophet, one that we still talk about thousands of years later!

QUESTIONS FOR DISCUSSION

* How do we learn to live with unfulfilled prayers?

* Do you feel that God sees your needs?

* Using Hannah as an example, how should we handle unfair accusations or harsh words?

* How do we keep bitterness from taking hold of us when we see others enjoying the blessings we long for?

Eli

Rumors and Responsibility

"Rumors, they are only rumors," Eli muttered as he strode up the hill in Shiloh. His long legs used to take the incline easily, now he panted a little. He pursed his lips wryly. It seemed that he was aging faster—if that were possible. The first streaks of grey had appeared only a few years ago, now his beard was almost white.

He adjusted his linen ephod as the entrance to the enclosure came into view. He squinted at the bustle in the courtyard. The pleasing fragrance of incense and seared meat filled his nose. Though his eyesight wasn't what it used to be, he could discern his two sons busy at work, overseeing the sacrifices. He frowned.

Surely the rumors about Hophni and Phinehas were no more than unfortunate misunderstandings. He couldn't believe that his sons were actually stealing from the Lord. It was ridiculous! No man—no priest! —would ever dream of taking the Lord's portion for himself. Eli had raised them to be men of God, hadn't he?

He shifted uncomfortably. It was true their mother had accused him of being indulgent, and that indulgence had only grown when his wife died and the young boys were left motherless. Others had complained about the boys' youthful pranks, yet, wasn't a father supposed to love his children unconditionally?

He drew a deep breath and strode through the courtyard towards the tent of meeting. He felt eyes on him. He blinked the clouds from his vision and saw a woman smiling at him from beside the flaming altar. She had a young boy's hand in her grasp. Eli smiled absently as she pointed towards Eli and the boy lifted his chin and stared with wide, expectant eyes. Beautiful curls touched the child's narrow shoulders.

Eli stopped before the bronze pool. The sunlight reflected off the polished metal and cast sparkles of light onto his clothes as he leaned forward and ceremonially washed his hands and feet to purify himself before he served the Lord.

He murmured the prayers, and as he stepped back and turned, he jumped as he came face to face with the woman and the little boy.

"Peace be on you," he stammered.

The woman's smile wobbled as she looked at him, and her eyes drifted over his face. He frowned a little, confused. She sounded disappointed as she said, "You don't remember me, do you, my lord?"

Eli looked at her again. "I'm sorry, no."

The woman glanced down at her son, a child who couldn't be more than three or four years old. The boy stared openly and Eli felt strangely exposed before this child's measuring gaze.

The woman's soft tones were hard for his dim ears to discern, and he leaned forward as she said, "I suppose our meeting meant more to me than you." She looked up and smiled, though tears shimmered in her eyes. "I was here, alone, praying just there—" she pointed to the entrance of the tent of meeting "—and you thought I was drunk."

Eli furrowed his brows as flickers of faint memory teased the corners of his mind. "I think I remember."

"Well, you told me to go in peace, and said that the God of Israel would grant my petition."

Eli nodded politely.

The woman held her son's hand in both of hers as she said, "The Lord answered my prayer, so I am here to fulfill my vow. My son Samuel is to be dedicated to the Lord all his life. He shall not touch strong drink, nor shall a razor touch his head."

Eli blinked. What was the woman getting at? "So you've come to make a sacrifice for your firstborn?" That was the usual way of the people. The firstborn of the womb belonged to the Lord, and they were bought back with a sacrifice.

"I have come to bring him to you, " she said, "so you may raise him up to serve the Lord."

Eli stared at this barely weaned child and felt his limbs grow cold. A child for the tent of meeting? He had raised his own children here in the tabernacle enclosure, but that was years ago. Now his sons were long since grown and married. How could he take responsibility for one so small at his age?

The rumors of his sons' transgressions shot through his mind again. The man who summoned him had angrily accused his sons of sending their servants after him to take more than their allotted portions as priests—stealing right from the cooking pot. That, combined with tales that his sons were sleeping with the women who served at the doorway to the tent of meeting ...

Eli folded the thoughts up and tucked them away as one does a blanket. He saw the woman was waiting with a mixture of emotions shifting over her face. The child looked hesitant. The youthful innocence in Samuel's face tugged on the old man's heart. He could not refuse the woman, not when she had made a vow to the Lord.

Feeling nervous, he crouched, his knees popping as he brought his eyes level to the boy's. He held out a wrinkled hand, and the young boy glanced up to his mother before reaching out to set his chubby fingers in Eli's palm. Eli closed his hand over the youthful warmth and looked up at the mother.

"Does he understand what is happening?"

"He does," the woman said, swallowing hard. "I have often spoken to him of this day, and have prepared him for his life here."

The little boy lisped, "I will work for 'd Lord."

Eli's heart swelled at the simple, trusting words, nodded once, and rose back to his feet. This woman was trusting him with her prayed for —and obviously loved—child. The responsibility weighed on his shoulders as the woman knelt and wrapped her son in a tight embrace.

The woman rose and rested her hands on her son's curls as she spoke a prayer of thanksgiving and hope in the Lord. Eli felt the hair on his arms stand up at her ardent voice, and when she reached the end of her prayer his mouth went bone-dry as she said,

"Those who contend with the Lord will be shattered;

Against them He will thunder in the heavens,

The Lord will judge the ends of the earth;

And He will give strength to His king,

And will exalt the horn of His anointed."

The woman smiled and hugged her son again as Eli sifted her words. There was no king, not in Israel. Did this woman prophesy?

His eyes were dragged to his sons. Did they contend against God? He refused to follow that thought any further and pulled back to the present.

"My husband goes back to Ramah, but I shall see Samuel again when I return." She gently pushed her son forward, and he came and stood at Eli's side, slipping his hand into Eli's grasp again.

Eli, feeling stunned by the unusual turn his afternoon had taken, watched silently as the woman hurried out of the courtyard with her chin down.

He turned and looked down at the staring child who watched him with wide, damp eyes. "Well, now," he said kindly. "Let's see about finding you a place, shall we?"

Read this story for yourself in 1 Samuel 1:19-2:11

STORY COMMENTS

Hannah's faith to give what she loves to the Lord is truly humbling. I doubt she knew about the rumors of Eli's sons, but if she did, she still trusted Eli to raise her son to serve the Lord.

The book of Samuel opens in a time when "there was no king in Israel; everyone did what was right in his own eyes." (Judges 21:25) Eli is the priest, and his sons serve the people by assisting with sacrifices. This was a holy task, not to be taken lightly.

God had called Aaron's descendants to serve in the temple. God set aside portions of sacrifices to be dedicated to the priests. After all, they need to eat too.

Some of the priest's portions included:

* The breast of a wave offering and the thigh of heave offering (Exodus 29:27-28)
* A portion of grain offering (Leviticus 6:16-17)
* The skin of a guilt burnt offering (Leviticus 7:8)
* The priest who presents the offering gets the grain offering that

is baked or prepared in a pan or griddle (Leviticus 7:9)
★ Grain offerings mixed with oil or dry, belong to sons of Aaron, to all alike (Leviticus 7:10)

The other parts of the sacrifices belonged to the person who offered them, to be taken home and eaten. Or they were exclusively for God, such as the fat and certain organs.

> "You shall not eat the fat of ox, sheep or goat, whoever eats the fat of the animal from which an offering by fire is offered to the Lord, shall be cut off."
> - Leviticus 7:22-25

Hophni and Phinehas are stealing from men and from God! God will not let this stand, and through Hannah's words we get the first warning of coming judgment. One that Eli should heed.

The other sin these brothers committed was sleeping with the women who served at the doorway to the tent of meeting. Who were these women, and what did they do?

I tried to dig up some solid answers, but I couldn't find anything conclusive. This phrase is used only one other time, in Exodus 38:8, describing how the laver of bronze was made from the mirrors of women who served in the doorway of the tent of meeting. Mirrors in ancient Egypt were made from highly polished bronze, and these women gave up their mirrors to make this important vessel for the tabernacle.

These women might simply be coming to pray, like Hannah. Perhaps Hophni and Phinehas promised answers to prayers in exchange for sex. Perhaps these women served by baking and frying the grain offered in sacrifices, or by weaving, cleaning, fetching water, and other important tasks that kept the tabernacle functioning.

Or, perhaps these women were dancers, like the women from Shiloh mentioned in Judges 21:19-21.

Whatever their reason for being near the tabernacle, it is clear they were not to be used as prostitutes like the pagan cults who used sex for worship.

I found it intriguing in this story, and in the story of Hannah, how these women are right before the door to the tent of meeting. The

Jerusalem Temple in the first century had certain divisions, and a woman could not approach the Court of Israel (where the altar was) without a purpose, such as coming to bring a sacrifice. It seems in the Old Testament, there may have been less gender separation in worship than in later Jewish culture. Interesting thought to ponder

Questions for Discussion

* This is the second time one of Hannah's prayers are recorded. This one bears a striking resemblance to another woman's famous prayer. Read Mary's Magnificat in Luke 1:46-55 and see if you can see the similarities.

* Have you ever seen an indulgent parent that spoils their child and the child ends up suffering for it?

* We know that God loves us, so why isn't our life always easy?

* Do you think we would be better people if life was never difficult?

* What hardships do you feel God has used to teach you something and made you better because of it?

Samuel

CALL IN THE NIGHT

Samuel rolled up the raw hide to take to the tanner. Hophni wiped his forearm across his damp forehead and nodded once to him, flicking the sharp blade in his hand dismissively. Samuel scampered out of the enclosure, eager to be away from the priest. He didn't like Hophni, or his brother Phinehas. He had overheard Eli chastising them many times, and yet they continued to do whatever they pleased.

Samuel loved Eli as if the man was his own grandfather, yet as Samuel matured he saw a weakness growing in the aging priest like a tumor. Samuel had laid upon his mat many a night and pondered, why didn't Eli do something about his sons? Wouldn't it be better for everyone if he removed them from their positions? The greedy, self-indulgent sons of Eli mocked the tabernacle and its holy worship. Yet, Eli did nothing but talk, talk, talk to his sons, and they just rolled their eyes.

He shrugged one of his long braids over his shoulder as he arrived at the house of the tanner, a burly man who reeked of the concoctions he used to cure skins into leather.

The tanner grinned when he saw who had arrived on his doorstep. "Welcome, Samuel," he said. "The same order as usual?"

"Yes, please." Samuel handed over the sheepskin and spun around to go.

"What's your hurry?" the tanner chuckled.

"I've got more chores to do," Samuel said simply, and the tanner grinned wider.

"You're a good boy, Samuel. I've never seen you shirk your duties, not even once. Everyone says what a well-mannered, respectful young man you are. Your mother must be proud."

Samuel swallowed around a lump. Yes, his mother was proud of him. Hannah told him so every year when she traveled to Shiloh to sacrifice. She always brought him a new linen ephod, a replica of the robes the priests wore. She had other children now, but every year when she came, they spent days together. Just her and him. They would sit side by side, mother and son. She would wrap her arm around his shoulder and he would lean into her, breathing deep the fragrance of her skin and her long hair. Nothing smelled as lovely as his mother. Then she would tell him the story of her prayer for a son, and God's answer, and how she had dedicated her firstborn to serve the Lord for all his life.

Sometimes, after she left, Samuel wished she hadn't dedicated him to the Lord, and that he could go home with her to live with her and his father, Elkanah. He would lay in his bed with the tears hot beneath his lids and his throat clawed by sadness. He would press the new ephod into his face, trying to find a trace of her scent.

The sadness didn't last. Life ministering before the Lord was all he knew. Within a week or two after his mother's visits, he was back to his old self, playing with his friends, learning from Eli, and doing his chores. Like he should be doing right now. He shook off his thoughts.

"Peace be on you!" Samuel nodded at the tanner and dashed back up to the tabernacle enclosure. He fetched and carried for the rest of the day until the sun began to sink and it was time for his supper.

He ate his bread and meat with Eli, and washed them down with water. Eli drank wine. The liquid was a beautiful color, and Samuel was curious to know how it tasted. Yet, it was forbidden to him, part of the vow his mother had made. His life belonged to the Lord.

As his ravenous appetite was sated, Samuel noticed at last that Eli had hardly touched his food.

"What's wrong?" he asked, scooting closer. Eli's clouded eyes turned his way, his gaze sliding over him as if trying to focus on his face. "I had a visitor today. A man of God."

"A man of God!" Samuel exclaimed. He had never seen a prophet, they were very rare these days. "What did he say?"

Eli sighed and set aside his bowl. "Word to dry the marrow from my bones and harden my muscles like leather. I don't know what to do, my boy," Eli said, and his voice trembled weakly. "I am just an old man … they don't listen to me anymore …"

Samuel knew then that the man of God had spoken against Hophni and Phinehas. He crawled right up to Eli's knee and leaned upon his lap. He didn't know what to say. He didn't want to tell Eli that it would be all right, for how could it be? So he laid his head upon the elderly man's knee and let Eli run his weathered hand over his long braids. The braids showed everyone that the young man was dedicated to the Lord, and Eli seemed to take pleasure in remembering Samuel's devotion.

"Clear away the meal, say your prayers, and then it is time for bed," Eli said at last.

Samuel dutifully gathered up the dishes. He said his prayers the same way he had every night as long as he could remember. Then he took himself to his pallet in the large communal tent beside the tabernacle. It was set apart for the priests' use and divided into areas for different families. Samuel heard the other children getting ready for bed too, their mothers singing to them, or scolding them to settle down.

He crawled under his blanket, weary from his day's labors. Despite the noise, he fell asleep almost at once.

Samuel!

Samuel sat up and replied automatically, "Here I am!"

He felt disorientated. It was dark now, and all the chatter and bustle was gone. He could tell by the feel of the air that the hour was late, closer to dawn, when the lamps would need to be refilled in the temple. Who had called him? He stood up, shivering slightly as the blanket fell to his feet. Eli must need him. He left his little area and went to the room where the men slept. He went to Eli's place.

"Here I am, Eli," Samuel whispered. Eli's even breath caught, and Samuel realized he should have been able to tell that Eli was sound asleep.

"What is it?" Eli asked, his voice gravelly with slumber.

"Didn't you call me?" Samuel asked, his brow furrowing.

"No, I did not call, my son. Go lie back down."

Samuel obeyed, feeling perplexed. Had he dreamed the voice?

He had just shut his eyes when he heard the voice again.

Samuel!

He hastened back to Eli and said, "Here I am." Eli once more sent him back to bed. Samuel worried. Some men lost their minds when they grew old. Did Eli call for him and then forget?

Samuel!

Feeling frustrated, Samuel obeyed at once and went to Eli. This time Eli sat up when Samuel said, "Here I am, because you called for me."

Eli didn't answer at once this time, and Samuel waited to see what the elderly man wanted.

"I think I know what is happening, my son," Eli whispered eagerly. He was wide awake now. "Go back and lie down. If you hear Him call you again you shall say, 'Speak, Lord, for Your servant is listening.' "

Samuel was puzzled, but he obeyed. He lay on his back on his pallet, staring up into the murky shadows of the tent roof.

Samuel! Samuel!

Samuel felt the hair on his arms rise up, and he sat bolt-up in bed. It was almost as if the voice came from the tent of meeting, where the ark rested in the Holy of Holies. His mouth dried, and he barely managed to whisper, "Speak, for Your servant is listening."

The voice spoke in the stillness of the night,

Behold, I am about to do a thing in Israel at which both ears of everyone who hears it will tingle.

In that day I will carry out against Eli all that I have spoken concerning his house, from beginning to end.

For I have told him that I am about to judge his house forever for the iniquity which he knew, because his sons brought a curse on themselves and he did not rebuke them.

Therefore, I have sworn to the house of Eli that the iniquity of Eli's house shall not be atoned for by sacrifice or offering forever.

The voice fell silent and Samuel sat alone, feeling the darkness pressing against his eyes and wrapping around his shoulders. The voice, the one who had called him—it belonged to the Lord! His mind spun at the implications. The Lord spoke to men of God, to prophets and prophetesses, not to boys like him! What did this mean?

He lay wide awake for a long time, full of fear that the Lord had chosen to speak to him, and the even greater fear for what Eli would say when Samuel told him what the Lord had said. Eli knew that his sons were wicked. Yet, he had not done a father's duty to restrain them, nor a priest's duty to cut them off from the people.

What exactly had the man of God prophesied to Samuel's guardian?

What would happen to the house of Eli? It couldn't be good.

Samuel felt pity and sorrow for the elderly man who had raised him. A chill ran down his spine and he shivered. He rolled on his side and pulled his blanket up to his ears. The Lord had spoken to him, but a small part of his boyish mind couldn't help but wish that the Lord had chosen someone else.

Read this story for yourself in 1 Samuel 2:18-3:15

Story Comments

Samuel was a special, set apart child from his birth. He had restrictions put on him like a Nazarite ("one separated"). He couldn't cut his hair and he couldn't drink wine. (Numbers 6:2-5) The mighty Samson was another such Nazarite from birth. (Judges 13:5)

Right after we hear the negative report of Eli's sons in scripture, we have this phrase:

> "Now the boy Samuel was growing in stature and in favor both with the Lord and with men."
> - 1 Samuel 2:26

This phrase is used in the scriptures for another special child.

> "And Jesus kept increasing in wisdom and stature, and in favor with God and men."
> - Luke 2:52

Was the author of Luke trying to tell us something, by drawing the reader's attention back to the book of Samuel? Read the next story to learn more!

Questions for Discussion

★ How would you feel if God spoke to you personally?

★ How would you react if you were told to give a negative prophecy to someone you loved?

★ What are the differences in the way Samuel served versus how Hophni and Phinehas served?

★ Why do you think Eli didn't do more to stop his sons?

Shiloh's Fall

DROPPED FROM FAVOR

He ducked as a blade whistled over his head, and then thrust his spear forward, catching his opponent in the gut. The Philistine's eyes bulged with surprise as he fell to his knees. Eben yanked the spear backward and wrinkled his nose at the stench of death.

He glanced around himself. He had been pushed little by little to the back of the fray where the battle was dwindling.

He looked up the hill where his countrymen were fighting. It felt like they were losing badly but they couldn't be, not when the ark of God was here. The priests Hophni and Phinehas flanked the ark of the covenant, the golden chest swathed in layers of curtain, skins, and brilliant blue cloth. He had heard stories of the ark that resided in the tabernacle, but Eben had never expected to see it himself.

When the ark had come into the camp the men had cheered, their moral instantly renewed. Surely the Lord would fight for them if His ark was here! Even now, when hope seemed lost, God could rout their enemies.

Yet, God was not intervening. His eyes flicking wildly, Eben could only see a hundred or so of his countrymen, and they were being pushed back closer and closer to the ark, men crumpling as the Philistines cut them down.

Eben moved to join them but felt someone grab his leg. His heart leaped into his throat. He jerked free and raised his spear, but when he looked down he saw his commander lying in the churned up grass.

"Joash!" Eben gasped. Blood spilled from a severe laceration in the older man's thigh. Joash was one of the men who led the Benjamites into battle. Eben hesitated, torn between helping his commander and helping his fellow soldiers. The battle on the top of the hill was drawing nearer and nearer to the ark, and more Philistines were joining the fray.

He stepped towards the ark.

"Wait," Joash groaned. "The battle is lost."

Eben's stomach fell, but he shook his head in defiance. "No, there is still a chance!"

Joash squinted at the hill, his face pale from blood-loss. "We were thirty thousand. Now we are a hundred. It's over. You must run to Shiloh. Tell them all is lost."

Eben felt heat rise up to his face and rage poured into him like fire. "No!" Joash was wrong, they could still win! He began to run headlong towards the ark, jumping over fallen enemies and countrymen alike, dodging the sharp edges of spears and blades. Men groaned and reached for him, crying for help, but he would not stop.

He had spanned half the distance when a great roar of victory filled the air. He stumbled and stopped. He saw Hophni and Phinehas holding out their hands, pleading for their lives. He jerked instinctively as swords were thrust into their stomachs. The priests dropped to the ground, dark blood staining their white linen ephods.

The Philistines surrounded the ark. "We have defeated the Israelites and their God!" they chanted, gripping the ark's poles and turning it a victory circle.

Eben felt cold. The ark was captured!

He dropped his spear and tore at his clothes. The words of his commander echoed in his mind. Without a second thought, he turned and ran. He had to warn Shiloh.

At first he sprinted, but as soon as there was a little distance between him and the Philistines, he dropped to a steady jog. He paced his footfalls to his breath. He would need to maintain this speed for miles over grassy slopes and rutted roads.

Though his heart pounded and sweat dripped down his back, his mind was free to wander—and regret.

What had they been thinking, taking the ark from its sanctuary? It had not been moved in hundreds of years, not since the days of Moses and Joshua. Had they really thought they could force the Lord to help them? He felt shame in each jar of his bones as he raced through the ripened autumn grass.

It was hours later when he stumbled into Shiloh. The men at the gate rose to their feet when they saw him. He dropped to a knee before them, his muscles quivering with weariness.

"Bring wine!" someone yelled, and a wineskin was thrust before him.

He took a swallow of the rich drink and wiped the back of his hand across his lips.

A grey-haired man stepped forward, hands outstretched in supplication. "You've come from the battle." It was not a question.

"I have," Eben nodded once. "It is lost." The man's eyes widened and he took an involuntary step back. He cried out, "And the ark?"

Eben gathered a handful of dust. He poured it over his head in an outpouring of grief. "The Philistines took it."

The men at the gate began to wail, tearing their clothes and sprinkling dust on their heads. Eben groaned to his feet and continued past them. He had to find Eli. Eli needed to know.

The word spread like wildfire through the city, and as Eben ascended the hill to the tabernacle, a great keening rose up behind him like the sound of a thousand funerals.

Eli was sitting in his usual seat near the road where he could hear the news of the city. His ancient face was lost in wrinkles, and his eyes were milky-white. A young servant attended him. Eben's heart turned over at the prospect of giving the terrible news to the elderly man.

"What is happening?" Eli cried out. "What is causing this commotion?"

He summoned his breath and his courage and hurried forward. He stopped before Eli and said, "I am the one who came from the battle line today."

Eli's brows twitched, but he straightened his bowed shoulders. "How did it go, my son?"

Eben hesitated, and then answered, "Israel has fled before the Philistines and there has been a great slaughter among the people."

Eli paled, and his servant gasped.

Eben knelt at the old man's feet and spoke to the ground between them, "Your two sons, Hophni and Phinehas are dead."

The priest moaned, a hand fluttering to his forehead. Though he looked grieved, he did not look surprised. Eben paused, drawing courage to give the most terrible news of all. "The ark of God has been taken."

The look on the old man's face was a mask of unimaginable horror. Eli wailed and threw his hands in the air. Eben lunged forward as the old man swung backward, but he wasn't fast enough. Eli hit the ground with a sickening crunch of bones.

The servant, already distraught, leaped forward to his master.

"He's dead!" the servant gasped, and ran into the tabernacle enclosure, screaming like a madman. "He's dead! They're dead! The ark is lost! We are all lost!"

Eben shook his head and hastened after the hysterical young man, hoping to find someone to help. Shiloh was in grave danger from the Philistines. Now that the Philistines had the ark, there was little doubt that the holiest city in Israel would be their next target.

If only Samuel was here to lead them, but he had left the tabernacle service years ago when he had grown, and now spent his time judging the people in various cities. Everyone knew that God was with the seer, Samuel, and it was clear that God was with Shiloh no more.

A woman's scream tore the air, and he turned to see the gibbering servant was giving the news to a pregnant woman. Eben pressed his lips together.

"Phinehas is dead? My father-in-law is dead?" she gasped. Her face drained of blood, and then she doubled over, gripping her round middle with both hands. A stream of water hit the dirt at her feet as she let out a shriek.

Other women came running to her aid, and the wailing woman was half carried into the priest's quarters.

The other priests came hurrying forward in their white ephods, question in their faces. Elbowing the blubbering servant to the side, Eben told them as quickly as he could all that had happened.

The priests shook and trembled but moved into action, beginning to gather and secure the holy relics and utensils. Long ago the tabernacle had moved from place to place. If they were lucky, they could move it once more.

Exhaustion finally took him, and Eben slumped to the ground. Everyone was dashing around in various states of usefulness, but he let himself drift into a strange, dreamless sleep.

He was roused by a shake on his shoulder and a woman's voice saying, "Here, you must eat."

Eben looked down and saw a chunk of bread pushed into a bowl of stew. His stomach growled. He accepted the food and began to eat. The woman stood beside him, her arms wrapped protectively around her chest.

"How is the baby?" Eben asked when some of his gnawing hunger was soothed.

Her gaze shot to his like she was trying to read something in his face. "The baby is fine, but the mother did not survive."

Eben swallowed his stew painfully. Another loss for the bleak day.

The woman had tears running down her cheeks as she said, "She had time to name him before she died. She named him Ichabod."

Eben stiffened. Ichabod. No glory.

The woman sniffed. "She said the glory has departed from Israel."

Read this story for yourself in 1 Samuel 4

STORY COMMENTS

To fully understand this story of the capture of the ark, we need to hold the previous stories in our mind. The people had the ark of the covenant in Shiloh, but the priests were not honoring it with proper service.

Eli knew his sons were stealing from God and sleeping with the temple serving women, but he did nothing to stop them. Sure, he scolded and pleaded with them, but he didn't remove them from their prominent places in service. Eli's sons Hophni and Phinehas should have been spiritual leaders, but instead, they became the rope with which the people hung themselves.

Years before this story, Eli was warned what would happen to his sons. He received the word from a man of God. (1 Samuel 2:27-36) The unnamed man asked Eli how he could honor his sons above God? The man of God told Eli that his sons would both die on the same day and that God would break the strength of Eli's house.

Then the prophecy was repeated when God spoke to the boy

Samuel. (1 Samuel 3:11-14) Still, Eli did nothing.

Because the people were not worshiping God as He had commanded, God withdrew from Shiloh and allowed the ark to be captured. Even when the ark was returned to Israel seven months later, it didn't go back to Shiloh. While we don't have a written record of what happened, the city disappeared from history and Shiloh became a symbol of what happens when God takes away His blessing.

Years later, the ark was in the glorious temple of Solomon, but once again the people refused to serve and honor God. Jeremiah said to them,

> "Will you steal, murder and commit adultery and swear falsely, and offer sacrifices to Baal and walk after other gods that you have not known, then come and stand before Me in this house, which is called by My name, and say, 'We are delivered!' —that you may do these abominations? Has this house, which is called by My name, become a den of robbers in your sight? Behold, I, even I, have seen it," declares the Lord.
>
> But go now to My place which was in Shiloh, where I made My name dwell at the first, and see what I did to it because of the wickedness of My people Israel. And now, because you have you have done all these things … I will do to the house which is called by My name, in which you trust, and to the place which I gave you and your fathers, as I did to Shiloh."
>
> - Jeremiah 7:9-14

The people did not listen, and the temple of Solomon fell. The people were taken captive. The ark was carried away and is lost to this day. (2 Chronicles 36:18-19)

Fast-forward centuries later. The people were freed from captivity. Their temple was rebuilt. The sacrifices were being offered, the festivals were being celebrated, and more people knew the Torah than perhaps ever before in history. Yet, once again the people in charge were not following God the way they should. A revolutionary rabbi comes into the temple court and quotes this scripture to them from Jeremiah.

(Matthew 21:13)

These scribes, teachers, and priests knew their scripture. Jesus was using the words of Jeremiah to warn them. Yet, once again, they refused to repent and change their ways, and the second temple fell in 70 AD.

Questions for Discussion

* I love how the Bible builds on stories of the past to teach people. How can we apply this story to our lives today?

* Can we do good deeds yet not be honoring God in our hearts and actions? Read 1 Corinthians 13:2b

* How can we be sure that we are doing God's work in the way He desires?

* How can we show love for God and for each other in our daily actions?

* How were Samuel and Jesus alike?

Samuel

GRIEF AND HOPE

His arm jerked. He looked back and saw the heifer had found a tantalizing bit of grass and was munching away. Samuel sighed, allowed the cow a moment to get a good mouthful, then tugged on the lead. Taking the heifer along had been God's idea. He tipped his head up and raised his shoulders at the heavens.

"Your plans are always good, but just once, can't they be easy too?" He chuckled to himself and kept walking on the dusty path through the hill country. Samuel was on his way to Bethlehem, and for the first time in years, he journeyed with a light and eager heart. He felt hope flutter in his pulse and strengthen his bones. The sky felt bluer today and the bird song was sweeter. God had a plan and things were about to change.

He had received his first word from the Lord as a boy. From that day forward, he had felt the Lord's presence go with him. Every year he made a circuit of the land and the Lord helped him judge the people. Sometimes God wanted Samuel to speak for Him, to be His voice—His prophet.

Once, Samuel might have felt a glimmer of pride at being chosen, but in the last few years his calling had worn him down. He was tired of warning and teaching and the thick-skulled people learning nothing.

The people were foolish and hardhearted. They couldn't seem to grasp who God was. If they couldn't figure out who God was, how would they ever understand who they were supposed to be?

Samuel couldn't help but feel responsible for the people. When the people did wrong and God came against them, he felt their sin like a boulder in his stomach. He was their prophet and judge. He wished he could lead them as easily as he did this heifer.

As if in response to his wishful thoughts, his arm jerked again as the heifer turned to another juicy plant. He looked up to heaven and shook his head with a rueful laugh.

Samuel knuckled his lower back as he tugged on the lead. With every passing year, his age sat a little heavier, and he was no closer to a quiet retirement than he had been a decade ago. He scratched his beard. It was more silver than brown. Did prophets ever grow old in peace? He had hoped his two sons would be judges in his place. Unfortunately, they didn't have the moral strength to be leaders. He had learned from Eli's mistakes. His sons were no longer in power.

God had sent Saul to him, and Samuel had anointed him as king—the very first king of Israel. Yet, the man appointed to govern the people had been a disappointment, to say the least. Samuel felt a wave of grief wash over him, and he had to stop for a moment to let it subside. "How did it go so wrong, Lord?" he murmured.

How long will you grieve over Saul, since I have rejected him from being king over Israel?

Samuel shook off his mood. God had sent him here to find a man named Jesse. God had chosen a new king from among Jesse's sons.

"Let him be as You said, Lord, a man after Your own heart," Samuel prayed. He didn't have many years left, and he wanted to leave the people in good hands.

He strode up to Bethlehem. Flocks of sheep and goats wandered the green slopes, guarded by shepherds with their long staffs. As he approached the city of shepherds, he heard the chatter of children as they dashed about in play. They saw him and ran hooting and hollering back to the city to spread the word: the Seer had come.

Before Samuel reached the city, a delegation of local elders came forward to greet him, worry on every face. They inclined their heads respectfully. "Samuel, we weren't expecting you! Do you come in peace?"

Samuel's lips twitched. A few fiery accusations and his reputation had become fearsome. He held out a hand towards the heifer. "I am here in peace. I have come to sacrifice to the Lord. Consecrate yourselves and come with me to the sacrifice."

He glanced around and found the man he sought. "Ah, Jesse. I want you to come as well, and bring your sons." Jesse creased his sun-browned forehead at being singled out, but he nodded.

Samuel sacrificed the heifer the way he had learned in the tabernacle courts. He burned the Lord's portion on a stone altar and had servants prepare the rest of the meat as a meal for the people. The local wives worked together to provide bread, curds, fruit, and skins of wine. The young men constructed an open-sided shelter while the young women hung lamps and spread out mats and cushions. By the time twilight fell with refreshing coolness, it was time to eat.

Samuel sat under the shelter and watched the people arrive. The men were all freshly scrubbed and wearing clean clothes. He perked up when he saw Jesse lead his family to the feast. Samuel beckoned for Jesse to come to him. The eldest son was on his father's heels, a tall and handsome man. Jesse introduced him, "This is my firstborn son, Eliab." The eldest son wore his position like a mantle. Samuel thought, 'Surely this is the one the Lord will choose!'

Do not look at his appearance or his height, for I have rejected him. God sees not as a man sees, for man looks at the outward appearance, but the Lord looks at the heart.

Samuel nodded to himself, accepting the wise words of the Lord. He looked at Jesse. "Show me your other sons." Eliab's face soured with jealousy and he stepped back.

Jesse, still having no idea what Samuel was up to, beckoned to his next oldest son, Abinadab. Samuel looked him up and down, and he shook his head. "The Lord has not chosen this one either."

Jesse's forehead was damp with perspiration as he brought his other sons to stand before Samuel, not knowing what the Seer sought. The other people at the feast kept glancing their way, but Samuel ignored them. Soon seven young men had passed by, and Samuel had heard God reject them all.

"Are these all your children?" Samuel asked Jesse.

Jesse's ears turned crimson. The man held out his hands and said, "There is actually one other, but he is the youngest. He is tending the sheep."

"Well, send for him. We will not sit down until he arrives."

Jesse hastily sent someone to fetch his youngest from the pastures, and then stood awkwardly with his sons while they waited. Samuel knew they were dying of curiosity, but he stayed silent.

At last a young man came running up. He was ruddy and handsome, with beautiful eyes. Samuel felt a stirring in his heart at the youth's open, honest expression.

Arise, anoint him. This is the one.

Samuel rose with a popping of joints and went to the young man, who was looking confused and unsure.

"What is your name?" Samuel asked.

"David, son of Jesse."

"Kneel, David," Samuel said.

David knelt, and Samuel opened the horn of oil and poured it over David's hair while his elder brothers looked on in surprise. The liquid shimmered in the lamplight. David instinctively spread out his hand to catch the drips in his palm. He was stunned for a moment, then tipped up his face to stare at Samuel in wonderment.

A feeling of calm certainty washed over Samuel. The Lord had a plan for this one. Samuel touched David's shoulder and whispered the words his mother had prophesied years ago, "The Lord will give strength to His king, and will exalt the horn of His anointed."

Read this story for yourself in 1 Samuel 16:1-13

Story Comments

We've come full circle in this story, all the way back to when Hannah brings the little son she prayed for to Eli, to dedicate the child to the Lord. She is overcome and says a prayer, but there seem to be tones of prophecy in her words.

Standing in Shiloh, Hannah prays: "Those who contend with the Lord will be shattered; Against them He will thunder in the heavens."

In the story of Shiloh, we read how God allowed the ark to be captured and the city to tumble from favor—all because the people were not worshiping God as they should. The main culprits were Eli's priestly sons, Hophni and Phinehas, but Eli had failed his job both as father and priest by allowing his sons to continue in prominent leadership positions in the tabernacle. Eli had been warned by both a man of God and the boy Samuel. Instead of changing his ways and removing his sons, he simply accepted the Lord's judgment and dies the same day as his sons.

Hannah also prayed, "He keeps the feet of His holy ones."

Before the fall of Shiloh, Samuel was already known for having the spirit of the Lord on him. It says that "All Israel from Dan even to Beersheba knew that Samuel was confirmed as a prophet of God." (1 Samuel 3:20). This phrase mentions a city at the northern edge and a city at the southern edge of the promised land, so it means the whole country knew that Samuel was a prophet.

At some point Samuel leaves Eli and the tabernacle. We don't get to hear if he left on friendly terms, or if he was relieved to leave the tabernacle where the sons of Eli were exploiting God and the people. I suspect it was the latter.

We learn in 1 Samuel 1:15-17 that Samuel has a house in Ramah, the same place his parents lived. He gets married and has sons. Every year he would travel a circuit to Bethel, Gilgal, and Mizpah, and he would judge Israel there.

We almost see history repeat itself. Eli's sons did not follow God, and Samuel's sons Joel and Abijah are determined to go their own way too—accepting bribes and perverting justice. The people are upset and ask Samuel to appoint a king for them instead. It seems from 1 Samuel 8:7 that this hurts Samuel's feelings. However, Samuel has more strength than Eli. He takes the problem to the Lord. Soon after, Saul is anointed as king.

At first things go well with Saul, but it doesn't take long for Saul to start doing things his own way, against the will of God.

Imagine Samuel at this point. He is old. He is tired. He has given himself to the Lord all the days of his life, and he has to be wondering, why can't the king do the same? Who will judge the people when Samuel is gone?

The ringing note of Hannah's prayer calls out, "And He will give strength to His king, and will exalt the horn of His anointed."

Remember, Hannah said her prayer before there was any king in Israel!

Samuel has lived through the apathy of Eli, the sinfulness of Hophni and Phinehas, the greed of his sons Joel and Abijah, the willfulness of

Saul, and now, at last, he anoints David, a king who lives in the people's hearts, even today. He was not a perfect king, of course. He messed up big time and had to repent of his sins. Yet, this young boy is anointed by the hand of Samuel and the will of God. God sees David as a man after His own heart.

QUESTIONS FOR DISCUSSION

* Have you ever worked hard in service for God and yet felt like it was all falling apart?

* Samuel was a man of God, yet his sons did not follow his footsteps. We cannot control our children, but what can we do to help them become men and women after God's own heart?

* God passes over Jesse's older sons in favor of David. Can you think of other Bible stories where someone who was not first-born is honored above the others? Is there something we should learn from that?

David

After God's Heart

His muscles were taut with anxiety as the arrow whistled through the cool morning air and planted itself deep in the gravely soil. As the boy scampered to fetch it, Jonathan called, "Isn't the arrow further yet?"

David's heart dropped like a stone, and his shoulders slumped. It was the code the two men had worked out among themselves three days ago. Saul still wanted him dead. Swallowing around the lump in his throat, he lifted his head from the brittle grasses to take one last look at his best friend. They had planned it all out ahead of time. Jonathan was supposed to leave now and go back to his father, and David was supposed to flee. His limbs felt as if weighed down by heavy armor. How could he turn and run away from his family and friends?

He was surprised when Jonathan did not walk away, but instead handed his bow and quiver to the lad and sent him back. David rose slowly to his feet. The two friends looked across the field at one another. Homesickness punched David in the gut, even though he hadn't left yet. Jonathan was not only his best friend, he was his brother-in-law, his family. There was no brother he'd rather have by his side in a crisis—but Jonathan couldn't go with him this time. He was the son of the king, the one who would have taken up Saul's throne—

if Samuel had not anointed David instead. If David had known how much it would cost, would he have knelt and allowed the old prophet to pour the horn of oil over his head?

He stared at his best friend and saw his expression was deeply troubled. Jonathan had his father's good looks and his height, standing nearly a head taller than other men. It was Jonathan's birthright David was usurping, yet Jonathan had never shown a hint of jealousy. Gratefulness surged in his heart, and David dropped to his knees. He bowed low to the ground three times.

Jonathan walked forward, then ran the last few paces and wrapped David in a crushing hug. His voice was partially muffled as he spoke, "My father is mad with jealousy. When I tried to defend you, he threw his spear at me. You have no choice, you have to go."

David felt tears coursing down his cheeks, and when Jonathan released him at last, he saw his friend was also weeping. David kissed his best friend's cheek like a brother, and wept all the harder.

Jonathan put a steadying hand on David's shoulder. "Go in safety. Remember the vows of loyal friendship we swore before the Lord, that He will be between me and you and between our descendants, forever. Now go! Before someone sees you."

David clasped Jonathon's shoulder one last time. Painfully, he turned and fled, dashing his tears away with the back of his hand. He would not allow himself to look back. If he did, he might not be able to go on.

He walked mindlessly for a time, his thoughts focused on what he was leaving behind. As the distance fell away, he began to rouse himself. Where would he go? He could not go back to his childhood home in Bethlehem, that would be the first place Saul would search for him. Gravel crunched under his sandals as he walked steadily, trying to plan. He would need to keep moving. He would not be able to settle down, or word would get back to the king.

He shook his head, for the first time in his life frustrated that he was so well known. Would he spend the best years of his life as a wanted man, eking out a beggar's existence until Saul grew old and died? Was his future as bleak as the sun-bleached rocks in the wilderness?

Samuel said he was to become king, but the prophet had not told him how it would come to be. Should David confront Saul in arms? Seize power for himself? Surely men would rally to him! Yet, men would rally to Saul too. Fighting for rule could tear their nation apart.

David frowned.

His steps slowed, then stopped altogether. He stood in the road with his arms outstretched. He lifted his face to the sun and let out a slow breath. The day was as quiet as when he had been alone in the fields with his sheep and his lyre. He had sung praises to God in those simpler days. He remembered how the olive oil had felt as it slid over his hair. He remembered seeing it drip down his brow and landing in the dust at Samuel's feet, and how his heart had pounded wildly. God had declared that a shepherd boy would be king!

Standing exposed in the middle of the road, his head told him to push on, to keep running, but his heart bid him to wait. He knew deep inside that he was on the cusp of a dramatic change in his life, and he waited to hear the will of the Lord. He heard the cry of birds, and felt the wind toss his clothes.

What kind of king would he be? Saul had also been anointed by Samuel, but had lost favor with God when he became determined to do things his own way. If David wanted to be a righteous king, his foremost concern had to be pleasing God. He felt calm wash over him. He opened his eyes, and looked back to the city, feeling resolved. Saul would not die by his hand. He would trust God to deal with Saul in His own way.

David whispered a song, like he had as a boy. "The Lord is my light and my salvation; Whom shall I fear? The Lord is the defense of my life; Whom shall I dread?"

He turned and faced the wilderness, and strode forth with confidence.

Read the story for yourself in 1 Samuel 20, and Psalm 27

STORY COMMENTS

I wonder what was the greater challenge for David, facing down Goliath or living with an uncertain future?

With Goliath, the goal was clear. Strike down the giant, win the battle. But with David's dealings with Saul, David had to live day by day in uncertainty. He knew he would be king someday, but how? When?

He had people giving him all sorts of advice about how to end up on the throne, even offering to kill Saul for him. Yet David withholds his hand and waits for God. This is in direct contrast to when Saul had started to do things for himself, which cost him everything.

David is called a man "after God's own heart", and it is his faithfulness to God's will, even while struggling in the wilderness, that inspires us today.

QUESTIONS FOR DISCUSSION

★ What is your wilderness?

★ Maybe you feel God telling you to do something, but aren't sure how to go about it. How can you decide when to wait and when to act?

★ David didn't do his trials alone forever, he drew faithful companions to his side. Who do you have to journey through your struggles with you?

★ If you haven't found a group of believers to help you through life, what is holding you back?

Psalm 18

THE LORD CAME DOWN IN A STORM

I fled into the mountains, hoping they would not find me among the crags and caverns. Yet, they chased and hunted me, and now I stood with my back to a sheer stone wall. They spread out in front of me like a pack of lions, ready to tear me to pieces. My only light was the cold shards of stars above.

I was trapped, utterly trapped. In my terror, I felt as if cords broke through the cracked earth beneath my feet and captured me. Icy cold and reeking of death, they bound my legs, trying to drag me down to Sheol. The putrid bands of fear twisted around my chest and arms. I knew I had only moments to live.

My enemies' gloating roiled over me like a mighty wave of the sea, striking me forcefully and rising higher and higher, threatening to cut off my breath. Powerless to move, my eyes flitted back and forth on their shadowed faces. I was surrounded by people determined to kill me. Helpless in the face of so many foes, I did the only thing I could. I tipped back my head and cried out for help to the Lord.

I felt a quiver beneath my feet when He heard me, a tremor that went straight to my heart with hope. The pebbles rattled on the dry earth and the air was seared like hot metal. The craggy mountains around us shook with His anger. His rage sent rocks cracking and tumbling, the rumbling filling my ears. I felt the hair on my arms rise up, and I trembled at His might. I looked at my enemies, and their eyes were white with fear as they quailed.

As one we all turned our faces upwards, and we saw the proof of His anger. Churning smoke billowed from His nostrils. He opened his mouth and fire shot forth, searing the sky with His power. The heavens themselves bowed away from His presence as He came down. Thick darkness surrounded and concealed Him as He flew on the wings of the wind. As we strained our eyes against the blast of wind, we saw the darkest torrents of water and the thickest clouds of the sky were His hiding place.

The Lord spoke, and it was like thunder. Helpless, we clapped our hands over our ears as the sky echoed with His might. From beneath my fingers, I heard a piercing whistle as coals of fire sliced through the air and slammed into the ground. I could feel their heat as they passed, and my nose twitched with soot. Hailstones began to fall among the coals, and my enemies dropped their weapons and threw their hands over their heads.

As if they could shield themselves from His wrath.

The Lord sent his arrows and my foes cried in terror and turned to flee. Lightning struck again and again, and I had to squeeze my eyes shut to keep from being blinded. It grew quiet. Slowly I opened my eyes and saw my enemies were finished.

I felt myself being drawn up by the Lord, lifted away from those who had hated me, who had surrounded and overpowered me, who would have killed me. I was carried away from the sharp mountains to a soft, open valley. After months of hiding in dust and rock, I felt sweet grass beneath me and drew deep the fragrance of wildflowers.

My enemies had been strong, but the Lord is my rock, my shield, and my fortress! He rescued me because He loves me.

Read this story for yourself in Psalm 18:1-19

STORY COMMENTS

We are told to think of God as our father, but a father plays many roles, doesn't he?

When you were a child, sometimes you wanted to curl up in your parent's lap for a cuddle, and sometimes you wanted them to charge in and rescue you. This story reflects the desire of rescue for the Psalmist.

Perhaps you've never been surrounded by physical enemies. (I know I haven't!) The author of this Psalm knew what it was like to face death and have to rely on God to save him. The language is poetic, like many of the Psalms. It does not describe a real storm but encapsulates the emotions the author was feeling in his trials. In that sense, his cry for help in time of trouble is applicable to you and me.

It's good for us to remember that when we cry out, God *does* hear us. When we are sick, or worried, or lost, or suffering, or grieving, and we pray to him, He hears! True, He doesn't always ride in on a storm to save us. Sometimes my prayers feel unanswered. If you feel the same, please remember that God loves you, and someday, somehow, things will be made right for those that trust in Him.

Questions for Discussion

* Hero movies are super popular right now! Disaster breaks out, and the costumed heroes run into the chaos to fight evil and save the day. Do you think of God as your hero?

* In what ways, big or little, has He worked to save you or someone you love from physical, emotional, spiritual, or mental harm?

* And, on the other side, in what ways has He enabled you to be the hero?

* How can we rescue others with the love of God?

Michal

Heartache and Pride

She arranged her robes carefully as she reclined on the couch, though there was no one to admire her regal figure or the way her hair rippled in lustrous waves over her shoulder. She tossed her head and sniffed, the dainty noise the only sound in the empty room.

Everyone else was gone, gone to fetch the ark of the covenant. The other wives and concubines had left in a whirlwind of noise and excitement, but Michal had refused to go out with them.

Abigail had frowned at Michal's stubbornness, but she refrained from voicing her objections. The other women didn't quite know where to place Michal in the hierarchy of wives.

Michal plucked at the soft linen of her dress and scowled. She knew where she belonged. She was the daughter of King Saul, the first king of Israel! She was the first wife of David, no matter what strange circumstances had waylaid her marriage, or the numerous wives David had taken since—women chosen for their beauty, their wisdom, or their political importance.

Michal's stomach clenched. For which of those three reasons had David chosen her? Considering all that had happened, she knew he couldn't have married her for love.

The unhappy thoughts drove her from her couch. She went to the polished copper circle that hung on the wall and examined her reflection. The years had slipped by since she was an innocent princess giddy with love for a handsome young warrior. Her bitter father had hoped she would be a stumbling block to David and had demanded a high, grisly, dowry—one hundred foreskins of the Philistines. She had chewed her nails ragged waiting for David to return, hoping her father's plan would fail. Despite her father's wicked hopes, David had triumphed, and she had been overjoyed to wed the most famous man in the land.

Michal shook her head at her golden reflection. What a naive girl she had been! She, a princess, had been swept off her feet by the bold courage of a young shepherd boy.

The faint bugle of trumpets wafted through the open window. She sighed and walked languidly to look out, resting her elbows on the windowsill and cupping her chin in one hand. The smoke of multiple sacrifices was dark in the sky outside the city. David was being careful to show the ark the proper respect, especially after what happened last time.

The trumpets sounded again, closer. She could hear the people cheering. As the procession drew nearer and nearer, she could hear the instruments and was reminded of a bridal procession. She swallowed hard. Twice she had heard the music played for her own wedding. Once for her wedding to David, and then again when her father had given her to Paltiel.

She knew her father had arranged her second marriage to spite David. She had cried and pleaded when her father told her what he had planned, but eventually reasoned herself into acceptance. She had saved David's life once, though her risk clearly meant nothing to him. Hadn't she waited and waited for David to come back for her, languishing alone with rumors of her husband's new wives to cause her pain? If David had forgotten her, why should she remember him? In the end, she had gone to Paltiel willingly.

Paltiel had been a good man, and she had been his only wife. She had been cherished as a wife deserved—until David had imperiously sent for her. He had been painfully cool in his summons, with no words of love or longing. No, the new king just wanted what was rightfully his, no matter how Paltiel had wept.

Now, she was one of many wives in a large household, and a childless wife at that.

The trumpets were nearly deafening now. Michal, despite herself, leaned out the window to take a look. Priests came first, wearing their elaborate garments and each blowing on a long, silver shofar. More priests followed, carrying a large, covered object on long poles. There was a great distance between them and the people, for this was the ark of the covenant with the testament within and the mercy seat above—it was a holy object. The ark was swathed in layers of cloths and skins, but she knew that it was overlaid in pure gold.

The people followed, cheering, singing, and waving branches in the air. Children raced eagerly around, and women shook tambourines and danced with each other. One man, wearing nothing but a linen ephod, was apart from the others, whirling and leaping like a mad man, his skin glistening and his hair damp with sweat. She opened her mouth to laugh at this strange parody of a priest, when the man threw up his face and she recognized him.

It was David. Her mirth vanished and she clutched at windowsill for support until her knuckles hurt.

The mighty warrior, winner of battles, King of Israel, was dancing like a fool before the people. He spun in a wild circle, and the people cheered. Did he think they approved? Didn't he know they were laughing behind their hands at him? Her lip curled with disdain as she blushed for him, and for herself. This was the husband she had been forced to accept? She turned angrily away from the window.

Michal brooded alone in the women's room as the ark was safely placed in the tent David had pitched for it, and even more sacrifices were offered. She knew David was handing out bread and cakes of fruit to the mob, and the common people went home happy.

Twilight was falling when she heard voices coming back into the palace. She rose at last, adjusting her dress and necklace. She left the women's quarters and slipped down the stairs to the great hall where the servants were bustling around lighting lamps and laying out refreshments. She paused in the shadow of a pillar.

The rest of the household were gathered. The women were resting weary feet on couches, pulling off dusty shawls as servants brought them basins of water so they could wash. Children laughed and stuffed themselves with treats, and babies were nursed. Everyone was tired but very happy.

Michal felt on the outside of the bright family circle, all alone in the shadows. For a brief moment, she regretted her refusal to accompany the other women to the sacrifices, but it was swiftly smothered as David strode into the room, smelling heavily of sweat and incense. David began to greet his wives and children one by one, blessing them. He didn't look at all regal. No, he had reverted back to the simple shepherd boy. She sneered at him.

Michal, in the shadows, was almost forgotten in the blessings, but she stepped forward at the last minute. David saw her and smiled, but it didn't soften her heart.

She gave an exaggerated bow and her words dripped with sarcasm. "How the King of Israel distinguished himself today!" The room fell silent, and her heart beat wildly, but her tongue was like a runaway horse. "He uncovered himself today in the eyes of his servant's maids, looking just like one of the fools!" She trembled as heat surged through her veins, but lifted her chin as everyone stared at her.

David weighed her with his eyes. His tone was measured as he said, "I danced before the Lord, who chose me above your father and all his house, who appointed me ruler over the people of the Lord; therefore I will celebrate before the Lord." Michal's cheeks burned at the reminder of her family's fall, and David's voice rose in volume. "And I will be more undignified than this, and I will be humble in my own eyes—yet with those maids you mentioned?" He gestured back outside. "With them, I will be distinguished." She stared, wordless, and he turned away without blessing her like the others.

Michal felt nausea wash over her, and she fled from the room. She held her pride in front of her like a shield, justifying her words, but regret batted it to the side like a trained soldier. Oh, what had she done?

Read this story for yourself in 1 Samuel 18:20-28; 19:11-17; 25:44; 2 Samuel 3:13-16; 6:12-23

STORY COMMENTS

It's much more enjoyable to study women of upstanding character, but the flawed women have a lot to teach us.

Yes, Michal was prideful and rude to her husband the king, but I feel sympathy for her. Though she loved David, her father wanted him dead. She was betrothed because King Saul hoped that David would die fulfilling the bride price, and then given to another in the hopes it would insult David and invalidate his claim to the throne. Her second husband seemed to love her, yet she was taken away from him—once again in the name of politics. Did she feel loved and wanted for herself?

David was good at many things, but relationships do not seem to be one of them! I doubt Michal had the happy life she imagined for herself. I myself have said my fair share of rude and mean things when my pride is wounded or my feelings are hurt. It's not something I'm proud of, but I can empathize with Michal's foolish words.

Michal looked at David's worship and despised him. He wasn't acting the way she thought a king should act and she was likely embarrassed by him. Her focus was on the wrong place. Instead of joining in the people's praise to the Lord, instead of filling her heart and mind with things above, she was focused on what she saw as her husband's faults. It makes me look inside and wonder, how many hurtful words would have gone unsaid if my focus was pointing in the right direction?

Michal's story ends with the sad words, "Michal the daughter of Saul had no child to the day of her death." Was this because of the distance caused by a loveless relationship, or because the Lord wanted to be sure that we all knew the cost of mocking those who worship with their whole heart? What do you think?

David was willing to look like a fool for the Lord. There are many times when we are forced to look ridiculous for our faith. Sometimes, we even look down on our fellow believers for doing faith in a different way than us. I think the story of Michal is telling us to pay attention to where our focus is. The story would have been much different if Michal had entered into worship instead of dwelling in her pride.

QUESTIONS FOR DISCUSSION

★ What advice would you have given to Michal?

★ Have you ever said something you regret in a moment of anger or embarrassment?

* Have you ever been made to look foolish because of your faith?

* Have you ever held back from doing something God would approve of because of your own embarrassment?

Elijah

BREAD AND RESURRECTION

His eyes followed the thick walls of the city. Zarephath. A city of Sidon, near the great salty sea. A city of foreigners. He chewed his lower lip and felt a pang of homesickness. Why did the Lord send him here, to people who did not know the Lord?

Then again, it felt as if the Israelites did not know God either. That was why Elijah had stood before Ahab, the idol-worshiping king, and declared that there would be no rain or dew until Elijah said otherwise. Ahab and his wife Jezebel had laughed in his face and jeered at his back as he strode away.

For months now the drought had continued, and God still didn't return the rain to the land. Elijah doubted the king and queen were laughing now. He sniffed to himself. Let them pray to Baal, their pagan god of rain and prosperity! They would go unanswered. Let them worship at the Asherah poles. The false fertility goddess would give them nothing.

He could hear chatter as the people went out of the city gates in small groups to tend to fields, gardens, and herds.

It would be good to be among people again, even foreigners, he thought begrudgingly to himself. A man could only last so long with just his own voice for company.

He saw a stranger walk by, eating his meal as he went. The sight of fresh bread made Elijah's mouth water. Not that he had gone hungry. The Lord had provided for him in his hiding place by the brook. Ravens had come morning and evening, carrying bread and meat. Not fresh, not hot, but it kept him full. The Lord provided, though sometimes in strange ways!

Like now. When the brook had dried up the Lord had sent him here, to find a widow among a people that were not his own. Strange ways indeed. His eyes flicked over the little flocks of laughing women walking with their baskets and water jars. How would he know the right one?

He walked slowly, subtly examining every face. His attention was caught by a young woman who came out of the gate alone, head bowed as if the world rested on her shoulders. She had no happy companions with her. He moved closer and saw her face. Tears leaked down her thin cheeks. Though she was young, sorrow sunk her eyes into shadow. She followed the edge of a grove of trees, gathering up sticks.

The quiet voice inside told Elijah,

this one.

Elijah approached her, and she glanced up at him. Her eyes were wary, and she quickly brushed her cheek dry with her sleeve. "Peace be on you," he said.

Her face softened slightly. "And on you, traveler. I can tell by your accent that you are not from here. You're an Israelite, aren't you?"

"I am. From Gilead."

"I've heard stories of your people." Her head tilted as she considered him, her gaze thoughtful as she added, "And your God. Why are you here?"

Elijah smiled, but he simply said, "I have traveled far. Please, would you bring me a drink of water?"

The woman's cheeks lifted slightly into a sad smile, and her gaze seemed to look past him, perhaps to happier times. She whispered, "It has been far too long since I have had a guest to serve." She nodded, her eyes returning to Elijah. "Please, wait here. I will bring it."

As she stepped towards the city, he asked, "Please, can you bring me some bread too?"

The widow paused and slowly turned back to him. He saw the tears spring back to her shadowed eyes. "As the Lord your God lives," she said, "I have no bread, only a handful of flour and a little oil." The prophet was surprised that this foreign woman believed in the God of Israel. She held out her arms, making the dry sticks clatter. "I am gathering wood to bake the last loaf of bread for my son and me." Her features wavered as she said, "We shall eat it, and die."

Elijah's heart went out to her, his throat tight at the picture of the last meal of a widow and her child. She was on the brink of starvation. He had been told the widow would provide for him, but she was destitute! She could not feed herself, never mind a homeless prophet.

He searched his heart for God's will. God had said the widow would provide. So he spoke with confidence, "Don't be afraid. Go, bake your bread. But first, make me a little bread cake and bring it out to me." She bit her lip. He could see her desire to be a good hostess, yet this was her last meal, and he was a stranger.

Elijah saw another stick on the ground, picked it up, and handed it to her with an encouraging smile. "The Lord God of Israel has said, 'The bowl of flour shall not be exhausted, nor shall the jar of oil be empty, until the day that the Lord sends rain on the face of the earth'."

Her eyes opened wide. She wavered only a minute, but then nodded once and hastened into the city. Elijah wasn't sure, but he thought he had discerned a spark of hope in her eyes.

He waited for what felt like a long time. He began to think the widow had decided to ignore his request and his promise. Finally, he saw her coming out of town. A small boy followed on her heels, a thin child around four or five years old. The woman served Elijah first, handing him a small loaf and a jar of water. They sat together.

"Here, Kit," she said, and passed her son the bread. Elijah noticed she gave her son far more than she ate herself. Kit cradled the brown bread like it was a treasure. Elijah watched the boy eat the coarse barley loaf as if it was a honeyed wheat cake.

Elijah talked with the boy and was immediately taken with his cleverness and spirit. The mother watched the prophet and the child chat like old friends, and she smiled. When she finished her meal, she rose to her feet.

"Please, come be my guest in my home while you are here," she said. "If it is as you say, we shall all have food to eat." He saw her eyes glance to his belt, searching for a bag of coins. There were none. She creased her brow, but said nothing.

Elijah grinned at the little boy and ruffled his hair. "We shall eat fresh bread every day!" The boy laughed and jumped to his feet, believing the prophet with the simple faith of a child.

Elijah went with the widow and her son to their humble, two-story home. She gave the prophet the upper room, with a small window overlooking the sea. He took the opportunity to kneel in prayer to the Lord.

As the time for the evening meal approached, he heard her cry out in alarm. He raced down to the lower room, and saw her standing with the flour jar in her hands.

"It was empty this morning, I swear it!"

Kit ran to peer in the jar, then stared at Elijah with wide eyes. He held out an accusing finger. "He put it there!"

Elijah chuckled. "No, young man. God put it there."

Every day their jar of flour was filled, and the flask of oil never emptied. The widow kept asking if Elijah was sneakily replenishing the stores, but he only shook his head and answered, "The Lord has done it." She pursed her lips but did not argue.

Elijah found Kit to be a wonderful boy, and he spent many hours playing and talking with the fatherless child. This was a definite improvement from his days alone by the brook!

His heart felt light as he ducked under the doorway a few weeks later, and he called out a happy greeting.

Silence greeted him with cold heaviness.

He felt instantly that something was wrong. His pulse fluttered. His eyes darted across the room, and he saw the widow sitting in the shadows, cradling her son in her arms. Kit's lips were slack and blue. His hand hung loosely by his side. The widow sat with tears running down her face, silent agony in every line of her body.

Elijah felt as if all the air was sucked from the room, and his throat burned as tears rose into his eyes.

Kit was dead.

"Why?" she whispered. Her eyes seared him. "Why?!" she wailed, her voice shattering like broken pottery. "Why have you come here? Did you seek out a foreign widow, Man of God, so you could put my son to death?"

She began to shake with sobs. Elijah, hardly knowing what he was doing, rushed to her. He reached out his hands to take the child. She met his gaze, her eyes dark pools of pain. Her grip tightened for a moment, but then she relinquished the one she loved most into his arms. Elijah's heart broke for her. She had lost her husband. Must she lose her only son too?

Elijah carried the child to his room and laid the boy on his bed. He knelt beside the child and felt sorrow and confusion rise up in his chest. He raised his hands and cried aloud, "O Lord, my God! Would you bring this calamity on the poor widow who shelters your prophet, by causing her son to die?

He bowed forward, lying his head on the boy's chest, resting his hand on his forehead, and feeling sorrow and pain shoot through him like a spear. Three times he bowed over the child, and then he sobbed, "O Lord, My God, I pray to You, let this child's life return to him."

At once, Kit's chest rose, and his eyelids fluttered. Elijah sat back on his heels, his face breaking into a smile so wide it hurt his cheeks. Joy tumbled through his heart like the crash of the waves on the sea. He scooped up the child and raced down the steps.

He called out as he ran, "He's alive! See, he's alive!"

The mother cried out and leaped to her feet. She ran forward, taking her son into her arms. Her sobs of sorrow turned to tears of gratefulness. She kissed her son repeatedly until Kit complained and pulled away.

It was many minutes before she could speak, her voice thick with emotion. "Now I know that you are a man of God. The word of the Lord in your mouth, is truth."

Read this story for yourself in 1 Kings 17

STORY COMMENTS

This story always fascinated me. God provided not only for Elijah but for a Phoenician widow and her son as well. Why did God choose this widow in particular? We may never know. Perhaps it is because of the hint of belief we hear in her conversation with Elijah.

I would bet that the woman believed in the Lord all her life after this, and raised her son to believe in Him also. This story seems to be reminding the Jewish people that God wanted to bring all nations to Him, not just Israel.

We are powerfully reminded of this desire for all the nations again in Matthew 15:28. Jesus goes to Sidon, just like Elijah, and meets a woman who pleads for him to heal her daughter. She believed in him and even called him the Son of David—one of the few to honor Jesus that way in the gospel.

My imagination is stirred to think that perhaps the seeds Elijah planted in that widow's heart grew into a family that believed in Israel's God. A foreign family that longed for the Messiah just like the Israelites.

Questions for Discussion

* The widow stepped out in faith and shared her last meal with Elijah. All she had was the word of a stranger that there would be food for the next day. Would you have done the same?

* Has something been pressing on your heart, but you've been hesitant to give it up? Time, money, food, service, friendship—they are all valuable commodities that God loves to see us share.

* Have you ever seen faith from previous generations work in your life today?

* What legacy of faith do you hope to pass on to your descendants?

Elijah

FIRE AND RAIN

The sun shone starkly in the cloudless sky, marking midday. The orb beat down upon a strange scene unfolding on Mount Carmel. Undulating cries rose into the air. Rivulets of sweat tracked down dusty brows and soaked the tunics of the dancing, wailing, and pleading prophets. The teeming mass of pagan worshipers circled an altar and swayed like a wave of wind through the brittle grass.

Elijah crossed his arms and watched Ahab, King of Israel. The king stood with his feet spanned wide, his hands clasped behind his back, evoking a posture of confidence. A closer look showed his lips were pressed together and pale, and his eyes were lined with growing concern.

The gathered crowd observed closely. For them, this day would decide who they worshiped. Their feet shifted nervously on the rocky soil, and their eyes darted back and forth between the nine hundred and fifty prophets of Baal and Asherah, and the lone prophet of God, Elijah.

Elijah sighed with exasperation as he watched the sons of Israel. Their doubt was their downfall. Their worship of a bloodthirsty, pagan god of fertility had brought drought and famine on the whole land.

God had been clear, 'No other gods before Me.' Their idolatry could not go unanswered. God had spoken through Elijah, and at Elijah's word, the rain had ceased to fall for three, long, dusty years. Elijah frowned at the false prophets. Flies swarmed over their sacrificed ox. The blood had crusted and the edges of the meat were dry and shriveled from hours under the hot sun.

"Oh, Baal, answer us!" they cried hoarsely. "Send down your fire and show your power!"

Over and over they shouted and wailed. Elijah shook his head at them.

"Better speak up!" Elijah cupped his hands around his mouth and shouted, "He must be far away and can't hear you. I'll bet he's on a journey! Louder, louder!" One of the priests glared his way.

Elijah laughed at him and glanced to the young man beside him, his only ally. He spoke out the side of his mouth, "His temper is nearly hot enough to burn up the sacrifice, 'eh?"

The young man snorted behind his hand.

Still, the false prophets danced and leaped about, their feet kicking up dust that parched their throats.

Elijah crossed his arms and leaned on one leg. He called again, "Maybe Baal is napping. You need to wake him up!" An idea struck him as funny, and he jeered, "Maybe he's on his way, but stepped aside to relieve himself!"

The prophets became even more frenzied, shouting to drown out Elijah's sarcasm. One pulled a knife from his belt and slashed his own skin before passing the blade to those next to him. Soon the dirt was splattered with droplets of blood.

The afternoon passed. One by one the false prophets began collapsing with exhaustion and the heat. The sons of Israel had long quit standing. They sat on the coarse ground, watching grimly. Ahab's face was purple with anger, but he said nothing. Elijah nodded to himself. The point was made.

"Enough!" Elijah shouted, and the dozen remaining prophets quit their choked cries and feeble dance. Their bodies were caked in sweat, dust, and blood. Elijah's lip curled. Fools, the lot of them. He swept his gaze over the people. "Gather near!" he called to them, and they rose to their feet and came closer.

Under the eyes of the sons of Israel, Elijah reassembled the altar to the Lord that had been torn down. He lifted the last, heavy rock, and it settled with a satisfying clunk. He stepped back, dusting off his hands, and cast his eyes over the crowd. After today, there would be no doubt. "Let's dig a trench," Elijah said to the young man near him. Together the men dug until they had encircled the low altar while the people murmured to one another.

"Bring the ox," he commanded his servant, and the young man led the beast up the mount. Elijah slaughtered it and arranged the wood and meat on the altar. Sticky blood coated his arms. He glanced at the altar of Baal, buzzing with flies.

He scanned the sons of Israel, who waited to see what would happen. His eyes landed on their weak king, the petulant monarch who did whatever his pagan wife wished. Elijah's stomach tightened. He couldn't let the people continue their headlong tumble into sin. They had to know who was the true God, the One that deserved their worship. Three years of drought had not been enough. He nodded once to himself. Today, they would believe.

Elijah looked at the people and pointed at a handful men. "Bring four large jugs of water." The remnant of a river was nearby. Elijah waited until the four men returned. Elijah gestured to the sacrifice and the wood and commanded, "Pour it on." Raising brows, the men obeyed. Elijah nodded. "Again."

He sent the men back twice more until the wood was soaked and the trench was filled with water. Then the men set down their water jugs, doubt on every face.

"You will want to step back," Elijah said to the men with the jugs, the corner of his mouth teasing upwards. They glanced at his face, and then quickly scampered to stand with the rest of the gathered crowd.

Elijah surveyed the drenched altar, then spread out his red-stained hands and lifted up his voice so all could hear his prayer. "O Lord, God of Abraham, Isaac, and Israel, today let it be known that You are God in Israel. Let these people know that I am Your servant, and have only done what You have asked of me." He closed his eyes and drew a deep breath through his nose. His heart beat wildly in his chest. "Answer me, O Lord! Answer me, that these people may know that You are Lord and that You have taken their heart back again."

A roar filled the air. Elijah's hair was blown back with heat and wind. He opened his eyes and saw a ball of fire had fallen from the sky and landed on the altar. His skin tingled with the heat, and an exultant grin spread on his face as the fire consumed the water soaked offering, the wood, and even the stones on which the meat had laid. His heart cried out, Yes, God, You are worthy of our worship!

The crowd fell on their faces in fear and worship. Their voices rose together as they cried out praise and repentance.

The sacrifice consumed, Elijah turned his gaze on the cowering prophets of Baal and Asherah. There was no hint of amusement or humor in his voice as he shouted, "Seize them! Don't let any of them escape!"

The prophets turned to Ahab and pleaded with him, but the sons of Israel, blazing with zeal, rushed past their helpless king and captured every false prophet. Elijah led the way and the people followed him down to the river, dragging the prophets of Baal and Asherah. He had every pagan prophet put to death. He felt no remorse for the cruel men who commanded the sacrifice of children in exchange for rain and crops.

The sons of Israel went back to their homes, talking eagerly about what they had seen on the mountain. Elijah knelt and washed in the sluggish river. The ripples beneath his arms turned red.

Shaking the droplets from his hands, Elijah looked at Ahab. The king was standing near his chariots and servants, staring at the ruin of his wife's cult. He was probably afraid to go home.

Elijah strode over, crossed his arms, and said, "Better go eat something, I hear the sound of rain." Ahab's eyes flicked to his. Three years ago Elijah had stood before Ahab and Jezebel and promised there would be no rain or dew until he said so. And it had happened as he said. Ahab nodded once and walked grimly away.

Elijah called his servant and strode back up the mountain. Dusk was falling, but the air smelled cool and fresh. He almost didn't recognize the scent of rain.

Elijah was bone-tired. He slumped to the ground, bent his knees, and rested his brow on them, his back aching from butchering the oxen and lifting the heavy stones. "Go," he said, his voice slightly muffled. "Look over to the sea."

"There's nothing," was the reply.

"Go look again," Elijah said. The reply was the same, but Elijah kept sending him. The seventh time the young man ran back eagerly.

"I saw a cloud as big as my fist coming up from the sea."

Elijah chuckled. "Better go warn the king. Tell him to take his chariot at once, or the storm will overtake him."

The young man hurried to obey, and Elijah rose to his feet. He felt the wind strike his face, and it was damp and sweet. He breathed it in deeply. Dark clouds gathered, and a grey sheet fell across the land, moving towards him with a roar.

Rain, blessed rain!

He had missed the sound of it! He pictured the streams laughing with tumbling joy as they were filled, and the grasses and trees lifting up their leaves to praise the Lord. Joy for the power of God rose up in his heart, and Elijah laughed and laughed.

The rain swept closer. He belted up his tunic and raced down the hill, his feet as swift and light as the wings of an eagle.

He felt as though God's own hand was on him; he had never run like this in his life! He flew past Ahab's astonished servants. He soon caught up to Ahab himself, who leaned forward, snapping the reins of his horses, driving them faster and faster, his robes flapping behind him.

Elijah passed the king and laughed as Ahab cried out in shock.

"I'll see you at Jezreel!" Elijah teased over his shoulder, and he ran the miles in the power of the Lord of Israel.

Read this story for yourself in 1 Kings 18:19-46

STORY COMMENTS

Elijah seems almost wild, doesn't he? As the only remaining prophet of the Lord in a land corrupted by idol worship, he faithfully carries out God's plan—with his own humor and a good touch of sass.

Sometimes when we read the Bible, we can miss the humor and individual personalities, and form a mistaken idea that the men and women lost their individuality in serving God. This idea can make us believe that we don't have the right personality to serve the Lord. We forget that God called people who enjoyed jokes, had interests, hobbies, skills, and flaws—just like us! Elijah is a prime example of how God uses all kinds of people, big personalities and all!

QUESTIONS FOR DISCUSSION

* Read Exodus 20:3. When God laid out the ten commandments, what topped His list? Why?

* What does idol worship look like in the world today?

* Do you ever feel that you don't fit the model of a Christian? Why?

* What do you think God looks for when He calls people to serve and act for Him?

Elijah

FAILED MINISTRY

His sandal caught on a rock, and he stumbled, scuffing his toes and drawing blood. He cried out in frustration, "Why does everything have to be so hard?"

He limped to the shade of a juniper tree and threw himself down on the dirt. His head ached and his stomach was sour.

God had answered his prayer just a few short weeks ago and had sent down blazing fire to the altar, showing the people that God, not Baal, was the one true God. Elijah's heart had leaped with joy, hoping that this was the beginning of change. That joy had been short-lived.

Sulky, weak-minded King Ahab had gone home to his powerful wife, Jezebel, and tattled on Elijah as if they were boys who had scrapped in the market.

One of Jezebel's men had sought out Elijah and told him the heavy news: Jezebel absolutely refused to believe that it was Elijah's God who had returned the rain. From her throne, her eyes flashing, the queen had declared that the deaths of Baal's prophets had soothed the fertility god's wrath. Baal had ended the three-year drought. Baal, not the Hebrew God, had sent the rain. From between bared teeth she had sworn to kill Elijah before the next day ended.

Elijah had heard the messenger with a sinking heart. He fled with his servant, running south to hide in the land of Judah.

He had left his servant in Beersheba. He would be safe enough there, and honestly, Elijah needed to get away from him. Elijah could not bear how the young man looked at him. His gaze was warm with trust that Elijah could do anything.

Elijah scoffed to himself as he rubbed his wounded toes. Elijah could do nothing. Nothing! No matter what he did, Jezebel and Ahab hardened their hearts and kept leading the people to ruin. Elijah might as well be speaking to the wind for all the good it did!

Elijah, sitting in the earthy scent of dirt, felt his chest tighten until he was forced to yell or suffocate. A cry ripped from his throat, sharpened with anger, rough with bitterness, and rising at the end with anguish.

"Just let me die, Lord!" he pleaded, covering his face. "I can't do it!"

Tears burned in his eyes, hot and salty. They trickled down his cheeks, but he let them fall. He was a failure, an utter failure. What use could God have for him?

At last, exhausted, he found comfort in sleep, still lying beneath the tree.

He felt a hand gently shake his shoulder. A calm voice spoke, "Arise, eat."

Elijah sluggishly lifted his head. It was dark now, but the ground was still warm, so it was not long past dusk. There was a ruddy glow before him. He scrubbed a hand over his eyes and saw a cluster of hot stones. His first thought was that his determined servant had found him, but he looked around and saw no one. Sitting up, he saw a bread cake was baking on the stones. It smelled like manna from heaven! He took it, juggling the hot cake between his hands until it had cooled slightly. He ate it all, his stomach calming. As his belly filled, drowsiness stole back over him.

When had he last eaten? He wondered dully. He had been too full of fear for his life to pause for such a common need as food.

There was a jug of water nearby. Without pausing to wonder at its mysterious appearance, Elijah quaffed several swallows then fell back to the ground. Sleep dragging him under like an anchor in the sea.

Again, he felt a gentle shake rouse him from his dark dreams. This time, he opened his eyes at once and saw a stranger before him in the pale rosy light of dawn. Elijah knew, somehow, this was a messenger of the Lord.

The angel said, "Arise, eat, for the journey is too great for you."

Elijah swallowed hard, feeling bitterness at the back of his throat. Too great? His job was impossible! He would teach a mountain to fly before he convinced Ahab and Jezebel to repent! His failures sat on him like a fever, dulling his mind.

He opened his mouth to demand why God was bothering with him. Surely this angel could do God's will much better than an aging prophet. Before he could speak, the messenger of the Lord left. Elijah sighed.

Elijah found another bread cake hot on the stones, and the jug of water was refilled. Despite everything, God had brought him breakfast. Elijah ate and drank. As the good, sweet loaf settled in his belly, he felt an overwhelming urge to go to Horeb, the mountain of the Lord. He needed to know. Why did God continue to provide for the failed prophet?

He decided the bread given to him by the Lord must have been blessed. On its sustenance, he walked forty days to the mountain. He avoided people, skirting around villages, farms, and towns. If he couldn't avoid someone, he wrapped his mantel over his head and strode with the hunched pose of someone who wished to be left alone. Jezebel surely had men out hunting for him. He tramped steadily with only frustration, self-pity, and bitterness for his companions.

He arrived at the foot of Mount Horeb at last. Long ago, the prophet Moses had met God on this mountain. Elijah twisted up his mouth. Moses had certainly enjoyed better results with his mission than Elijah. He was still not entirely sure why he was driven to come to this craggy mountain with two peaks. All he knew was he needed answers. Didn't he deserve answers?

He climbed the mountain until he found a cave. He threw himself down inside the cool, comfortless cavern. It smelled stale. Stale like Elijah's abilities. Perhaps he should stay here for the rest of his days, he thought sullenly. If the Lord did not choose to feed him by ravens, widows, or angels as he had before, he could just lie down and starve.

The sun tracked across the sky, but Elijah stayed in his gloomy cave and did nothing. As the hard ground made his backside ache, and hunger grew in his stomach for the first time in a month, his bitterness turned to anger. Like a hot coal in his chest, his anger burned hotter and hotter. He needed to know what the point of it all was!

At last, the Lord spoke to him.

What are you doing here, Elijah?

Elijah, swamped by a barrage of pained emotions, cried out, his words tumbling one over the other, "I have given everything for You, Lord! The sons of Israel have torn down Your altars and killed Your prophets. I alone am left, yet they seek to kill me too."

The voice spoke again, but this time it radiated with authority.

Go forth, and stand on the mountain before the Lord.

Fear spiked through Elijah, and instead of obeying, he drew back from the mouth of the cave in terror. Regret for his accusatory words struck him like a blow. He trembled head to toe. The Lord was coming!

A howling wind began to blow past the mouth of the cave, creating an avalanche of thundering boulders, but the Lord was not in the wind.

The earth began to shake beneath his feet, rocks rending with ear-splitting cracks, and threatening to collapse the cave, but the Lord was not in the earthquake.

Brilliantly white fire shot past the mouth of the cave; the heat blazing over Elijah as he threw his hands before his face and cried out for mercy. Yet, the Lord was not in the fire.

The heat left, and all Elijah heard was the whisper of a gentle breath. Sweat broke out on his brow and he felt his stomach turn to water. He knew that the Lord was here. He couldn't look on the Lord, the host of hosts, the creator of the universe, the master of all! How had he forgotten the great authority behind his words? How had he gotten so twisted around to believe that it was his own deeds that would make the difference?

The Lord waited.

Elijah wrapped his mantle around his head, covering his face. He dragged his hands along the wall of the cavern until he found the entrance.

The voice demanded, *What are you doing here, Elijah?*

Elijah opened his mouth and said the same words he had before, but they were not angry, nor accusatory. The reminder of God's power had burned away his self-pride. He was just a man. If he did as the Lord commanded, that was enough. It wasn't up to him to win over the people's hearts. It wasn't his job to bring Israel back to the Lord. That was God's job. He was only the messenger. Yet his heart turned over with sorrow, and as he repeated himself, it was a plea for help.

"I have given everything for the Lord. The sons of Israel have torn down Your altars and killed Your prophets. I alone am left, yet they seek to kill me too."

There was a moment of silence, then the voice came softly.

Go, back through the wilderness to Damascus. I want you to anoint Hazael king over Aram; and Jehu king over Israel, and Elisha the son of Shaphet you shall anoint as prophet in your place. The one who escapes the sword of Hazael, Jehu will put to death. The one who escapes Jehu, Elisha will put to death. Yet, I will leave seven thousand in Israel, all the knees that have not bowed to Baal, and every mouth that has not kissed him.

The Lord departed.

Elijah did as he was told, and set out at once. As he strode back the way he had come, he felt like a different creature. He walked straight-backed, his mantle thrown over his shoulder. He was a wanted man in a world gone crazy, but the Lord had a plan. Elijah drew a deep breath and let thoughts of himself blow away in the breeze.

He wondered about this 'Elisha' God had mentioned. What would he be like? It would be good to have another prophet to work with him! Hopefully, the man wasn't a crazy old fool like someone he knew all too well. For the first time in over a month, a smile split Elijah's face, and a chuckle rumbled from his chest.

Read this story for yourself in 1 Kings 19

STORY COMMENTS

I don't know about you, but I have definitely fallen into the trap of believing that my actions or words are what matter. I pray and pray for some good thing, and yet get a no. I speak up and share my faith, and yet nothing changes. I start to feel like a failure. I forget my job isn't to save, but to follow in faith, and share the good news.

Ahab watched as Elijah prayed and a firebolt shot down from heaven that burned not only the sacrifice but the rocks too! It wasn't proof enough for stubborn Ahab. If a show of God's power wasn't proof enough, isn't it beyond silliness to think that our words or deeds will make the greater impact? We sometimes need a reminder, like Elijah, that God is the one with all the power.

The story mentions seven thousand who did not worship Baal. Elijah was so focused on the fact that the king and queen refused to repent, that he forgot about the thousands who were faithful! People who would listen and heed the word of the Lord. People his words had encouraged and taught.

We can't always see the fruit of our labors. So isn't it better to trust and obey and let God sort out the rest?

QUESTIONS FOR DISCUSSION

* Why do you think God picks flawed humans to carry His message instead of always sending angels?

* Do you believe God can use you?

* Atheists refuse to believe in God, declaring there is no proof that He exists. The people of Israel witnessed a startling miracle from heaven, yet only a fraction of them believed. Why?

* Do you ever feel like your own ministry is failing? What do you do?

* How can we encourage one another to keep serving God even when things look bleak?

Gomer

Unfaithful Wife

"You said you loved me!" she cried out, twisting in his iron grip. He grabbed a fistful of her hair and dragged her the last few feet to the slave-traders block.

What she could see of his face was coldly angry, his beautiful features transformed into a cruel, unfeeling mask. She painfully remembered the tender caresses, the sweet whispers of promise, the delight of new gifts, and the feeling of his fingers intertwined with hers as they ran laughing from her husband's home.

She had left her younger two with her eldest son, a boy of ten. Hosea must have been surprised to return home and find her gone. A flick of guilt touched her heart. She hadn't even left the children with a scrap of bread in the house. She had no thought for them when her lover had appeared in his luxurious clothing, smelling of sweet oils. He had promised her a life far from drudgery and hard work. Like a trapped bird, she had burst from her cage.

"You were meant for more than this," he had whispered, putting a bracelet on her arm. "Come away with me, and I will treat you as you deserve."

Now her lover was impassive to her plight and tired of her. Not content with simply turning her out of his home, he was determined to make a profit. He had dragged her from her bed, through town, and to the auction block. He cast her down, and her knees jarred on the wood.

He spoke to the slave-trader. "I have one for sale, a seasoned harlot."

The man glanced her over with a curled lip. "She doesn't look like much."

Gomer's head dropped in humiliation, and hot tears burned the fresh cut on her cheek.

Her lover laughed. "She's well enough, take a look for yourself."

She cried out as he grabbed her thin garment at the neck and ripped the robe from her back. She begged for mercy as he heaved her, naked, to her feet. The crowd laughed at her. There was a time when she could have undressed boldly before a room of men with a wink and a seductive smirk. No longer.

"She's too old!" one shouted.

"She's obviously suckled babies!" another jeered, and Gomer squirmed and pleaded, trying to cover herself with her hands. All she got was a switch against her backside and a command to stand still.

"How much for this one?" the slave trader called over the taunts. "If you don't want her for your bed, send her to your fields!"

Gomer fearfully scanned the hard faces, wondering who would take her, and what toil and suffering she had ahead of her.

"I will give fifteen shekels of silver, and a homer and a half of barley," a voice called over the crowd.

Gomer gasped. She knew that voice. As men laughed at the ridiculous price for a used-up whore, her eyes flicked over them until they landed on the face she knew.

"Hosea," she whispered in disbelief, tears starting afresh.

Relief, joy, guilt, shame, and fear tumbled through her as the slave trader quickly called out, "Sold!"

Gomer felt her arms released, and she dropped to the ground gathering the tatters of her clothes around her. She watched with wide eyes as Hosea came forward, and paid the price to the same man who had tempted his wife away from her hearth. Hosea looked at her, and she automatically recoiled in fear before realizing there was no hatred on his face. Was that tenderness in his eyes? It couldn't be!

"Let's go home," he said quietly, and turned away from the slave market. Gomer gulped back the tears that refused to cease, and hastened after him without a backward glance for her former lover.

This was the second time Hosea had taken her home. The first time he had come to the whore-house and chose her out of all the girls. She had never understood why he wanted a harlot for a wife. She had been content for a time with the home and the children—until boredom and dissatisfaction had crept in. She had chaffed beneath household responsibilities, looking longingly back on the days when she had laid on cushions and been plied with wine and coins in exchange for her body. Time had distorted her memories as she swept and sewed until the blessings of home seemed stale and oppressive.

She looked on Hosea's broad back as he led her home. The man was a prophet of God. Why did he care for his adulteress, harlot of a wife? Why had he rescued her from slavery after all she had done to hurt him?

He glanced back and saw her limping in her bare feet. With love and compassion in his gaze, he swept her up into his arms and carried her home.

Read this story for yourself in Hosea 1-3

STORY COMMENTS

The story of Gomer is much more than it appears. In it, we see our own weaknesses and our need for rescue.

We learned the idea of being redeemed in the story of Ruth. The God-fearing widow is redeemed by Boaz and finds a home, a people, and hope for the future.

Gomer is not so lovable. She is a prostitute before her marriage to Hosea and ends up running back to her old life by taking up with another man. What were you thinking, Gomer?

And poor Hosea! God tells him to marry a prostitute, and then he is told to go and love his adulteress wife! Why would God ask him to do that?

"For the land commits flagrant harlotry, forsaking the Lord." - Hosea 1:2

The people were not interested in following God, and they ran after idols who gave them the lifestyle they thought they wanted. God was using Hosea and his cheating wife as a truth-teaching story.

Chapter two of Hosea speaks of the unfaithful wife who ran after her lovers thinking it was they who blessed her with bread and water, wool and flax, oil and drink. God says,

> "She does not know that it was I who gave her the grain, the new wine and the oil, and lavished on her silver and gold, which she used for Baal. Therefore I will take back My grain at harvest time, and My new wine in its season, and I will also take away My wool and My flax given to cover her nakedness ... and I will put an end to all her gaiety ... I will destroy her vines and fig trees of which she said, 'These are my wages which my lovers have given me' ... I will punish her for the days of the Baals when she used to offer sacrifices to them."

This story is about more than Gomer, for she represents God's people. We want all the blessings of God while playing the adulteress with the world.

So does God take away Israel's blessings simply for revenge and retribution?

No! The rest of chapter two speaks of God's heart for His people.

> "I will allure her, bring her into the wilderness and speak kindly to her. Then I will give her vineyards ... she will sing there as in the days of her youth ... as in the day when she came up from the land of Egypt ... and I will abolish the bow, the sword, and war from the land ... I will betroth you to Me forever ... Yes, I will betroth you to Me in righteousness and in justice, in lovingkindness and in compassion, and I will betroth you to Me in faithfulness ... I will say to those people who were not My people, 'You are My people!' and they will say, 'You are my God!'"

When we look around and consider judgment and suffering, we need to keep this picture of Gomer and Hosea in our minds, because this is the story God wanted the people of Israel to keep in their heads as they ran laughing into destruction, declaring God was a myth and that they knew better.

I want to be clear here, that I do not think that all suffering is because the person deserves it. Innocent people suffer daily, and they have done nothing to warrant it. (John 9:1-3) God will see the wrongs made right someday, I am confident of this. (Revelations 21:4) I also don't believe God tricks us or tempts us to sin. We listen to the deceiver and run into sin all on our own. (1 James 3:13-14).

We see that in history God used suffering to bring His people back to Him. We see it over and over again after the exodus from Egypt. Perhaps when our lives fall apart, it is a time for us to grow closer to Him.

QUESTIONS FOR DISCUSSION

* Can suffering ever lead to good?

* Is it an oxymoron to speak of the God of Love causing suffering?

* Why do people want to deny that it is God who gives us blessings?

* Why do we turn to the world for our joy instead of God?

* When Hosea comes for Gomer, does she feel that she deserves his rescue?

* How should we feel when God forgives us for all of our wrong-doings?

Jonah

MERCY FOR NINEVEH

His lip curled as he paused outside the city gates, staring at the images that flanked the wide opening. They were disgusting—men's heads atop winged bulls. An unnatural and idolatrous image that showed the depravity of a nation who did not know the true God. His feet planted wide in defiance, Jonah glared at the city as he was jostled by the noisy crowds that pushed their way forward with their heavy carts loaded for trade.

A patrol of soldiers marched by wearing short, scarlet tunics, iron swords belted at their hips, and cypress wood spears in their fists. Their shields were painted red. The color of blood. The soldiers glanced at Jonah, seeming to sense the loathing rising out of him like steam from a pot. A quick glance up and down showed them they had nothing to fear. The prophet was dusty and thin from travel, his sandals badly patched and his traveling bag flat and empty. It had been a long trek from the coast of the Mediterranean to Nineveh's gate, around five hundred miles of dusty roads. He had plenty of time to regret his reckless and failed flight to Tarshish, and more than enough time to practice the message he was about to deliver.

"Are you sure this is what you want, Lord?" Jonah murmured. God didn't answer, but Jonah could almost feel the Lord's displeasure at

Jonah's continued resistance. The message hadn't changed.

Arise, go to Nineveh the great city and cry against it, for their wickedness has come up before me.

Jonah breathed deep through his nose and instantly regretted it as the stench of the overfilled city gagged him. Grunting, he lifted a heavy foot and walked through the gateway in the fortified walls.

He followed the crowded road and passed the inns. Women hung out of the windows, flashing skin and waving coyly at the weary travelers below. Jonah snarled at them,

"The Lord has heard of your wickedness, and He shall reveal your disgrace to the world! In forty days, Nineveh will be overthrown!"

The women paused at his words, but he didn't stay. He marched deeper into the city of sin. The road led him into the market. The crack of whips and the wail of men made his blood boil. The callous citizens of Nineveh strolled by the slave traders without care, blind to the plight of those who were being sold to the highest bidder.

He cringed at the sight of the wide-eyed children being held back as their mother was shoved to the front of the crowd. These people were the spoils of war, captured by the vast Assyrian army with their chariots and cavalry—the greatest, most brutal army in the world.

Jonah glanced around, his pulse pounding in his veins. He saw a wagon being unloaded and leaped onto the back, raising his voice above the clamor. People turned to look at him.

"You wicked and cruel people! The Lord, the God of Israel has seen your depravity! He has heard the cries of your victims and the cracks of your whips! The Lord will come upon you and in forty days, this city will be no more!"

He expected jeers, but instead, he saw mingled curiosity and even a touch of worry. He railed on them for an hour, hurling words like arrows and insults like spears. He expected any minute that the scarlet soldiers would march up and arrest him, but they didn't come. He almost wished they would. At last, his throat hoarse, he leaped off the wagon and shouldered his way deeper into the city.

The stone houses he strode by were rectangular and made of stone. There were no windows, and their roofs were flat and covered with earth. Jonah grunted. They were virtually fireproof, an important feature in a crowded city, but he trusted that God would see every one knocked to the ground. He stomped by women on their way to the well, boys playing in the streets, men with their long beards and tall hats striding by in business.

He cried out as he walked, "Forty days and all of Nineveh will be overthrown!"

He came to one of the seven temples dedicated to Ishtar, where people were lining up to bring their offerings of animals, trinkets, and money. The air was thick with the scent of smoke and perfume. He trudged up the wide steps, ignoring the glares of the priests as he blasted the people who brought tribute to gods of stone and clay.

"The Lord will cut down your idols and your images! In the houses of your gods, He will prepare your graves!" The supplicants stared at him as he lashed out at Ashur and Ishtar, Nabu, Sumnuah, Marduk, and all the other fickle gods that the Assyrians believed controlled love, war, harvest, and learning. Again Jonah expected someone to rise up and hustle him away, but no one stopped him as he prophesied their imminent doom.

Jonah continued his march through the city until he had rained down words like brimstone on every market and the steps of every temple.

He slept in the streets and ate little, refusing to find comfort within the walls of this city—the city that sent out its people into the world with its lies of idolatry and love of wealth and war. Jonah had seen their influence among his own people, and how his countrymen admired the brilliance of the greatest civilization the world had ever known. Yet, under that brilliance, Jonah knew the Assyrians were walking corpses, spewing uncleanliness and death on everyone they touched.

Jonah was surprised that the people stopped and listened to him. He began to see men appearing in sackcloth.

On the third day, Jonah was shocked to hear the king's messengers on every street corner calling out, "Your king and his nobles have decreed that no man, beast, herd, or flock may taste a thing. Do not let them eat or drink water. Both men and beast must be covered in sackcloth, and let men call on God earnestly that each may turn from his wicked way and from the violence which is in his hands."

Jonah saw it and was worried. Surely God wouldn't be swayed by this last minute change of heart, would He? And sackcloth on their animals? These people were ignorant of anything to do with the God of Israel, foolish and knowing nothing about true obedience.

Yet, he felt something had changed in the city, something beyond the fact that traders were not funneling through the gates. Something louder than the bleating of hungry flocks of sheep and lows of confused cattle.

I have relented concerning the calamity I declared. I will not do it.

Jonah felt all the air being sucked from his lungs, quickly replaced by a burning sense of injustice. He turned in a slow circle on the street, glaring at everything he saw.

"How can you spare them? How can you forgive them?" All the emotions he had felt as he boarded the boat in Joppa flooded back. "Isn't this what I said while I was still in my own country? I tried to avoid this by fleeing to Tarshish!" Bitterness tightened his heart. "I knew You are a gracious and compassionate God, slow to anger and abundant in lovingkindness, and one who relents concerning calamity."

He felt rather than heard God ask Him why he rejoiced over compassion for Israel but felt only loathing when God showed it to other nations.

Jonah didn't want to hear it. He tipped back his head and roared at the sky, "O, Lord, please take my life from me, death is better than this life!"

Do you have good reason to be angry?

Jonah gritted his teeth. He had every reason! Why had God sent him here? He didn't want to be the tool of forgiveness for Assyria, he wanted to be the herald of their end. They deserved death for all they had done! They were a stinking refuse pile of the worst of humanity, sending their putrid rot down the streams of the world and contaminating it with their disease, reaching even into the hearts and homes of Israel. They needed to be wiped out for the good of his people!

At last, Jonah made it through the city. He took himself to the east and fashioned a shelter. He wanted to stay and witness the calamity that would rain down on Nineveh. This surface repentance wouldn't last, and then God would give them what they deserved. Would it be fire and brimstone like Sodom and Gomorrah? Would it be plagues like Egypt? Would the city crumble like the walls of Jericho?

He sat outside his meager shelter. It did little to protect him from the heat of the sun.

One morning when he unrolled himself from his cloak and went to his usual sitting place, he saw a leafy plant had shot out of the ground overnight. He smiled, pleased, and sat in the shade, enjoying its shelter as he pictured all the ways Nineveh might be destroyed. The next morning, however, the plant shriveled, and Jonah grumbled. A hot wind blew in from the east, and the sun beat on his head. His head pounded with a headache and he felt nauseated, too ill to even go for water. Why had God brought him here? To kill him instead of Nineveh?

"Oh, just let me die!"

Do you have a good reason to be angry about the plant?

"Yes! Enough to die."

You had compassion on the plant for which you did not work and which you did not cause to grow, which came up overnight and perished overnight. Should I not have compassion on Nineveh, the great city of one-hundred-twenty-thousand people who don't even know the difference between their right hand and their left?

Read this story for yourself in Jonah

STORY COMMENTS

Why was Jonah so hard-hearted against Nineveh? Nineveh was a great city in the superpower of Jonah's day, Assyria. At least at one point, Nineveh was the capital city of this country of wealth and influence. Assyria did not believe in God, and this country was intent on expanding its borders through war, trade, and their own culture— putting smaller countries like Israel at risk of being taken over by assimilation or force.

We know from the Bible that the gods of Assyria had infiltrated Israel. Ishtar was the Assyrian goddess of love and war. In Canaan she was called Ashtoreth, Ashtaroth, or Asherah, and she was often depicted as the consort of Baal, though her depictions change throughout generations.

* As Ashtoreth, the goddess of Assyria is a huge stumbling block for the Hebrews.

* Not long after taking the promised land, the Hebrews began chasing other gods including the Baals and the Ashtaroth. (Judges 10:6)

★ Solomon turned away from following only God and turned to other gods, including Ashtoreth. (1 Kings 11:5)

★ In a great show-down where the prophet Elijah proves who is the real God with fire and rain from heaven, we see the four-hundred-and-fifty prophets of Baal bested. We also hear mentioned four-hundred prophets of Asherah. (1 Kings 18:19)

Every time the people turn away from following God, God has to do something to turn them back to Him. He lets them be taken as captives, or they lose battles, or they have drought and poverty. In the case of Solomon's idolatry, soon after the king's death, the united country of Israel splits in two, and a once united people of a great country are now splintered and depleted.

No doubt, Jonah does not want his people to suffer similar fates because of Nineveh. He wants to snuff out the source of idol worship and corruption to protect his own people. We can get that. We try to protect our own loved ones from bad influences that might harm them.

However, God seems to have a plan beyond the borders of Israel. In a stunning show of compassion, God sees the repentance of Nineveh and forgives them. Though Nineveh eventually falls to Babylon in later years, this generation in Jonah's day is allowed to live. If they had continued on their path of repentance and changed their ways, perhaps Nineveh would never have fallen.

The story of Jonah ends with a question. I think this so that the reader pauses to ask themselves the same question. We are eager to accept good things from God for ourselves and our loved ones, but we have less compassion for those who are cruel and corrupt. We might say it is natural to despise the vile people of society, but as we see in the story of Jonah, forgiveness is given to *all* who truly repent and ask for forgiveness, no matter what they did before. This is a hard teaching for those who have suffered at the hands of evil. We see it in the anger of the prodigal son's brother in Luke 15:11-32.

Yet, Jesus reinforced the road of compassion in his teachings to love our enemies and to pray for those who hurt us. (Matthew 5:43-47) He showed it in his forgiveness and acceptance of those that society thought unlovable, and in his healing of those outside the Jewish people, and in his message of forgiveness on the cross. (Luke 23:34)

This compassion makes an impact on the early church, as we can see when Stephen emulates Jesus during his own death. (Acts 7:60)

Questions for Discussion

* What do you think about the ending of Jonah's story? Did this surly prophet find compassion for Nineveh, or did he go home with bitterness and hatred in his heart?

* Are there some people who don't deserve forgiveness?

* Have you ever had to forgive someone who has done something truly awful?

* Have you ever experienced forgiveness?

The Exile

JUDGMENT FOR JUDAH

Can stone burn? It seems as if it could. Billowing black smoke was choking out the air, obscuring the great building. Teran coughed and squinted blurry eyes, trying to find his father. Fear clutched his young heart as he called, "Papa! Papa!"

When the trumpet sounded, his papa had rushed to the temple with the other men determined to keep the Babylonians out of the holy building. It didn't seem like it had worked. Teran had escaped his mother's clawing hands and had ran down the clogged streets to the courtyard where the great temple stood. The towering building was engulfed in flames that licked up the sides and rose to the heavens, trying to scorch the sky.

A few dozen priests feebly battled the seasoned warriors, but even a young boy like Teran could see they were losing. They were half-starved from the siege, and it was too late anyway. Too late to save the temple. Too late to save Jerusalem. Maybe too late to save their lives.

Teran darted around the courtyard searching for his father. The smell of smoke and blood burned his nose. Bodies lay everywhere, but he didn't look at them. His father would not be one of them. Hopelessness began to rise as he ran and ran without seeing the comforting frame of his papa.

Sick with smoke and worry, he stumbled to a stop. Panting, his gaze was dragged towards the roaring, crackling flames.

He was right before the temple, staring into a blazing furnace. The doors, already stripped of their gold veneer years before, were cracked and charred. Though the house of the Lord burned now, it had been pillaged years before, the golden articles stolen from the nave and the treasury. Still, to the young boy it felt as if the ancient temple was Jerusalem. If it was lost, so were they all.

The heat licked his face, but he couldn't seem to look away. He stood transfixed as the flames ate away the cedar lining of the house of the Lord. His boyish mind struggled for understanding. Shouldn't God put it out? It was His house after all. Maybe He needed water. The Great Bronze Sea was to the side, dark with patina that no one had polished away for long years. It was full of water, or at least it was supposed to be. Did anyone remember to fill it? His father sighed that the temple services were but a parody of the days of glory long ago. Bitter at the loss, he had taught Teran how things were supposed to be.

The lessons didn't matter now, Teran realized with a heavy feeling. The temple was gone. There would be no worship, no sacrifices, and no atonement.

He swallowed hard as one of the massive doors broke off its hinge and fell in a blaze to the ground. For one, terrifying moment he saw straight through the temple to where the smaller doors had been left open to the inner sanctuary, the Holy of Holies. He couldn't breathe. No one was supposed to see in there. No one but the priest could look, or they might be struck dead. His eyes smarted from the smoke but he couldn't blink or turn away. The golden chains were broken. He could see the massive cherubim. Their outspread wings were wreathed in brilliant red flames, melting gold dripped down like tears. The corners of his vision grew dim.

With a jolt that felt like someone was pulling his stomach through his feet, he was spun around.

"Teran! What are you doing here?"

He looked up into the face of his father. There was blood dripping from a gash under his father's eye. He stared at it, unable to look away.

"Teran!" his father gave him a shake and his teeth rattled in his head. He blinked rapidly. His papa was alive! He choked back a sob as he jumped into his father's arms.

"You're okay!" he gasped, wrapping his arms around his father's neck.

"Yes, but we can't stay here. We have to get your mother and sisters. The city has fallen, my son."

Teran squeezed harder. Would they all be killed, abandoned here like the bodies that filled the courtyard?

"They're taking captives," his father said. His voice sounded strange —a mixture of relief and suffering. "We can survive this, Teran. We can live, all right? Just keep your head and stay with me. Do you understand?"

"Yes, Papa."

His father turned, still holding him in his arms, and Teran was once more facing the heat.

Teran still couldn't understand. "Why doesn't He put the fire out?"

"Who?"

"God. Doesn't He want His house?"

Teran's papa was silent for a moment. "He's not there, Teran. God is not contained in a building."

"But it *is* His house, isn't it?"

"It is where we came to meet with Him."

"And now He's gone?"

His father grunted. "Yes, son. But we left Him first."

"What do you mean? We're still here."

His papa sighed. "Don't you remember, son?"

Teran's mind felt as scattered as the ashes that drifted through the courtyard. He couldn't seem to pull any thoughts together. "No, Papa."

"God told Solomon that if the people turned away from God's commandments and worshiped other gods, that He would uproot us from the land and that the house which He consecrated for His name would be uprooted from His sight."

Teran's eyes caught shifting movement, and he saw Babylonian soldiers were watching them. He clutched his father tight with fear, but then he saw that the tips of their swords were pointing at the ground. The Babylonians were letting them leave the courtyard with the other survivors of the battle.

Teran's papa looked back at the temple, his voice hitching as he quoted,

"As for this house, which was exalted, everyone who passes by it will be astonished and say, 'Why has the Lord done this to this land and to this house?' And they will say, 'Because they forsook the Lord, the God of their fathers."

This story is imaginative,
but drawn from the true history of the Bible.

★ You can read a description of the spectacular temple, including the cherubim and the sea of bronze in 2 Chronicles chapters 2-5. (This was about 970-931 BC)

★ Read about Hezekiah stripping gold and silver from the temple in 2 Kings 1:14-16.

★ Read about the burning of the temple and the exile to Babylon in 2 Chronicles 36. (This was about 601-587 BC)

STORY COMMENTS

Strange as it may seem, this story is important to understanding the good news of Jesus. This is one of the bleakest points in the history of God's people, but one that pointed them toward true worship and an everlasting kingdom more glorious than anything they could imagine.

When Solomon dedicated the temple some four hundred years prior to the exile, the presence of the Lord descended on it.

The priests could not enter the house of the Lord because the glory of God had filled it! Imagine! (2 Chronicles 7:1-3) God appeared to Solomon at night and told him that if the people humble themselves, seek His face, and pray, God will forgive their sin and heal their land.

But the people rebelled after Solomon died, helped in part by Solomon's own sins.

The land fractured into two kingdoms. Kings rose up who did not seek God's will, and injustice and pain were the result. Instead of turning back to God for help, they bowed down to idols and made foolish alliances with other kingdoms. They turned away from the real worship that would bring blessings to them and their land.

When God had enough of their cruelty and wickedness, He allowed the Assyrians to take Israel captive, and then later the Babylonians carted away Judah.

You could call this a national time-out for Judah. They are left to stew in Babylon. They need to figure out where it went wrong, and to decide if they want to repent and renew their relationship to God.

After seventy years of captivity, a Persian king defeats Babylon and decrees that the captives are free to return home!

Many, but not all, go back and rebuild the temple with plenty of hardship and setbacks. It's finally complete, but it's a shadow of the greatness of Solomon's temple. The people are confused. Didn't the prophet Haggai say that "the glory of this house would be greater than the former"? (Haggai 2:9) Not long afterwards, prophecy dies out. The country is jerked one way then another by foreign countries who fight over her.

The people who live near this temple are left wondering: Are the promises made to Abraham and David null and void? Will all the nations be blessed through Abraham's seed? Will God establish a Davidic king upon the throne like He promised? Will God forgive them and heal their land?

These questions are still on the minds of the people in the first century. We see Matthew open with this profound statement that would have stirred the people's hearts to remember the promises: "The record of the genealogy of Jesus the Messiah, the son of David, the son of Abraham!"(Matthew 1:1)

God had a bigger plan than they knew. A plan to save not only the exiles, but the whole world! A cosmic rescue plan that began in Bethlehem, in a manger, with a little baby.

QUESTIONS FOR DISCUSSION

* How do you think the people felt at the fall of Jerusalem and the temple? Do you think they were shocked that God let this happen?

* What Bible stories have you read that point forward to Jesus and the Kingdom of Heaven?

* Was Jesus coming to earth a last-minute decision or a

long-term plan?

Daniel

In the Hands of the Lord

.

Iron fists gripped his forearms, hustling him down the stony path behind the palace. Lush greenery flourished in the tended grounds, pristine pools reflected scarlet skies, and brilliant blooms crowded around elaborate statutory. The pathway continued past this tamed beauty and towards the stark prison.

Daniel swallowed hard. He knew he was not destined to languish beyond bolted doors. His fate was behind the stone prison—in the place where traitors to the crown met a violent end.

The guards pushed him roughly, even though he didn't resist them. As they rounded the prison, Daniel saw men in fine robes and gold necklaces positioned so that they had a clear view as he was shoved and jostled. Every face was cruelly smug.

Fools! He thought angrily to himself as he shook his head. They were so concerned with their own position as satraps over the kingdom, so jealous of his favor with the king, that they were blind to the true source of Daniel's wisdom and understanding.

Daniel's eyes were drawn inexorably to a hole in the ground. It was only a little wider than a man and gaped like a black, hungry mouth. He did his best to smother the tremble that ran down his limbs. He knew what was down there. He summoned every ounce of his courage.

His friends had walked away unharmed when King Nebuchadnezzar had thrown them in the fiery furnace. Like them, I am in your hands, Lord, he prayed.

Standing near the opening was Darius himself, king of the Babylonians, the Medes, and the Persians. Below his golden crown, his eyes were sorrowful. Daniel knew the king regretted his decree that no one could pray to any god save the king. His kingly pride had played right into the satraps' hands.

Shadows stretched long across the stony ground as a rope was fastened around Daniel's waist.

Darius stepped forward and put a hand on Daniel's shoulder. He spoke gently, "Your God, whom you constantly serve, will save you."

There was a shifting, jealous movement among the satraps. Did they fear the king would recant his decree? They relaxed when the guards pushed Daniel towards the hole.

Daniel's heart rose to his throat as he sat on the edge, cringing as he dangled his feet into the black void. He could hear a low rumbling, and the hair on his arms stood on end. The guard gave him a shove and he slipped forward, the rope jerking painfully under his arms. He hung, suspended in space, and fought the panicked urge to draw his feet up to his chest.

He desperately prayed, "Protect your servant, Lord!"

He was lowered until his sandal-clad feet felt the uneven ground beneath him, and the rope slackened above. There was a whisper as the rope fell down beside him, and Daniel's pulse flew. He looked up, and the last thing he saw was King Darius' strained face before the grating of rock shut out the last rays of sunlight.

Daniel stood stock-still in utter darkness. The smell of lush greenery was lost, leaving only the musky scent of animals in the chill air. His pulse pounded in his ears, but not loud enough to hide the padding of heavy paws circling him. He felt a puff of hot breath against his hand and stiffened. A cold sweat broke out on his brow. The pacing continued, surrounding him, with low growls on every side.

He braced as if for a blow, his heart hammering as he wondered what it would feel like for a lion to tear out his throat.

If this is to be my fate, Lord, let it be quick.

Minutes passed. Something enormous brushed past him, making him jump. Then the noise moved away. He heard the shifting of the huge beasts, and then it was quiet, except for the sound of soft breathing.

Daniel stood stock still for what felt like an eternity, until exhaustion crept up his limbs. As quietly as he could manage, he slid the rope off of him. He crept backward carefully, tottering on the uneven rock until he felt cold stone behind him. Feeling better with something at his back, he slid slowly down into a crouch.

True sleep was impossible, but in the complete blackness, vivid dreams wound in and out of his mind as if he skimmed on the surface of slumber.

He was lost in one of these vivid moments when the scrape of rock jerked him alert. He threw a hand up to hide the brilliant light and saw the cave mouth was opening.

"Daniel! Daniel!" the king's familiar voice cried anxiously. "Has your God saved you? Has He delivered you from the lions?"

Daniel lowered his hand and saw the interior of the cave for the first time. Across the small expanse, three sets of yellow eyes were fixed on him. Tawny tails flicked, whiskers twitched, and padded claws tensed upon the stone. Daniel could see ribs clearly. These giant predators were kept on the cusp of starvation. Yet, they did not move. Terrified exultation rose up within him as he gazed on the beasts with whom he had spent the night, and he stood slowly.

"O King, may you live forever!" Daniel called. "My God sent His angel and has shut the lions' mouths. They have not harmed me! God has found me innocent of any wrongdoing towards Him, and towards you, O King. I have committed no crime."

Daniel heard commands being issued, and a rope snaked down into the hole. His eyes fixed upon the lions, Daniel went forward cautiously and tied the rope around his middle. As the rope strained and lifted his feet off the ground, Daniel looked upwards to the bright morning sun and sent up a grateful prayer.

Read this story for yourself in Daniel 6

Story Comments

Daniel's story happens during the period of Judah's exile. He was a man of God living in a world that did not believe in God, and why should they? From the Babylonian perspective, they were the superior people with the superior gods. The Babylonians had conquered the Jewish people, surely that proved that their god was stronger?

As we have seen, God sometimes allows His own people to stumble, lose a battle, or be taken captive to show them that they can't rely on their own strength. Though God did not approve of Babylon, and His prophets (including Daniel) proclaimed her imminent doom, God still used this godless nation to serve His purposes: the discipline and correction of His children.

I find Daniel's actions and words interesting in this story. He speaks well of and to the king. He does not waver from his faith, which is what lands him in the lion's den. However, he does not actively seek to overthrow the throne either. As a commissioner, Daniel is a man of high position, and he uses his skills for good—even as an exile.

QUESTIONS FOR DISCUSSION

* Have you ever found yourself in a situation where your employer or your supervisor was difficult to respect?

* How can Daniel's example teach us to act as people of faith in a world where our boss might not be a believer?

* Do you think Daniel's open faith had an impact on King Darius?

* Read Matthew 5:3-12. Can you see any similarities between these traits and the life of Daniel?

Esther

FOR SUCH A TIME AS THIS

Trembling from head to foot, Esther paused before the engraved doors that led to the throne room. Two eunuchs stood on either side, their eyes fixed forward, waiting to see if she would dare bid the slaves to open them. Drawing a shaky breath, she reached up a hand and adjusted the narrow circlet that rested on her glossy hair. Her fingers fluttered to make sure her necklace was straight, her dress smooth, and that every bit of silk and finery was perfect. If the king did not find her lovely and extend his scepter in welcome to her, her raiment would become a funeral shroud.

"Open the door," she said in little more than a whisper.

"My Queen, are you certain—" one of the eunuchs began, but she straightened her shoulders and spoke louder.

"Open the door!"

The double doors were pulled open on their oiled hinges, and she stood facing the great throne room. Chatter hushed as faces turned her way in shock.

She stepped into the opulent room—uninvited and uncalled for—and dropped her gaze humbly. She walked forward in a whisper of silk, her embroidered slippers peeking out from her long skirts as she moved. The hair on her arms stood on end, and fear clawed her insides even more than the hunger of her fast, but she kept going until she was just before the raised throne. She saw only the king's feet, she dared not look any higher. A long moment of silence followed where all she heard was her hammering heartbeat.

"Queen Esther," a soft voice spoke above her bowed head, and she slowly lifted her chin until her eyes met that of her husband, the ruler of one hundred and twenty-seven provinces, the wealthiest, most powerful man in the world. She dragged her gaze to his hand and saw his golden scepter stretched towards her. She smiled weakly in relief. His gaze softened. He had not spoken with her for over a month. His dark eyes caressed her face and traveled over her frame. She knew he thought she was beautiful.

"What is troubling you, Queen Esther?" he asked, setting the scepter down. His hand stroked his oiled beard, and the other rested on the arm of his throne. "What is your request? Even up to half the kingdom it shall be given to you."

Esther's heart leaped within her breast. She gathered her thoughts and took a deep breath, ignoring the calculating eyes of the men of the court. She had planned this carefully. She couldn't ask what she desired, at least not yet. She was about to play the most dangerous political game of her life.

She bowed low. "If it would please the king, may the king and Haman come to a banquet I have prepared for him."

The king smiled and inclined his head. Dismissed, Esther walked backward from the throne until the king nodded, then she turned and left the room in a flutter of skirts and nerves. When she was out of the room, she nearly ran to her apartments, her mind flying. Hathach was waiting. The deep creases on his dark face smoothed when she nodded.

"The king is coming for a banquet," Esther said with forced calmness. "Summon the best food and wine from the kitchens."

Hathach grinned and strode from the room.

She turned to her gawking maidservants.

"Hurry, girls, hurry!" Esther reprimanded them.

The maids collected themselves and leaped into action. They drew couches close together and heaped them with silk cushions. They lit fragrant incense, the musky scent quickly permeating the air. Two of the maids trotted into the room with arms laden with fresh flowers for the vases.

The room was a flurry of movement, but Esther stood apart, praying for wisdom and guidance. The lives of her people depended on her. She went to her table, withdrew the parchment from where she had hidden it, and read again the genocide orders prepared for the Jews. Haman had poured honeyed lies into the ears of the king, and now the king's seal on the wax permitted the slaughter of every Jewish man, woman, and child on the thirteenth day of the twelfth month. The parchment trembled.

Esther stuffed the royal decree out of sight and put her face into her hands. She was only an orphan. She had been raised by her cousin in humble circumstances—a girl without a noble background, untrained in the intrigues and politics of court. She didn't even belong here. Her people had been dragged from their homeland as plunder and were scattered throughout this foreign land where the inhabitants bowed to false gods.

Did God truly see one such as her? Would He help her save His people?

"Perhaps you had been raised to royalty, for just such a moment as this," her cousin Mordecai had said.

"Your majesty," Hathach said, and she lifted her face. He was a devoted servant, and he smiled kindly on her now. "The king approaches. Prepare yourself."

Esther drew a deep breath and tried to stifle her nerves. She placed herself gracefully near an urn of flowers, the light of a lamp illuminating her gown and flickering off her jewels. When the king entered the room, she was the first thing he would see.

"Smile, your majesty," Hathach whispered.

Her heart in her throat, Esther smiled graciously as the doors were thrown open, and the king and the murderous Haman strode into her apartments.

The platters of food were ravaged, the wine drunk, and through the billowing curtains, the night was growing late. The king leaned forward and toyed with the bracelet on her wrist. She had been as affectionate to him as she dared—laughing with him and serving him food with her own hand. She could see how taken he was with her. He smiled, brushing a finger down her arm. She saw the signet ring on his hand and suppressed a shudder. It was the same one that had pressed the wax, sealing the fate of every Jew in his realm.

"Now, what is your request? Even up to half my kingdom, it shall be given to you."

Esther's eyes darted to Haman, who sat in regal repose, basking in the luxury of a private banquet with the king and queen. He was the one who had convinced her husband that the Jews needed to die. If he caught on to what she was trying to do … Her nerve faltered.

"If I have found favor with my king, and if it pleases you, come again tomorrow, to another banquet," Esther said, smiling at the king from under her lashes while berating herself for her cowardliness. "Then I will make my request."

The king chuckled, his eyes lingering on her lips. "As you wish."

The next morning, Esther heard a banging noise from outside her window. She went into the gardens outside her rooms to see what was happening. Before her eyes spread the houses of those in favor of the king—the largest and most ornate belonged to Haman, of course. Practically on his front step, something tall was being constructed, over fifty-feet high.

Esther turned to one of the maidservants who were dusting the room. "What is Haman building?"

The maidservant looked humbly to the floor as she replied, "Gallows, your majesty. He plans to hang the Jew, Mordecai, on them tomorrow. Haman has sworn to all his family that he will have no pleasure in life until the man is dead."

Esther's eyes widened, and she turned quickly away from the maidservant to hide her face.

Only her cousin Mordecai knew her Jewish background, and that her true name was Hadassah. Out of the entire palace, he alone understood that Haman's orders for genocide included the queen. Bile rose up into her throat. She clutched her hands and stared at the grim construction. She couldn't waver tonight.

As the moon rose pale in a purple sky, the king and Haman came again to her apartments. Again she served them choice foods and wine. She had musicians play quiet music, and was as charming as she was able. The sight of Haman turned her stomach. She hated watching the blood-thirsty brute revel in his position and prestige.

As the meal ended, her anxiety was at a fever pitch. The food she had eaten tried to rise back up her throat. Her cheeks felt aflame and her tongue was thick and clumsy. She swallowed hard. She had to be brave and wise. This night would decide the fate of thousands of lives

—and her own as well.

The king leaned back on his cushions, satisfied and happy. "So, Queen Esther, what is your petition? Up to half the kingdom, it shall be yours."

Esther dropped her gaze to her trembling fingers. She tightened them upon her knees and swallowed hard.

Her voice wobbled in her own ears. "If I have found favor with the king, my request is that my life be given to me, and the lives of my people." The king stiffened, then sat up straight. Drawing her courage, she raised her eyes to beseech the king, and pleaded, "For we have been sold, I and my people, to be annihilated."

His gaze narrowed and burned with anger. Was it against her? She held her breath as he cried out, "Who has presumed to do such a thing?"

Esther's gaze fell on Haman, and he widened his eyes. This was the moment that could decide everything. She raised her chin. "Haman has ordered this, he is a foe and an enemy!" She took the parchment she had secreted behind her shawl and passed it to the king. The king scanned the document then glared at his advisor.

The blood rushed from Haman's face, and he clutched his chest. Haman opened and closed his mouth like a fish in a net. The king cast his cup angrily aside as he stood to his feet and stormed into the gardens.

"Your majesty! My Queen!" Haman's voice pleaded, and she turned away from him, anger and fear coursing through her veins.

The king's wrath was kindled, true, but had she said and done enough? Would the king intercede on her behalf? Would he choose her over his right-hand man? She felt Haman move to her couch, and he grabbed her arm, trying to turn her face to him. "My Queen!" Haman whimpered.

A kingly voice rang through the room, "You would dare to assault the queen, with me in the house?" Haman realized his error and scrambled away, bowing with his face to the floor. Esther rose gracefully to her feet, moving away from Haman. The king's eyes were dark as flint, and just as hard. He snapped his fingers. Harbonath, one of the king's eunuchs, came forward and bowed low.

"What do you know of this?" the king demanded.

The faithful servant extended his hand to gesture out into the gardens. "If it pleases your majesty," Harbonath said. "Behold, the gallows Haman constructed, fifty-feet high. He made them for Mordecai."

"For Mordecai!" The king's eyes burned down on Haman, who flinched as if whipped. "You mean the man who saved my life from assassins? Who, this very morning, was given a robe and a ring, and whom Haman led through the city in honor?" Haman sunk even lower to the floor, utterly prostrate. Esther was surprised, she had known none of this. The king swelled with anger, and he held out an accusing finger. "Is Mordecai the reason you want the Jews exterminated? You told me the people you wanted dead were insurrectionists! Your pride has become your downfall, Haman!" The king turned to his servant. "Have Haman taken to the gallows he built. Hang him there."

Haman wailed as Harbonath and Hathach leaped forward and grabbed Haman under the arms and dragged him away, sobbing and pleading.

The king strode from the room after them, radiating anger.

Alone at last, Esther collapsed back onto the couch. Weakly, she sipped from her goblet to ease her parched throat. The secrets were out. King Ahasuerus knew Haman's treachery and Queen Esther's heritage. The decree for the annihilation of the Jews lay on the floor at her feet. Tomorrow she would go before the king again. She would fall at his feet and beg him to issue a new decree, one that would save her people. She rose and went out to the garden, where the night air was sweet. She moved to her knees and bowed her head to the one true God. He had delivered her cousin, herself, and all her people.

Read this story for yourself in Esther 5-7

STORY COMMENTS

Something you may notice when you read the story of Esther is that God is not mentioned explicitly anywhere in the book. At first, that struck as me as strange. But on a second read, I can see God's hand in the chance occurrences in the story.

This story falls historically after a number of Jews have returned home from the exile to rebuild Jerusalem. Not everyone goes home, however. Mordecai and Esther remain, and Esther the Jew is chosen out of all the beautiful girls. As queen, she is in a position to plead for her people's lives.

Mordecai, her cousin and guardian, saves the king's life by overhearing an assassination plot and passing the information through Esther. He is awarded the house and political position of the man who sought to kill the Jews

Esther and Mordecai work together to send another edict out that saves the lives of the Jews. None of this could have happened without Esther being taken from her home and crowned Queen, a fate she might never have chosen for herself.

Mordecai notices how these events have been orchestrated for their possible salvation.

> "And who knows whether you have not attained royalty
> for such a time as this?"
> - Esther 4:14b

Can we truly say that God is not in the book of Esther?

This story is written in a time of exile. The people are far from their homeland and possibly feeling far from God. It is comforting to read of God's continual presence in their lives—even when He seems silent, He is there.

QUESTIONS FOR DISCUSSION

★ Have you ever been frustrated by the silence of God when you longed to hear His voice?

★ Have you ever felt God's hand in the "chance" moments of your life?

★ Read Esther 4:10-17. Do you think Esther considered keeping quiet instead of risking her own life? How does this make you feel about her? What would you have done?

★ The exiles were going through a really tough time, yet God continued to care for and protect them. Have you ever felt something similar?

★ Read Mark 6:22-23. Does Herod's phrasing seem familiar? This has led scholars to speculate that this happened shortly after the festival of Purim, when the story of Esther was read aloud. Does Herod identifying himself with King Ahasuerus say something about Herod's opinion of himself?

Herod the Great

RISE TO POWER

Herod leaned against the balustrade. His hands gripped the polished stone. It was shady and cool where he stood, with the high wall at his back.

This was his moment. The one he had worked for since his youth. Of course, he hadn't gotten here on his own. With his thumb, he toyed with the two thick rings on his fingers.

His father, Antipater, had slipped through the waters of politics with the grace of an eel, avoiding every obstacle in the dangerous quest for power. Antipater wished to rule over the little parcel of land situated along two vital trade routes. Judea was also nestled against the Mediterranean, the sea that connected some of the richest parts of the world in commerce. True, Judea was fractured, but Antipater and his two sons had worked tirelessly to unite it under one rule.

After long years, their political labors had been rewarded. The golden moment had come when Antipater sent reinforcements at the crucial moment to Julius Caesar in Alexandria—giving the new ruler a victory. Antipater had been made a Roman citizen and procurator of all Judea. One of his first acts was to name his sons as governors. Phasael was put in charge of Judea, and to Herod, he gave the governing of Galilee.

It had been a dazzling political victory.

Antipater hadn't celebrated long.

Death had cut the party short. The memory made Herod tug on the neck of his tunic. Midway through a feast, Antipater had struggled to his feet, clawing at his throat as his face turned purple. He was dead a minute later. It was impossible to tell who had slipped him the poison. Herod and Phasael had all the kitchen slaves executed, just to be safe.

A jingle of chains drew Herod out of his reflection. His moment was coming, yes it was almost here! Down below in the courtyard of the garrison, a man was unshackled and stripped, his rich garments tossed among the jeering soldiers.

Herod watched as the trembling man was lashed hand and foot to a large wooden 'X'. The man blubbered and pleaded for mercy. The soldiers looked up at Herod. He gave them a thumbs down. They shrugged and turned back to their work.

How sweet it was, that he could strike both a political blow and a personal one.

Herod might not have more than a drop or two of Jewish blood in him, but he knew their history. He knew that the land had once been bursting with wine, plump with grain, and overflowing with olive oil. Long ago, the great kings and queens of the world had come to see King Solomon and marvel at his riches. The people had never stopped longing for a return to wealth but had yet to have a king worthy of leading them there. The people's rescue was at hand. He stroked his beard and smiled.

A whistle sliced through the air, followed by a scream of pain. A thrill raced up his spine. Every other noise faded beneath the shrill slice of the whiptail and the shrieks of a fallen king who knew he would receive no mercy.

Herod curled his lip at the man's sobbing. Was this the same man who had bitten off the ears of his own uncle? Antigonus had mutilated his own flesh and blood so that he could take the role of high priest as well as being king. Herod had to admire the man's willingness to do whatever it took to seize power by the throat. His admiration did not extend to clemency.

Herod watched as the man writhed and twisted to escape the bite of the whip. Herod drew a satisfied breath through his nose and caught the coppery scent of blood. Just a few moments more and then he could move forward with his own plans.

Visions danced in his head. He was determined to make the land great again. He would increase production and trade, build up the ports, bring Roman civilization to a country that had been juggled from hand to hand for far too long. His pulse quickened with eagerness to begin and his fingertips tingled in anticipation. The nation needed stability. Peace! He would show them what luxury was: bathhouses, gymnasiums, aqueducts, theaters, chariot races, he would bring them all! He would build a proper palace for himself in the city, a fitting raiment for the ancient Jerusalem.

He smiled. The screams were mere background noise to his grandiose dreams.

His father had found power as procurator but had succumbed to poison. His brother, Phasael, had been raised to ethnarch of Judea at the death of their father, but he was struck down in battle. Killed by the same man whose blood was now splattering the stone floor of the garrison.

Herod did not desire either fate. Nor did he believe he should meet it.

He had the support of Mark Antony, ruler of Rome. He had dined with the beautiful Cleopatra of Egypt in her summer palace, the air saturated with the scent of incense. He did not lack skill in diplomacy and politics. He rubbed his palms together. He would win these stubborn people, these religious fanatics, these Jews. And he thought he knew how.

The priests refused to believe in the existence of any other god, and even forbade the construction of other temples to their one true God, as they called Him. They hated the Jewish temple that had been built in Egypt and had destroyed the one in Samaria. No, their worship centered on this one temple in Jerusalem. Hadn't they lamented for years at its shabbiness compared to the jeweled and golden temple of Solomon? He slapped the stone beneath his hand. A complete refurbishment of their center of worship, that was the way to secure his throne. It would be the crown of the kingdom; one of the great marvels of the world!

As soon as one last piece of business was complete.

Herod looked down into the garrison courtyard. Red droplets sprayed the stone floor on either side of the executioner, splattering back in a V shape as the whip dragged one way, then the other.

Antigonus' back was a cross thatch of pulverized flesh. It made Herod's stomach turn to look at it, so he shifted his gaze to the witnesses instead. He had kept the numbers small. There could be no rioting, not during his ascent to power. No, the only witnesses present were Antigonus' family and the fallen king's most stalwart supporters. Their pale faces showed that they knew who was in power now.

Antigonus stopped sobbing at last, and his head lolled back as he sagged against his bonds. His lifeblood was nearly spent.

"Take him down," Herod commanded. He could see the family supporting each other. Antigonus' wife was near fainting, but she cried out as Herod coldly added, "And remove his head."

The soldiers untied the ropes and dragged the limp man to the chopping block. The executioner took up an ax. He looked up to Herod. Herod nodded once, and the ax whistled through the air and landed with a satisfactory thunk. As soon as he saw the head fall to the stone floor, Herod turned and left, feeling as if a weight had been removed from his own shoulders as easily as the king had lost his. He chuckled at his wit. It was time to get to work.

As he swept through the halls of the garrison, soldiers bowed their heads to the new King of the Jews.

The story of Herod's rise to power is not found in the Bible.
It falls in the history between the Old and New Testaments.
For source material I used *Backgrounds of Early Christianity* by Everett
Ferguson pages 411-414.

STORY COMMENTS

Did you know there is more than one ruler named Herod in the Bible? This is Herod, sometimes referred to as Herod the Great. His son, Herod Antipas, was the man who executed John the Baptist.

This story, though not found in scripture, lays a historical foundation for the world into which Jesus was born.

Herod, though cruel, was a shrewd and able man. He was able to unite and rule the shattered territories of the promised land as one whole country—something no one had done since Solomon. (2

Chronicles 10) He achieved his dreams of making the land prosperous and peaceful. He rebuilt the temple to become one of the marvels of the ancient world. Yet, despite all this, the 'King of the Jews' was not popular. Partly because he was cruel, partly because he was a "friend of Rome", but largely because he was not Jewish.

This is the Herod who is approached by the magi from the east. Imagine a ruler who has worked his whole life to get where he is, and yet feels the people's animosity against him. He has murdered his favorite wife and two of her sons to protect his throne from usurpers. It seems a man who has stolen a throne from someone else is always worried the same will happen to him.

This power-hungry king hears that mysterious men from the east are asking around Jerusalem, "Where is he who has been born King of the Jews?" (Matthew 2:2)

Herod knows that despite everything he has done, the people still cry out for a savior. Why? Their religion teaches them that a son of David will bring an eternal kingdom. They will never see Herod as a true king. I can see the jealousy blazing in his heart.

We know what happens next in the story. Soldiers are dispatched to Bethlehem with ruthless orders.

Herod does everything in his power to kill the Messiah. A wondrous time of hope is born, but evil lashes out.

This is the sort of king the people of Jesus' day knew. This is the kind of ruler people had come to expect: muscle and might, men clutching power with both hands. If it had been Jesus taking the throne and calling for Herod's torture and death, there would have been cheers of approval from the crowds. Jesus could have raised a sword and the country would have rallied around him.

That's not who Jesus was.

He died with a sign over his head mocking him as King of the Jews; a title that was last held by Herod. But he did not live like Herod.

This is the history I have in mind when I read Jesus saying:

> "You know that the rulers of the Gentiles lord it over them, and great men exercise authority over them. It is not this way among you, but whoever wishes to become great among you shall be your servant, and whoever wishes to be first among you shall be your slave; just as the Son of Man did not come to be served, but to serve, and to give his life

as ransom for many."
 - Matthew 20:25-28

And we know that this humble man, this servant, Jesus of Nazareth, is the king of the entire universe!

When he rose from the dead he told his disciples, "ALL authority has been given to me in heaven and on earth." (Matthew 28:18, emphasis mine) He lived his whole life for this purpose, keeping his eye on the prize. His journey to the throne was a bloody battle, but it was not fought against the kings of the earth, but against sin and death! (2 Timothy 1:10) Jesus fought for—and won!—the kingship of the kingdom of heaven.

If Jesus is King, that changes everything.

When my study group was doing our in-depth study of Matthew, we were struck over and over by how often Jesus teaches about the kingdom of heaven. That is the kingdom we need to be most concerned about, for that is where our citizenship is! (Philippians 3:20) Your life may be a daily struggle, my friend, but it is not where your story will end.

When the magi found Jesus and bowed before him with their gifts, they were just the first. A day will come when every knee will bow, and every mouth confess that Jesus Christ is Lord. (Philippians 2:10)

QUESTIONS FOR DISCUSSION

★ Herod made many changes to Jerusalem and the ancient land of Israel. Jesus would have seen evidence of Herod's rule his entire life. Do you think that impacted how Jesus viewed a godly kingship?

★ The kings in this story were willing to do whatever it took to take the throne for themselves. Have you ever steamrollered over others in your quest to fulfill your dream, or felt the effects of someone doing it to you?

★ How does the world's idea of power look different than

Jesus' idea of power?

★ Some people think Christianity is the gospel for the poor, a pleasing story to make the little man feel better about his fate as the powerful sit back and enjoy life. What do you think?

★ Can power and prestige bring lasting happiness?

★ Considering that Herod killed his favorite wife and two of his sons, did Herod enjoy his life as the King of the Jews, do you think?

Elizabeth

Preparing the Way

"Good-bye, and thank you for everything," Mary said, standing in the doorway. The young girl smiled on little John with the warmth of a woman who was carrying a child of her own. Elizabeth's throat tightened, and she held her miracle baby a little tighter.

"Must you go?" She reached forward and grabbed Mary's hand. "You would be safe here with me, you know. We would protect you." Her eyes dropped to Mary's middle. It was early yet. There was no visible pregnancy, but it wouldn't be long now.

Mary touched her stomach for just a moment. "The Lord will protect His servant," she murmured.

Elizabeth nodded. "I am sure he will. But Mary," she squeezed the smooth hand within her own wrinkled one. "That doesn't mean it won't be difficult." Elizabeth watched Mary's eyes begin to shimmer as the innocent girl swallowed hard.

"I know, but I feel like this is the right thing to do. My baby will need a father, and Joseph is a kind and righteous man."

"Yes," Elizabeth said. "But if he is too righteous ..." she couldn't finish, and instead dropped Mary's hand to tuck John's blanket a little closer.

"I know." Mary was serious. "If he sees me as an adulteress he may divorce me. As my pregnancy progresses, everyone will know exactly why he cast me off. I'll be disgraced. My own family might disown me." She lifted her little chin slightly. "I may even be stoned."

"No!" Elizabeth cried out. "That happens so rarely, nowadays." Still, even if Mary was not killed for fornication, life as an unmarried mother was a hard one.

Mary picked up her bundle but did not seem eager to leave. After all, what betrothed girl would be anxious to go home and tell her family that she was with child? Would they believe the young girl when she told them that she was yet a virgin? Would they sneer when she claimed she was with child by the Holy Spirit? Elizabeth chewed her lip.

More likely they would think Joseph had been too eager, but truthful Joseph would deny it when questioned. What then? Her family knew Mary's virtuous nature. Her parents knew she would not be impure—at least not by choice. Would they think she had been raped? The Roman soldiers stationed all through the country had reputations of lust and violence. Would this precious, innocent, young girl be subjected to derision and blame? Would the child be stigmatized as a Roman bastard? Elizabeth shuddered.

"I see the convoy," Mary said, glancing out the doorway. "I should hurry or I'll be left behind." Mary had two coins in her bundle, her fee for protection. The traders were able to make a little extra profit by delivering people safely from place to place.

Elizabeth gave the young woman a one-armed hug, John cradled between them. They both looked down on the child, shared a smile, and then Mary broke the embrace. Elizabeth watched her until her young cousin was lost from sight.

John squinted his eyes and opened his little red mouth in a cry of hunger. Elizabeth went into the house and put the child to her breast. As she nursed him, she traced his tiny ear, and let him wrap his little fingers around her own. She had never known love could be like this!

"Yes, you are my sweet baby, aren't you?" she crooned. "My own little son."

She was blessed. Utterly blessed. All her life she had longed to be a mother. She and Zacharias had waited in vain for years. God had heard their prayers, but He had waited until their bodies were old to answer them. An angel had visited Zacharias in the temple with the great news. The vision had left him mute, and he had stayed that way throughout her pregnancy. When the child was born and named, Zacharias' tongue was loosed and his first words had been ones of praise.

"Blessed be the Lord God of Israel!"

Elizabeth had been overjoyed to hear her husband's voice again, and then stunned as he prophesied over their little son,

"And you, child, will be called the prophet of the Most High; for you will go on before the Lord to prepare His ways; to give His people the knowledge of salvation by the forgiveness of their sins, because of the tender mercy of our God, with which the sunrise from on high will visit us, to shine upon those who sit in darkness and the shadow of death, to guide our feet into the way of peace."

It had been nearly four hundred years since the last great prophet had walked the land in power—leading the people, guiding the king, proclaiming God's will for those on earth.

She bestowed a loving smile on the infant. Would this tiny babe truly grow up to be a man filled with God's power? Would he be as great as Elijah? She stroked her son's smooth cheek as his chin bobbed up and down. In her motherly pride, she believed her son would do wonders.

Yet, there was bitterness to tinge her joy. Elizabeth's smile wobbled. Deep longing made her throat thick. She leaned forward and breathed the scent of John's head, still sweet from his birth. She was old, and he was so young! She hoped she would live long enough to see him become the man God wanted. She sniffed and shook off her melancholy. Either way, she was blessed to be the mother of a prophet —a prophet of the Most High.

Read this story for yourself in Luke 1,
and the prophecies for a great prophet in Malachi 4

Story Comments

God seems to enjoy doing the "impossible". Like Abraham and Sarah, God waits until Zacharias and Elizabeth are old before they are given a child. Does He want to remind us that He is always in control, no matter how desperate things seem?

Mary's betrothal to Joseph was as binding as marriage. She was already, technically, Joseph's. He would pay her family a bride price (the opposite of a dowry) and would go and prepare a home for her. He might have been doing just that when she was off visiting Elizabeth. When about a year had passed, tradition dictated that he would come and collect her. He would bring her under his roof and they would consummate the marriage.

If Mary was pregnant by another man, she would be committing adultery against her betrothed. A righteous man couldn't marry an adulteress. It would show dishonor to God's commandments. (Exodus 20:14) Adulterers were stoned in the Old Testament. (Leviticus 20:10) Mary had to trust that God would keep her safe and that He would protect her honor.

Luke doesn't tell us how Joseph took the news. Perhaps this was common knowledge to his intended audience, or maybe he didn't think it was important to the story he was telling. Luke is clear, however, that Joseph keeps his engagement to Mary. (Luke 2:4-5)

The timeline between Mary's visit by an angel and the trip to Bethlehem is not certain, though scholars can make some pretty good guesses. Even though Luke claims to tell the story in "consecutive order" (Luke 1:3), it is clear right away that he is still telling the story with his own emphasis. That doesn't make it any less true, but it means that he had certain points he wished to make, and he highlighted them. He doesn't describe Joseph's angelic visit, and he includes the story of John's miraculous conception and birth.

A large majority of scholars think Mary was there for the birth of John. Verse 56 works (in a literary sense) to tuck Mary out of the way for a moment, while Luke deals with Elizabeth, the same way John is tidily excused in verse 80. (John does not live in the wilderness for years before the birth of Jesus!) There doesn't seem to be any reason for Mary to stay for three months and then leave Elizabeth before this special moment occurs. If they weren't good friends before, these women are now bonded by miraculous events. Wouldn't Mary stay for the birth, and then likely remain for the naming too? It is very possible that Mary heard this wondrous prophecy of John and treasured it in her heart.

Each gospel tells a slightly different story. It isn't our job to mash them all together to make a "true" gospel. The early church certainly didn't bother with that, or we would have one gospel instead of four. If you read the books of the Old Testament you will also see stories repeated, and sometimes slightly different from each other. We need to take each book on its own merit and hear what the author is trying to tell us. By taking each gospel as it was written, we arrive at a beautiful, multifaceted knowledge of Jesus' life and God's plan for salvation.

I think that in his gospel account, Luke is emphasizing John's role as prophet of the Most High to anchor and empower Jesus' role as Messiah.

QUESTIONS FOR DISCUSSION

* Does it bother you that the four gospel accounts are not all exactly the same?

* In how many different ways was the Holy Spirit involved in paving the way for Jesus' ministry?

* Elizabeth finally had her baby, but she was an old woman. Do you think she struggled with bitterness that she had her child at last but her time was short?

* Have you ever had a long-anticipated joy end too soon?

* Can we learn to find gratefulness and peace even when joy is all too brief?

The Shepherds

Sign of the Savior

Caleb puffed out his breath and the vapor swirled in the starlight before vanishing. It was a cold one. And bright—unnaturally bright. His gaze was drawn to the brilliant star that hung like a lantern over the city of Jerusalem. It was new, of that he was certain. A man didn't spend his nights in the open air for years on end and miss a star like that!

"Maybe it's a sign of something?" he murmured aloud.

"Eh? What's that?" his brother, Micah, grunted, already half asleep. They were rolled in their blankets by the dying coals of a small fire, tucked up near the gate of the sheepfold. Within the low wall, the sheep were quiet and bedded down. If it got much colder, Caleb figured he would crawl right in there with them. It might not smell so fresh, but it would be cozy.

Caleb pointed, even though Micah wasn't looking. "That new star. Maybe it means something."

Micah raised a bleary lid and then let it fall again. "Nah. Go to sleep."

Caleb tried to settle down, but he felt wide awake. He puffed out another breath and watched as it veiled the twinkling stars before disappearing. A clank of crude bells caught his attention.

"Are you lazy bones asleep already?" a voice called. The brothers sat up. Two more shepherds were making their way up the slope in the darkness, leading their flock.

Caleb chuckled. "I thought you two decided to bed down in one of the caves. Where have you been?" He untangled himself from his blanket and opened the gate. The sleepy occupants hardly shifted as the new flock filed through the narrow opening.

"We were missing one at the count. Had to do a search," his friend, Isaac, replied. "We've got them all now." These sheep were destined for the temple, they couldn't afford to lose even one.

Caleb shut the gate after the last one and latched it. This sheepfold was shared between all the local shepherds. Together, they maintained the stone walls and used the protection as a way to keep the docile beasts safe from predators and thieves. Deeper in the hills, there were many caves that the shepherds used as well, especially during lambing.

The four young men lay down in a row near the gate.

Asher leaned towards the others. "So, what do you two figure? About the new star, I mean."

"It's nothing," Micah was quick to grunt. "Now let's sleep."

"I think it's a sign," Caleb staunchly declared.

Isaac replied, "I agree with you, Caleb. A star like that can't just be an accident. Of course, we'll never know what the sign is."

Caleb nodded. Somebody, somewhere, understood the meaning of that star. Maybe the astrologists in Egypt.

"And why shouldn't we?" Asher cried out, and Caleb could almost make out Asher's eyebrows touching his hairline with a look of imperious injury.

"'Cause we're only shepherds," Micah rolled onto his side with an exaggerated yawn.

Asher sniffed. "Why shouldn't a shepherd enjoy a hint of the mysteries of life?"

Caleb shook his head and was sure Isaac and Micah were rolling their eyes in the dark as they listened to the same old song, but Asher was just warming up.

"Wasn't the great King David only a shepherd?" Asher's tone was regal. "Didn't he compose some of our people's greatest songs while sitting in the hills with his flock scattered about? Aren't we all children of the Lord?"

"Yes, but –"

Asher held up his hand. "Where did this foolish notion come from that there are some who are more worthy than others to receive news from heaven?"

"Now, really —"

Asher smacked a fist into his open palm. "Who was Gideon before he led the men into battle? Who was Esther before she was called to save her people? Who was Samuel before he was called in the dead of night? Nobodies! Just plain ol' ordinary men, women, and children! Like us! Nobody is more or less than his fellow man. God can call or use just whoever He pleases, right?"

Chuckles rumbled in the darkness.

"Don't let the king hear that."

"Or the Romans!"

"Or the Pharisees and Sadducees."

More chuckles followed, and even Asher joined in.

It was quiet except for the shifting of sleepy animals. The men snuggled deeper into the blankets, tucking them right up under their chins. They all lay back and stared up at that strange, new star.

Was it a sign? Caleb wondered. Would they ever know what it meant?

A flash exploded the sky.

The men threw their hands before their eyes with a yell of fear. Caleb's heart galloped like a runaway horse, and he lowered his hand to see what had happened to the sky. It was as if the heavens were torn like a garment. Behind that cosmic tear shone a brilliant light that wavered like the sun on water—sparkling, rainbow light. There were thousands of figures moving in the light, coming forward in graceful swoops.

Coming towards them!

Caleb's mouth went bone dry, and he reached out to grip Micah's arm even as he felt Isaac grab his other arm. The four men huddled together and trembled as a whole multitude of beings filled the sky above their heads. They moved in perfect harmony, like a flock of sparrows. Caleb heard his friends' gasps.

"What's happening?"

"What are they?"

One of the beings came closer. Its face and clothes shone so brilliantly that it was hard to look right at it. Caleb wanted to flee, but he couldn't make his body move.

Micah croaked, "We're done for!"

The being spoke in a voice like rushing wind, "Don't be afraid! I bring you good news that will bring joy to all people. Today, in the town of Bethlehem a Savior has been born! He is Christ, the Lord! This will be the sign for you: you will find a baby wrapped in cloths and lying in a manger."

Caleb's mind was like mud. A savior? A baby? A manger? What?

The heavenly speaker retreated to join the others, and together the strange creatures began to sing glory and praise to God. The song seemed to suck the air from Caleb's lungs. Tingles ran up and down his arms, and the hair at the back of his neck stood up. It was as if his chest was filled with the same light that radiated from the celestial beings. It made him want to sing too, though he didn't dare add his rough tones to the voices that rippled like the finest bells.

As suddenly as they arrived, they left. The light vanished.

The shepherds sat in complete blackness, their eyes seared with the dazzling light. Caleb blinked and rubbed his eyes until he could see the starlight again. The strange, new star still gleamed. He realized with a jolt that the shining star might not be over Jerusalem at all. It could be hanging over Bethlehem, a little town just a few miles away from the holy city.

They looked at each other. A sheep bleated sleepily.

Isaac whispered, "Was that real?"

Asher shook his head. "Unless we all had the same dream."

"Were those … angels?" Isaac's eyes were wide in the starlight.

Caleb jumped as his brother punched him in the arm. Micah's tone was disgusted. "And you said you *wanted* a sign?"

Read this story for yourself in Luke 2

STORY COMMENTS

Matthew gives us the story of the magi with their royal gifts. Luke highlights a different group: a bunch of shepherds. Why did these shepherds get this heavenly announcement? Luke doesn't say why this particular group was blessed, but I think Luke would like us to recognize that Jesus came for every man, even those thought of as "nobodies". Jesus is profoundly interested in everyday people; they are who he likes to hang out with, and who he calls to be his disciples and apostles—people like you and me!

Some have suggested that the shepherds near Bethlehem were in charge of raising the sheep for the temple sacrifices. I wasn't able to find a reliable reference for this theory online, but considering Bethlehem's close proximity to Jerusalem, it is surely possible. If it's true, then the same men who birthed and protected sacrifices for years, are some of the first to come and see the new baby who would sacrifice himself for us.

I've found many different theories about the sign given by the angel: the baby wrapped in cloths and laying in a manger. Some have said that these cloths were a symbol of his burial. (Luke 23:53) That allusion can surely be made when you know the outcome of the story of Jesus, but, historically, there was nothing unusual about a baby being wrapped in cloths. Any mom of a newborn knows how much they enjoy being tucked up and snug after their months in the womb. Ezekiel 16:4 talks about what a good mother would do for a newborn: navel cord cut, washed with water, rubbed with salt, and wrapped in cloths. It seems to me like the angels were saying, "You will find a very young baby, lying in a manger."

Jesus isn't in that stable anymore. His earthly story might have begun there, but when we look at our nativity scenes we need to remember that this isn't the whole story. The story of Jesus' birth is just a chapter in an epic narrative that began long before that night in the stable, and one that continues today. We are invited to find ourselves in this story of Jesus, and be transformed in the process.

QUESTIONS FOR DISCUSSION

* The story of Jesus' birth is very popular around Christmas time, and even non-believers enjoy the story. Why do you think Christmas gets all the glory and the message of Easter is often forgotten?

* Why do you think God chose this humble birth for Jesus?

★ Do you think the shepherd's lives were changed by this encounter with the newborn messiah?

Simeon

WAIT ON THE LORD

He puffed a little as he ascended the steps, his sandals slapping against the smooth stone. There had been a time when he had skipped lightly up to the temple to pray, but those days were long past. Still, he hurried as fast as his stiff knees permitted, for a sense of urgency pressed on his chest and made his heart pound. It was like the feeling of rushing late to a feast—an eager expectancy mingled with fluttering nerves.

He tried to reason why he felt this way. He had attended prayers in the temple courts as the sun rose, and the almost painful ache had begun then. He had gone home among the crowds who were preparing for another busy day in Jerusalem, but the feeling had persisted until he could do nothing but rise and go back to the temple.

He entered through the southern gateway and emerged into a massive courtyard that he knew as well as his own street. He had come here to pray nearly every day of his life. The sound of the trumpets, the scent of roasted meat and sweet incense, the rising and falling of voices in prayer—usually these soothed his mind and brought comfort to his heart.

On impulse, Simeon turned and shuffled along the shadowy colonnade that bordered the courtyard, looking for his friend. Perhaps she could help him understand. He passed a few humble rabbis with their small gatherings of students. The most prestigious rabbis taught on the second floor in Solomon's Colonnade, but here you could catch a lesson on the law or the prophets just about any time of day. Simeon passed a man passionately crying out words of prophecy, and he felt the yearning in his soul deepen. The man spoke of the consolation of Israel. The desire for restoration tightened Simeon's chest and made tears prick in the corner of his eyes. Was it his lifelong dream that had brought him here today?

How long, Lord? How much longer do I need to wait? You told me that I would not see death before I saw the Lord's Christ. The corner of his mouth twitched. I am growing old, Lord. Though I am grateful for the years, I am more eager to see the Anointed One! Finally, he saw her face through the crowd. He breathed a sigh of relief and quickened his steps. He hoped she could help him. "Anna! How are you, my friend?"

"Simeon!" she looked up and smiled, her face crinkling into a thousand fine creases. "Why are you back so soon? You're here nearly as often as I am!" She laughed at her old joke, and he tried to smile as usual. Her eyes were as sharp as ever, and she took in his expression. "What's troubling you, my old friend?" she asked.

He rubbed the back of his neck, the joints popping. Now that he was here, he didn't know how to put it into words. "I'm not sure, it just feels like something is supposed to happen, or like I'm supposed to do something. It's hard to explain."

Anna smiled knowingly. "I know how you feel." Simeon was sure that she did, for Anna was revered as a prophetess. She never left the temple courts and had given herself to fasting and prayer ever since the death of her husband over fifty years ago. If anyone knew how it felt to be prompted by the Spirit, he was sure she did.

"What do I do?" He furrowed up his brow. "I feel like I need to be here, but I'm not sure why."

"Go," Anna nudged him with a wrinkled hand. "Go pray. I'm sure it will be revealed to you."

Wishing she could have given him the answers he craved, Simeon nodded and pressed a coin into her hand as he turned to go. The prophetess lived purely on the gifts of others.

Simeon walked across the courtyard, feeling the yearning within tug him forward like he was a fish on a hook. He looked around himself, hoping to find answers. People milled around the money-changer tables and purchased animals, grain, or wine for sacrifices. Coins were dropped into guarded boxes for the temple treasury—it took a vast sum to fund the national sacrifices and supply the priests.

He approached a young, commonly dressed couple who were waiting to purchase pigeons. The young woman held a carefully swaddled baby in her arms. Clearly, they were coming to offer the commanded sacrifice. He fondly remembered bringing his own infant son to the temple a lifetime ago.

He moved to pass them when he felt the longing in his heart switch directions, catching him off balance. He faltered and turned back. It was like nothing he had ever experienced before. He felt an overwhelming urge to go and speak to these strangers. They glanced up with uncertainty as he approached.

"Peace be on you," he said, his eyes dragging over the man's face for some sign, some clue about what the Lord was trying to tell him. For years he had waited for the Messiah, could this be the man?

"Peace be on you," the man nodded, his words tinged with a Galilean accent. Simeon felt nothing special when he looked on the man, and he turned to the woman. She held his eyes for only a moment before demurely dropping them to her baby. She gently bobbed as she shifted her weight from foot to foot, soothing her sleeping child.

"May I see your child?" Simeon asked.

The young woman's eyes darted up in surprise, but she turned her arms so he could see a round face with puckered pink lips. At the sight of the infant, his heart burst with inexpressible joy.

"Blessed be the name of the Lord!" he gasped. He reached out, and the stunned mother let him take the child into his large, gnarled hands. His skin tingled with anticipation as he held the sleeping baby. This was it! This was the moment he had waited for all his life!

He cried out in joy, "Now, Lord, You are releasing Your bond-servant to depart in peace as You told me I should! I have seen Your salvation, which You have prepared in the presence of all peoples, a light of revelation to the Gentiles, and the glory of Your people Israel."

The man's hand jerked to his wife's shoulder as if he needed support, and she automatically reached up to hold it, but her eyes stayed fixed on Simeon's face in amazement. Simeon saw the truth in her eyes. This couple was not shocked by Simeon's proclamation. They had known that their son was the Messiah. They were only surprised that Simeon knew it too.

He gazed on the child's parents and his eyes filled with happy tears as he murmured, "May the Lord bless you!" He blinked rapidly as he felt new words rising up in him like an overflowing river, and he locked eyes with the mother of the Messiah. "Behold, this child is appointed for the fall and rise of many in Israel, and for a sign to be opposed. And a sword will pierce even your own soul to the end that the thoughts of many hearts may be revealed." Her lips parted as her face paled.

"Praise the Lord!" a wavering voice cried, and Simeon turned and saw Anna had approached, drawn by the Spirit that filled her. Her soft, creased skin seemed to glow from within as she lifted her hands to the heavens and broke forth in a litany of praise and blessing. People stopped to watch what was going on, but Simeon only had eyes for the soft cheeks and downy head of the infant in his arms.

Read this story for yourself in Luke 2:21-38

STORY COMMENTS

It says in Luke that Simeon was devout and that the Holy Spirit was upon him. It had been revealed to him that he would not see death before he saw the Lord's Christ. What a wonderful thing to be promised! His people were crying out for a savior, someone who would reunite Israel into one whole kingdom. He would remove the pagans and their false gods, and restore Jerusalem and the temple to their full glory with a proper priesthood and a righteous king.

Yet, Simeon didn't know just when the Messiah would be revealed. I wonder how many years he had to wait. I always imagined Simeon's wait was like Abraham's—a yearning to fill a lifetime. And then, when it finally happened, was it as he expected? Did Simeon ever imagine God would show him the Messiah as a baby? Had he expected to see the Messiah as a mighty warrior striding into Jerusalem to seize the throne, or as a Spirit-led priest leading the people from the sacrificial altar?

Instead, he took the Messiah into his arms as an infant, an innocent child. Sometimes we have to wait a long time, but God always keeps His word.

When Simeon approached, Mary was purchasing animals for a sacrifice. She was fulfilling the purification and sin offerings of Leviticus 12:1-8 that were offered 40 days after the birth of a son. A new mother would offer a lamb and a young pigeon or turtledove, or if she couldn't afford a lamb, then two pigeons or turtledoves. It sounds like, from the quote Luke chooses, that perhaps she couldn't afford a lamb. It seems this is combined with the redeeming of a firstborn (Exodus 13:11-15) as I could not find a specific law laid out for the process of offering something to God to redeem a firstborn. Luke seems to be affirming that Jesus' parents were righteous, and that they kept the required laws for their son.

QUESTIONS FOR DISCUSSION

* What's the longest you've ever had to wait for something?

* Can you think of other Bible stories where God promised something, but they had to wait a long time?

* Why do you think God makes people wait?

* Mary and Joseph were careful to follow the spiritual requirements for themselves and Jesus. What can we do to ensure our children get the best start in a life of faith?

Matthew

CALL OF THE RABBI

If only he could go inside. He rubbed the ache within his chest and drew a deep sigh through his nose. He was standing at the doorway of his own community synagogue, but he didn't dare set a foot inside. He imagined himself slipping silently into the room, but he knew as soon as his shadow darkened the doorway, every eye would swivel his way and every face would darken with rage.

"Get that tax collector out of here!" someone would snarl, and he'd have to slink away as everyone muttered.

It was easier when Jesus taught outside, like when he had spoken from the hilltop. On that day, Matthew had slipped along the edge of the crowd until he could clearly hear the amazing words of this new rabbi. He had never heard anything like it before! The rabbi spoke like one of the sages in Matthew's scrolls, but with an authority that defied all convention.

With confidence, the rabbi had said, "Ask, and it will be given to you; seek, and you will find; knock and it will be opened to you."

Standing here now, on the stone steps of the synagogue, Matthew's eyes smarted with hot tears. He didn't dare knock on the door in front of him, and so he could not hear what Jesus of Nazareth was teaching today. The ache in his chest deepened until he felt his shoulders bow forward. Rubbing the back of his hand across his eyes, he turned and went back to his booth, defeated.

His co-worker, Aaron, scowled as Matthew slipped behind the counter. "You tried to hear him again, didn't you?"

Matthew nodded, dropping onto his stool and straightening the ledger unnecessarily.

Aaron clicked his tongue. "There is no place for you there. You know that, don't you?"

Matthew didn't reply. He knew it was true, but he didn't want to admit it. When he had accepted this job he knew things would be hard, but he had underestimated how painful it would be.

The job had become available at a crucial moment when Matthew was desperately in need of funds to care for his sick father. Aaron, the local tax-farmer, had taken pity on him and had gotten him the position of tax collector for the town of Capernaum. Some would have coveted Matthew. Though there were no official wages, it was a lucrative business—if you weren't afraid of getting your hands dirty. With his new job, Matthew had the money to summon the physician from Magdala, buy the medicine, and hire a local woman to nurse his father. Even so, the best they had been able to do was make his father comfortable until his death only a few weeks later.

Now Matthew was alone, in more ways than one.

"Cheer up," Aaron said, his tone softening. He offered an encouraging smile. "I'm sure there's nothing that rabbi will say that you can't read in one of those scrolls of yours."

"Mmm," Matthew murmured noncommittally.

Aaron clapped a hand on Matthew's shoulder. "I know, I'll go get us something nice to eat. All right? You'll feel better with a full stomach." Aaron hastened away to the market.

Matthew sighed after him. Aaron was as close a friend as Matthew had, but the men had very different hopes for their lives. Aaron wanted to be rich and happy. Matthew was of the tribe of Levi, the tribe that served the temple and the priests. He should be a scholar and servant of the Most High, taking his turn serving in the temple courts. His father had traveled once a year to take his turn singing on the steps of the temple and doing tasks around the compound, bringing an excited Matthew along once he was of age. But now his father was gone, and Matthew wasn't summoned to serve with the other Levites.

Matthew leaned on the counter with his elbows, dropping his chin into his cupped palms. There was a hunger in him that no delicacy from the market would ever fill. He needed to feel … accepted again. He needed to feel like he belonged with God's people.

Being a tax collector put Matthew on the same social level as the prostitutes in the brothel in Magdala. He was taking money from his own countrymen and giving it to Roman oppressors. Judas the Galilean said that giving tax money to Rome was selling themselves into slavery, knuckling under to Gentile pagans with their false gods. He said it was an affront to God. Judas' teachings had only served to make the people hate men like Matthew even more.

A hum of voices broke through his dull mood and Matthew tipped his head to glance down the road. He leaped to his feet, knocking his stool backward. Jesus was coming this way! Matthew knew he shouldn't be surprised. After all, this was a busy road with people coming and going all day, but his heart pounded against his ribs and his palms dampened. Jesus was going to walk right past and see him standing here —if Jesus didn't avert his eyes like everyone else. Matthew swallowed several times, his stomach writhing. He couldn't have felt more nervous if the governor himself was arriving to inspect his ledgers! He clumsily righted the overturned stool and sat on it, trying to look casual.

The crowd moved closer and closer and Matthew drummed his fingers nervously. Would Jesus look his way? Would Jesus despise him? Matthew recalled Jesus' words on the hill as if he had just heard them.

"You have heard it was said, 'You shall love your neighbor and hate your enemy.' But I say to you, love your enemies and pray for those who persecute you, so that you may be sons of your Father who is in heaven; for He causes His sun to rise on the evil and the good, and sends rain on the righteous and the unrighteous. For if you love those who love you, what reward do you have? Do not even the tax collectors do the same?"

Matthew dropped his gaze to the grassy slope, feeling ashamed that his trade was used to illustrate the lowest moral standard of the community. He wanted to throw off his career right then and there, but what would he do then? He was a leper to the community now. No one would hire him. If he bought a boat with his ill-gotten gains and returned to fishing, none of the men would work with him. The synagogue would not forgive him until they had publicly whipped him. Even then, the stigma of his career would haunt him forever. His head had stayed bowed as Jesus kept speaking to the people. Jesus began to instruct them on how to pray. One of the lines had struck to the heart of Matthew's soul.

"Forgive us our debts, as we have also forgiven our debtors."

Matthew owed the people a great debt for the money he overcharged. He imagined how it would feel to have his people's forgiveness and acceptance again. He wanted to be included in the synagogue and be able to worship and serve!

Jesus was nearly alongside his booth, and Matthew fidgeted with his pen. Part of him wanted Jesus to look at him, and the other part hoped Jesus wouldn't notice he was there.

The rabbi was almost directly opposite, talking with one of the local fishermen, Peter. Matthew had heard how Peter had become a disciple of the Nazarene, and he felt a pang of jealousy. If only . . .

Jesus turned his head, and his eyes locked with Matthew's. Matthew clutched the counter for support as Jesus didn't look away in disgust. The crowd around the rabbi looked confused at Jesus' pause, and one of the local Pharisees grinned—obviously eager for the setting-down Jesus was about to give.

Matthew yearned to say something, to ask Jesus if there could be forgiveness and acceptance for one like him, but his dry tongue was stuck to the top of his mouth.

Jesus smiled, and it deepened the lines around his eyes. He swung an arm, beckoning to Matthew. "Follow me!"

Matthew was stunned. "M-m-me?" He pointed to himself.

Jesus chuckled and nodded. Matthew scrambled around the booth, leaving ledger and pen behind as he went to stand on the outskirts of the crowd around Jesus. The Pharisee's gaze darkened, but Peter reached out and pulled Matthew among the disciples of Jesus.

"Welcome, Matthew," Peter said as Jesus began to walk forward again. He laughed at Matthew's expression. "You look astonished now, just wait until you see what else Jesus can do!"

Matthew grinned, hope dawning. He looked ahead and saw the sun glinting off Jesus' windblown hair. He felt the comradery of the men around him, and none of the seething animosity that he waded through on a daily basis. His chest swelled with emotion. Despite what Peter had said, he doubted he would ever feel more astonished and gratefully joyful than he did just now.

Read the inspiration for this story in
Matthew 9:9, Mark 2:14, Luke 5:27

STORY COMMENTS

Reading the above scriptures will show at once that I've invented a story for Matthew. While most of this short story is a guess, there are some historical facts woven throughout. Not all the apostles have their calling recorded. Matthew has his written in three of the gospels, so there must be something significant about the way he comes to Jesus.

It is interesting in the Bible how people often had more than one name. Matthew appears as "Levi" in the parallel stories, but seems to be one and the same man from the similarities of the accounts. In the first century, it was common to have a Greek name and a Hebrew name, and sometimes an Aramaic name too. The Apostle Peter is also called Simon and Cephas for example, and Tabitha is also called Dorcas. Understanding the history of names in the first century helps clear away some of the confusion.

In this story, I expanded on the theory that his name, Levi, implied he was from the tribe of Levites. This is not proven historically, but I used this in my story to show some of Matthew's frustration that he can't serve God the way he was intended to, in the same way that our own sins separate us from closeness with God. When we see Jesus call Matthew, he is not only giving the tax collector a chance of community again, he is giving him a way to serve God, something we should all crave.

You can read about the duties of the Levites in 1 Chronicles 9: 14-34, with the two main duties being singers and gatekeepers (Ezra 2: 40-42). *Backgrounds of Early Christianity* says that these duties rotated, and only "Four chief Levites were on permanent staff of the temple: two overseers of the musicians (one of instrumentalists and one of singers) and two overseers of the Levitical servants (a doorkeeper and a supervisor of those who did the menial work.) The Levites provided the music for the different services, certain physical and custodial duties, and police functions." - *Backgrounds of Early Christianity* page 566

You've likely heard how despised tax collectors were to the Jewish people in the first century. Even though this civil job was necessary in their current political circumstances, Luke tells us how they were lumped in with the "sinners" in 5:30; 7:34; 15:1; 18:11. Their name is next to the prostitutes in Matthew 21: 31-32. They were not welcome in polite society. *The Dictionary of New Testament Background* page 1165 says, "… the rabbis regarded as unclean any house entered by a tax farmer."

There were many types of taxes, both ones ordered by the Jews for the continuation of the temple services, and various taxes that were sent as tribute to Rome to fund projects and the army. Depending on where you lived, there was tax on land, trade, sales, houses within cities, crops, and by the head. Different types of tax-collectors performed different roles. The most lucrative positions were sold to the highest bidder, and that bidder would be looking to get a good return on their investment. These men were often called tax farmers, because they paid the taxes upfront from their own pocket, then set about collecting them in their various methods and with several employees. Many methods of gathering taxes were crooked, such as appraising the value of property or goods.

It would be stunning to a first-century audience that a tax collector became a disciple. That this former tax collector is later called an apostle was a striking message about the forgiving and accepting nature of God's kingdom, one that Matthew would never forget.

The story of Matthew shows that it isn't what we've done that matters, but what we do when we hear the call of Jesus.

QUESTIONS FOR DISCUSSION

* Why do you think Matthew's call to follow Christ is singled out among the disciples?

* Sometimes we realize we have headed down the wrong road in life or faith. How do we get back on the right track again?

* Do you think Matthew being a tax collector influenced the other disciples' views?

* Can you think of stories where Jesus welcomes other

tax-collectors, or uses them as examples in a story? How do you think that made Matthew feel?

The Poor Widow

HER LAST TWO COINS

She sat beside the front door of the house, her few possessions beside her. She wouldn't be able to sit here long. Soon the new inhabitants would arrive with their barrels and baskets. She could see them in her mind's eye—a young family perhaps, the mother carrying a toddler on her hip, her middle possibly round with her next child. The father would eagerly inspect the workroom, already calculating how soon he would be turning out the finest wares in Jerusalem. They would all be full of hope for the future. Hope she couldn't share.

She glanced up and saw her landlord striding towards her, his dark scribal robes flapping behind him.

"Aren't you gone yet?" he asked sourly. She scrambled to her feet, clutching her basket and bundle of clothes.

She looked up at him. "Could I have just a few more months, my lord? I've written my son again. Surely, this letter will reach him. Then he'll send me money or come and collect me." His bearded face was implacable. Her voice became a whisper, "Or even just a few weeks? Please, I have no family in the city."

His eyes were hard. "You had months to get your affairs in order. If I give you free housing, how long will it be before all my tenants are giving me a sob story and asking for their rents to be forgiven?"

Sob story? Her mind reeled at his callousness. Her husband had died and she was alone!

"My son—" she began, but he held up his hand.

"He wrote to me. He did receive your letter." Her heart rose, but the landlord's expression checked her joy. His next words crushed her hope. "He wishes to honor the Lord, so instead of sending you money, he is dedicating a large sum to the temple. The money will provide sacrifices to God. You should be proud. He has a pious heart."

She stared at him, stunned. She had heard of such "piety". Instead of honoring father and mother with care, sons and daughters gave money to the temple, and were praised by the scribes and teachers for their generosity!

But what of me? She wanted to cry, but bit her tongue. It was clear that her landlord had no intention of mercy.

The man checked the house inside and out while she watched dully. Was he making sure she hadn't taken anything? She was too weighed down to care. He came back to her and his frown deepened.

"You need to leave. Walk to your son, or take up lodgings with friends, or go beg in the temple courts if that's what you wish, but first of all you need to leave before my new tenants arrive."

"Yes, that would be awkward, wouldn't it?" she whispered. "Watching a penniless widow turned from her house." His expression darkened and she numbly turned away.

She stumbled down the warren of narrow streets in the Old City. The cobbled roads were clogged, and she was jostled one way and then the other as she drifted aimlessly. Glutted with pilgrims for Passover, the city was a sea of tired travelers and eager sightseers.

She should be preparing for the festival like everyone else. Instead, she was homeless and unwanted. A widow without anything to her name. Well, she had a little money. She reached into her basket and pulled out two coins. They were worth less than an hour's labor, and would barely buy enough food for her supper.

She reached the end of the street and looked up. Way up. From where she stood, in the lowest part of the city, the tall stone walls hid the temple from view. People walked up and down the staircases, busy with worship or admiring the gleaming marble temple ornamented with gold. This was where her son had sent the money instead of caring for her. This was where her landlord came daily to pray and teach in the courts as a devout rabbi. She laughed at the irony. The temple was the heart of her people's faith, yet this lifeblood would be fueled by her own loss. Her husband's death helped line the coffers that bought sheep and wine, grain and incense, fine flour and oil, all to be poured out on the temple altar and eaten by the priests themselves.

Her stomach growled, but instead of going to the market to buy a little bread, she found herself climbing the steps to the temple courts.

She went through the gate and into the enormous courtyard. She could hear the cooing of doves and the bleating of sheep. Men weighed out grain and wine for offerings. All of which cost money. The money changers counted out temple coins to replace the Roman coins. After all, you couldn't offer pagan money to God.

In an open space, an ornate wooden chest was flanked by temple guards with long spears. There was a narrow opening on the top of the box, and men with purses full of coins lined up to drop in their donations. It made a clinking noise as the coins fell one by one.

She looked down at her two copper coins. They had been minted a century ago under a Jewish king. They were acceptable in the temple. Though, who dared to give so little? It would be an affront.

She clutched the coins in her palm until the cold metal grew as warm as her flesh. It seemed unreal. How could little bits of metal determine whether she ate or not, whether she lived or not?

Her eyes rose over the donation box to the temple itself. It was God's dwelling place. The place of the great I Am. The God of Abraham, Isaac, and Jacob. The God of the rich patriarchs but of the poor commoner too. Some were born to a life of ease, and others to hard work. It was God who really decided a person's fate, wasn't it? It was God who raised or lowered His people. It was said that God would protect the fatherless and the widow.

She opened her palm and looked down at the two coins. She didn't know what she would do tomorrow. She didn't even know where she would sleep tonight. She closed her eyes.

"Do you see me, Lord?" she whispered. "Do you see this poor widow? I ask you to care for me, for no one else will."

She opened her eyes and joined the queue at the donation box, feeling very out of place. When her turn came, she felt the heavy eyes of the guards. She held her shaking hand over the little opening. It was the last of her money. Yet, what good was a little bread if she was alone?

"Bless me, Lord," she whispered. She tilted her open palm and let the two coins slide into the black crevice and disappear. They made the tiniest noise.

As she turned, she saw a man observing her. He spoke to his young companions and they looked her way in question. She blushed and hurried away and out of the courts.

Read this story for yourself in Mark 12:41

Story Comments

I've made up a backstory for the widow, but I believe I've based it on a historical situation, one that Jesus condemned.

Jesus is angered that the scribes "devoured widow's houses". (Mark 12:40) These rich men took with one hand and gave generously to the temple with the other. God is not pleased with this kind of worship. In fact, soon after watching these donations of money, Jesus prophesied the temple would fall. (Mark 13:2)

Jesus condemned the Pharisees and scribes in Matthew 15:3-9 for replacing the God-given law to honor parents with a man-made tradition that allowed that honor be given to God instead. While that doesn't sound so bad on the surface, this meant they were no longer honor-bound to care for their parents! It is ridiculous, to the point of seeming out-of-date and easy to skim over, but we need to be careful to hear the lesson for ourselves. We can't have true worship if we are running rough-shod over our neighbor. Yet, the scribes and teachers were trying to do just that.

The poor widow gave her last two coins and we sit in awe of her. If she gave out of faith, she is a woman worthy of being emulated. The usual slant of this story is about the widow's generosity, but I am intrigued by the opposite side. Should she have *had* to give her last?

What happened to her after this gift? Was Jesus praising her willingness to starve to death for the sake of giving to God? When the people were selling their possessions after the day of Pentecost, this was to create a community where all had enough, not that they gave away everything and then starved. (Acts 2:44-45)

Is the emphasis of this story on those who poured out donation money, but weren't giving anything worthwhile at all? They were forgetting the more important law of mercy. They should have been caring for this poor widow. Maybe they'd have less money for the temple, but they'd have done more for the heart of God.

Isaiah 58 talks about the sort of fast (a type of worship) God desires. "Is it not to divide your bread with the hungry, and bring the homeless poor into the house?" In Matthew 9:13, Jesus quotes Hosea 6:6 and says that God desires compassion, not sacrifice.

I think Jesus would say that we need to give generously without fear, but we also need to care for those who need it.

QUESTIONS FOR DISCUSSION

* Have you ever hesitated to tithe because you were afraid you wouldn't be able to afford rent or food?

* Does your church take care of its own members, making sure that people are given a helping hand when they need it?

* How can you find a way to help those less fortunate than yourself—in time or earthly goods?

The Paralytic

TRAPPED IN REGRET

The mat lurched to the side. Uriah wanted to fling out a hand to catch himself, but he couldn't move. He wanted to cry out a warning to his friends, but his tongue wouldn't obey. At last they realized he was slipping and quickly leveled the thin mat that had been his prison for over a year now.

"Sorry about that," his cousin said as he looked back and smiled encouragingly. "It's not much longer, don't worry."

Don't worry. He might as well have been commanded to stretch these shriveled limbs and run through the ripening fields. His starved eyes tried to see above the edge of cloth, and he swallowed with difficulty. He was always drooling, he disgusted himself.

Uriah had been so proud of his strength and bearing. The local girls had glanced his way when he passed, and he had laughed a little louder, spoken a little bolder, and thrust his chest out a little more. That was before. Before he had been struck down with a fever that ravaged his body for more than a week. He had barely managed to keep alive.

In his hazy memories, he recalled his mother and father speaking in hushed tones. He had heard them discuss calling a priest to rid him of the demon that was sapping his strength and stealing his words. He had trembled with aches and pain while voices were chanted for hours. He had closed his eyes with feeble hope for healing.

Unrequited hope.

His father journeyed to Jerusalem and offered sacrifices on his behalf in the temple. Meanwhile, his mother had to change his clothes like he was a swaddling baby. It was humiliating, and he didn't even have the words to cry out in anguish as his life was leached from his bones.

In the end he was left utterly paralyzed.

Living on sips of broth, his body shrunk. When his mother lifted his arm to wash it with a damp rag, he saw the limb had shriveled. His hand bent towards his wrist and his fingers were claws. He had closed his eyes, refusing to look, and tears ran unchecked down his cheeks to tickle his ears.

His father came home from Jerusalem and rushed into the house full of hope. His crushed expression when he saw his eldest son lying feebly on his mat nearly broke Uriah's heart. His friends stopped coming to visit. His younger siblings were scared of him. Even his parents seemed to forget there was a mind trapped within the lifeless body, and neglected to talk and share their day with him.

He had nothing to do but think and reflect on his life. A life of selfishness and of gluttony for every scrap of pleasure he could grasp in a hard world. He had cared little for the things of the Lord. He had attended Passover, kept the feasts, and attended synagogue, but he had been more delighted with meeting his rowdy friends than serving the Lord. The God of Israel was distant, untouchable, and little concerned with him. So why should he bother with God? Didn't the sun rise and spread over the land, even when Uriah shrugged off his faith? Didn't the Romans sacrifice at pagan altars, yet revel in wealth and superiority?

While he lay by the hearth, his mother often sang the lilting melodies he had heard his whole life. Heard, but not comprehended. With nothing else to do, he meditated upon the psalms she sang. Songs of hope, of redemption, of judgment for evil. He swallowed hard. He knew, deep inside, that he had no place in God's favor. He had play-acted faith, and his heart was far from the Lord.

The day came when something changed within. He longed to make it right, with an ache that clutched his chest and dug under his ribs. Yet, how could he? He needed to go to the temple in Jerusalem and offer a sacrifice for atonement. He needed to stand before the altar and watch the smoke rise up to God and know that God could see him and the repentance on his heart. He tried to beg his father to take him, but the words came out garbled. His mother shushed and tried to soothe him like he was an infant.

He had laid for months, wallowing in guilt for his sin, with no possible way to atone. Would he die with this burden upon his heart?

Then, this morning, his long absent friends had burst into the house. Their youthful steps and their tumbling words were a painful reminder of his own frailty. Did they realize how fortunate they were? They could go to the temple whenever they wished! Then he listened to what they were saying.

"There's a prophet with healing powers, and he isn't far! Can we take Uriah to him?"

Hope surged in his heart. If he was healed, he could go to the temple! His mother had frowned and looked at Uriah with concern.

"I'm not sure if he can manage even a short journey," she said. "He's just too frail."

Uriah's heart pounded, and he tried to plead her with his eyes. At last she relented, and his friends picked up the corners of his mat and carried him outside.

Now, the bright sunlight nearly blinded him. The fresh scents of growing life, the buzz of insects, and the call of birds assaulted his senses until he was dizzy. His friends chattered constantly, telling him all the things they would do when he was better. His heart lit up with hope at all they said, but above all, he wished to have his sins forgiven. He would live his life in faith, if only this prophet would give him the chance.

He could hear that they had entered a nearby town, and he recognized the market by a glimpse as they passed. The town was busier than he remembered, and the voices were excited.

"Let us through!" his cousin called ahead, then looked back over his shoulder with frustration. "The house is packed." They gently set him down.

They hovered outside, and Uriah's hope faded until he was sure he would be taken back home, laid at the hearth, and die. As an hour passed, and then another, he took comfort that his friends seemed undeterred. He saw them put their heads together and whisper.

Without pausing to explain to their paralyzed friend, they took up his mat and went around the back of the house. Uriah swayed side to side as they climbed up the stairs to the flat roof. He was laid on the thatched top, and thankfully his head was turned so that he could watch with wonder as they began to tear into the mud and straw, breaking a hole in the roof.

"Get some rope!" one called. Uriah's heart pounded with fear as they tied the ends to his mat, and lifted him to test the weight.

He wanted to cry out in protest as they shuffled sideways, and he could hear exclamations below him. He squeezed his eyes shut and prayed his friends would not drop him. He believed that if he fell, his frail bones would crumble like dust.

He felt something beneath him, and then he settled to the ground. He opened his eyes, and all around him faces peered down. He saw judgment, concern, pity, and surprise. He looked past them, up to the jagged hole in the roof, where his friends' eyes were shining with hope.

Then he saw another face, with eyes that pierced him to his very soul. The eyes of a prophet. Those eyes cut him open and laid bare his heart and saw every failing, and every prayer for the chance to atone.

The prophet grinned at the hopeful faces above him, then smiled down on the cripple at his feet. "My friend, your sins are forgiven."

Tears smarted his eyes as light poured into his heart and filled him from his head to the ends of his toes. He couldn't explain why, but he believed the prophet. He was forgiven, absolved before God. Tears ran unchecked down the sides of his face in gratitude. He felt that if he were to die now, he could die in peace.

The prophet's eyes snapped up, and his gaze was fixed across the room. "Why are you doubting in your hearts? What is easier to say, 'your sins are forgiven', or 'pick up your mat and walk'? So that you understand that the Son of Man has the authority on earth to forgive sins—" he looked down on Uriah again, and power seemed to radiate from him. "Get up! Pick up your mat, and go home."

Uriah's heart gave an enormous leap. His skin crawled as tingles ran up and down his limbs. He dared to twitch a finger, and felt it obey. He wiggled his toes, and they moved. Joy flooded into him. He smiled, and his cheeks obeyed. He rose up to stand and felt his muscles return to their previous vigor. He stood straight and tall, but not proud. Gratitude coursed through his veins now.

The entire room was silent as he rolled up his mat, tucked it under his arm, and looked for the door. He glanced to the side and nodded to the prophet, happiness instead of sickness choking off his words. He walked to the door, and the crowd pulled back. He stepped out into the sunshine and heard the exultant shouts from his friends as they scrambled down from the roof. He laughed aloud. God had seen him suffering on his mat, and had worked to bring him before this prophet. God is glorious!

Read this story for yourself in Luke 5:18-25

Story Comments

Every time I read this story, I wonder why Jesus forgives the paralytic before healing him. Jesus does a lot of healing, but it sounds like this forgiveness was a new thing in his ministry—it sure got the Pharisees grumbling anyway!

Perhaps the paralytic truly understood what I often forget, that the health of my soul is more valuable than my physical health. I can be in peak physical condition, but if my soul is rotten, what will be left when my body fades in bad health or old age?

In writing this story, I didn't give the paralytic a deep, dark secret either. I made him struggle with what I, and perhaps you, struggle with: Loving God with more than just outward righteousness, but with my whole heart, soul, and mind.

Questions for Discussion

★ How can we move beyond outward obedience to the Bible and hold it in our hearts?

★ Do you remember a time when you ached for forgiveness?

★ What do we need to do to be forgiven? (Read Acts 3:19, Ephesians 1:7-8, 1 John 1:9)

★ I assume you care for your body. You brush your teeth, shower, eat, drink, sleep, wear clothing to protect yourself from the elements, etc. What could you do today to care for the health of your soul?

The Prodigal Son's Brother
STRUGGLES OF THE OTHER SON

The master of the estate patiently watched the servant set down the wooden tray and pour the wine into the earthenware cup. The servant added a splash of cool water, swirled it around, and held it out to his master. The master sipped, nodded in satisfaction, and shifted so he could see down to the road where the heat shimmered over the crushed yellow rocks.

He was on the flat roof of his house, beneath a thick canopy woven of black goat's hair. From within the house, he could hear chatter and the rough brush of a broom on the stone floor. Women sat side by side in the courtyard below, grinding grain in their hand-mills. He could taste the dust from the wheat as it rose in a cloud. The wheat harvest was nearly in. His oldest son had been working tirelessly overseeing the harvest. He smiled with pride at the thought of his hardworking, loyal son.

He was so lost in his thoughts, he almost didn't hear the servant's sigh. He glanced over, and asked, "What is it?"

The servant flushed and cast down his eyes, but his voice did not waver as he said, "I am only grieved for you, my lord. Every day you come up here at midday, and you watch and you wait. Your pain hurts us all, my lord. The entire household aches for your loss."

The master sighed and took a long drink. "And you wish I would stop coming up here."

The servant framed his words with an apologetic smile. "That son is gone, my lord, and with the way he left …"

"You don't think he's coming back."

The servant shifted his shoulders slightly. "We just want you to be happy, my lord. You have another, more worthy son." The servant saw his master's closed expression, bowed his head, and left with the tray.

The master took another sip. He knew his servant meant well, but the man just didn't understand. There was a place in his heart for each of his children, and those spots did not shrink or disappear with time. Though his heart was full of joy over his older son, he would grieve his lost son for the rest of his life. He would never stop waiting and praying for his missing son's safe return.

He fixed his eyes down the road and kept vigil, like he had every day since his son had demanded his inheritance, sneered a good-bye, and left with his nose imperiously in the air.

His oldest son had been furious. "Why did you give in to his demands? Why did you let him go? You knew it would break your heart."

He had tried to explain. "You would have me make your brother a prisoner? No, my son. Love does not take away choice, no matter how it hurts." His son had frowned, unable to understand.

Something shifted on the road. The father set aside his cup, his heart leaping into his throat. Was that … ? He squinted his eyes and made out a familiar figure. He did not doubt for even a second, it was his son! He leaped to his feet, the cushion from his seat spinning to the floor. He rushed down the stairs as tears formed in the corners of his eyes. His son was home! The servants heard his reckless pace on the stairs and came running to see what was the matter. The father didn't care who saw his indignity as he leaped down the last three stairs and ran down the road.

He met his lost child on the road. The father's heart nearly broke as he saw his son was barefoot, his feet scratched and bleeding. His clothes looked like they might have been luxurious—several months and many washes ago. His bearded cheeks were sunken from hunger, and his hollow eyes were dark with remorse. He had suffered, and it hurt the father's heart.

His son opened up his mouth to speak, but before a single word could be uttered, the father wrapped him up in a warm embrace. The father felt bones from near starvation protruding beneath his hands. A choked sob rose in his throat.

The son pulled back from his father's love. His voice was husky as he said, "Father, I have sinned against heaven and in your sight; I am no longer worthy to be called your son. Just let me be one of your hired men, that's all I ask."

The servants were approaching now. Their eyes opened wide at seeing the selfish son being warmly embraced by the same father he had scorned. It seemed the son's hardheartedness was to be forgotten, lost in the father's joy.

The master called out to them, "My son was lost, and now he's found! Come, take my son to the house and get him washed and dressed. Give him sandals and a ring. We shall have a feast! Kill the fattened calf and we shall celebrate!"

The servants caught their master's pleasure and surrounded the son, laughing and talking all at once. The father beamed at the scene and followed the noisy crowd back to the house.

By nightfall, the feast was in full swing. The father was happy to see his restored son eating his fill, warm and dressed in good clothes. His son would heal from his ordeals, now that he was back where he belonged.

Yet, someone was missing.

The father went outside and found his eldest son sulking outside the door, still wearing his work clothes.

The father pleaded gently, "Won't you come into the feast?" The older son started at the sound of his father's voice and jumped to his feet. In the dim light from the doorway, the father saw resentment smoldered in his eyes.

His son's angry tone was tinged with hurt as he said, "Why are you celebrating *him*? He insulted you and squandered your fortune on prostitutes!" The older son's voice hitched with betrayal. "I have been here all the time, and have always obeyed you, Father. Yet, you never even gave me a goat to feast with my friends."

The father put his hands on his oldest son's shoulder. He was not embarrassed to plead with him. "My son, you have always been with me. All I have is yours." His son softened at the words, and the father tugged him towards the open door where laughter and music drifted out into the cool night. "But tonight we have to celebrate. Your brother was dead, and now he lives. He was lost, but now he's found!"

Read this story for yourself in Luke 15:11-32

STORY COMMENTS

This may be the most famous of Jesus' parables, even though it is only found in one of the gospels. I've heard it said that this story encapsulates the good news of Christ.

The story shows the forgiving nature of God. It is one of three parables given back-to-back in Luke 15, to illustrate to the judgmental Pharisees and scribes why Jesus was allowing the sinners to come near him. Each story has the theme of something lost being found. There is great rejoicing in each story when what was lost is recovered.

Yet, there is more here than just a story of forgiveness and hope for sinners. If that's all it was about, you could just omit verses 25-31 that feature the grumpy older brother.

I don't know about you, but at least a few times in my life I have felt sympathy for the older son.

The reckless, hurtful son is just as loved as the obedient, hardworking one. That feels amazing for the reckless son, but it feels unfair to the good son sometimes. This story is a typical case of the squeaky wheel getting the grease. And that's the emotion that Jesus is trying to handle here.

This story isn't just about forgiveness for a total screw-up. This story shows that there is no competition for favor in God's eyes. It goes back to the start of the chapter. The Pharisees were biblical scholars, the ones society looked to for moral guidance. Whether or not they were failing, at least they had been trying. Now, these irreligious people come in at the last minute, and Jesus welcomes them. The Pharisees are indignant. Is there no reward for hard work and loyalty? When we cross the heavenly finish line, is everyone handed a participation ribbon, no matter how they ran the race?

Jesus is saying that is the wrong question. The responsible brother was concerned for his inheritance when the wayward child was welcomed home with open arms. The father was saying, "Don't worry about that. Your inheritance is secure. Focus on what matters: the lost have been found!"

Despite the popular title, this story is not about one son, but two. While we may sympathize with the prodigal son, I'd like to suggest that the emphasis of this story is the prodigal son's brother. If we look at this in context, this story is being told in response to the Pharisees and scribes. Who would they have related to here? The older son.

This is not a story originally given to uplift the sinners (though who has not been gratefully warmed by this beautiful story of God's eagerness to love and forgive us, no matter our mistakes?), but to instruct the Pharisees.

The Pharisees should have been overjoyed that the sinful people were eager for the word of God. They were too busy sulking when Jesus welcomed the people who needed help the most. "Why do they get the party, when we've been working for years?" they wonder.

Does God love the sinners in this story, and despise the Pharisees? Of course not. In the parable, the father is seen pleading with his older son and keeping his promise of reward for his heir.

Sometimes, we throw the Pharisees under the bus and write them off as the bad guys. At least we aren't like *them*. The funny thing is, that's exactly what the Pharisees thought of the rabble surrounding Jesus. It's important that we take these lessons given to the Pharisees and make sure we don't fall into the same trap.

QUESTIONS FOR DISCUSSION

★ Who do you relate more to, the reckless son or the obedient one?

★ Do you ever feel like God loves certain types of people more than others? Does this story support or deny your assumptions?

★ If you've been a "good Christian" all your life, do you ever feel like your road to salvation is not as interesting as those who took the long route with all its bumps and potholes?

★ Do you have great regrets about your past sins? Do you struggle to feel forgiven?

★ How can life-long believers support and welcome those who are new to faith?

Herod Antipas

HAUNTED BY THE PAST

Pacing, pacing, up and down the cool inner halls of his palace. Despite being sheltered from the arid heat out of doors, sweat beaded on Herod's face. Servants scurried quietly past in their duties, afraid of being noticed when their master was in such a state.

He paused in his pacing as Alexander, his clean-shaven butler walked calmly towards him, followed by a shrinking servant girl carrying a platter and a smaller boy balancing a pitcher of wine and a goblet on a tray. The lad was concentrating so hard not to spill a drop that the tip of his tongue protruded.

"My lord," Alexander said smoothly. "Come, sit, refresh yourself."

"Refresh myself?" Herod roared, wiping the sweat off his upper lip. "There is no refreshment for me, haven't you heard? John the Baptist has risen from the dead! He is traveling about the countryside and cities performing miracles! Am I ever going to be rid of him? Will he come before me? Will he want revenge?"

"Bah," Alexander said. He took his lord and master's arm and led him into a side room where Herod's favorite items, treasures collected throughout his rise to power, were displayed. "This man you've heard of is named Jesus of Nazareth, and he is no threat to you. Look around you! You have the greatest friends in Rome for your own. What is a poor man from the backwoods to you?"

Herod allowed himself to recline on the plump cushions and arranged his rich scarlet robes. The girl came forward, holding the silver platter laden with chilled fruits. The sight of the silver platter made his heart turn to ice as he envisioned the head of John the Baptist being handed to Salome.

"Take it away!" he cried. "Bring me something else, but not on anything silver!" Flinching as if whipped, the girl quickly backed away. Alexander raised an eyebrow, but nodded his head and followed her out of the room, his loose robe billowing as he walked.

The boy, without someone to pour for him, stood still as a statue, holding his tray and looking as if he hoped Herod would forget he was there.

Herod groaned and leaned his face into his hand, the images of his wife's daughter and her flashing feet spinning before his eyes. Why had he promised her anything she desired? And before all his friends, too. He had been tricked! Tricked into killing the man the people considered a prophet. Herod himself had enjoyed listening to the tirades of the crazy man in his wild clothing. It had been true theater, like something from the days of old.

Of course, recently John had been a thorn in his side. Truth be told, he had wanted John dead and gone, but he had not wanted to be the one to do it. He needed the Jewish people to admire and love him. To know that he, and he alone, was the peacemaker between them and the crush of mighty Rome. If only John had kept his mouth shut about Herodias. His hand fluttered over his eyes. John had brought this on himself!

Now, this Jesus was gathering followers and performing miracles. What would this mean for Herod's reign? What would Rome think of him if they knew that there was yet another rabble-rouser gaining prestige under his very nose?

At last, Alexander returned with the girl, distracting the ruler from his brooding. This time she carried a large enameled plate with cold meats and soft cheese with plump grapes. She set the tray down beside him, and Herod reached out his jeweled fingers to rip a piece of meat. The flash of gold and rubies soothed him, as did a long drink of the excellent wine that Alexander poured for him.

He looked around the room at the treasures he had amassed and smiled, comforted. He was untouchable. He had the ear of everyone important. Who had John been? No one! What trouble had his death caused? None! The problem of the raving prophet was finished. He would handle this new annoyance with the same ease. This Jesus of Nazareth would be forgotten, old news, while he, Herod, was almost a god.

"Oh, my lord?" Alexander said calmly. "The disciples of that prophet came and asked for the body, I told the prison guards to let them take it. I hope that was pleasing to you?"

"Yes, yes." Herod waved his hand languidly, his foul mood washed away by his wealth and power. "That business is finished then."

"Yes, my lord."

Read this story for yourself in Matthew 14:1-12

STORY COMMENTS

This story is about Herod Antipas, one of the sons of Herod the Great. When Herod the Great died, the territory was divided between three of his many sons: Archaelus, Antipas, and Philip.

Archaelus got Judea and the rich plum of Jerusalem, but he was so violent that a delegation was sent to Rome to have him replaced. Judea was then ruled over by a governor—Pontius Pilate in the days of Jesus' trial and crucifixion.

Philip ruled the area north and east of the Sea of Galilee. He was an able ruler and managed to keep both his Jewish and Gentile subjects fairly content.

Antipas was given the remaining territories, including Perea and Galilee. He built a new capital city for himself on the southern end of the Sea of Galilee. The city was built on a graveyard, making it unclean for his Jewish citizens. Then he went and named it after a Roman ruler, Tiberias. This city gives a little picture of how Jewish this ruler was.

John the Baptist took issue with Herod Antipas' wife, Herodias, saying the marriage wasn't lawful. Herodias had divorced one of Herod's half-brothers, Philip, (a different Philip, not the ruler mentioned above) so that she could marry Herod Antipas. Herod Antipas, in turn, divorced his wife, Phasaelis of Nabatea, to marry

Herodias. The country of Nabatea was insulted, and the divorce eventually resulted in war and Herod Antipas' exile.

Herod Antipas is very interested in John the Baptist. In the scriptures we read that he wanted John put to death, and yet he feared the crowd. It says that he was grieved when Herodias' daughter asked for John's head.

We have a man who loathes John for the trouble he has stirred up and yet is fascinated by him. Herod Antipas can't have John spouting off against the validity of his marriage—especially when it's already a sensitive topic among the more upright citizens. Yet, killing a man perceived as a prophet might incite a riot, a state of disorder that Rome strongly opposed. Many a leader had lost his power when Rome had to forcibly restore the peace.

What was going on in Antipas' mind? I see Antipas feeling as though he has made it in society, and he is determined to keep on top. I see him putting his faith in earthly power and treasures, the opposite of what Jesus has been doing. Antipas is swayed by his own emotions and desires, making him confusing and fickle. Jesus is firm in his faith in God. Herod Antipas and Jesus stand in sharp contrast to each other.

Questions for Discussion

- ★ Have you ever done something you didn't want to do because of social pressure?

- ★ Where do you place your confidence? In the governments, institutions, and people of the world, or in God?

- ★ How can we have confidence in an unseen God when life is hard and the bad guys seem to be winning?

- ★ Have you ever had to stand up for what is right, even though it cost you something?

Martha

BELIEVER

She pressed her fingers to her temples, rubbing in a circular motion, her eyes closed. Light from the doorway flickered through her lids. More were arriving. The large house was filled to the brim with mourners. Their intentions were good, but she was exhausted to the core of her being. Drawing deep through her nose, Martha opened her eyes and adjusted her lips into a calm smile. She greeted the latest guests.

"I'm so sorry for your loss," they said in hushed tones.

Martha murmured politely and squeezed their hands. She offered them refreshments and moved away, her throat burning with suppressed tears. She would weep later when she was alone—not now before all these people.

A wail from the room above ripped at her heart. She moved towards the stairs, but ten mourners beat her there. Martha, hoping their sympathy would rouse Mary to exert herself, found a place to sit where the sunlight struck the floor.

Her own grief leached life from her bones, but caring for her sister had become a weight almost too much to bear. Her sister was inconsolable. Lazarus, their little brother, had been in the tomb for four days, but Mary had scarcely stopped her weeping. She slept in fitful naps and only ate when Martha pleaded. Mary ate as if the action was a dishonor to Lazarus' memory.

"How can you think of food at a time like this?" Mary's tone had accused. Martha had not answered. Food was like ash in her mouth, but she knew her duty. Her younger sister was so unlike her. Martha was logical. Mary's passions were a raging fire—warming and wounding in turn.

Martha took comfort in the embrace of sunlight that fell across her lap. Mary's turbulent emotions would temper in time. The mourners would go back to their homes, and the sisters would pick up the pieces of their lives and move on.

Yet, Martha swallowed hard, she would have to live with the knowledge that all of this could have been prevented. Her dear brother Lazarus could be alive and well right now, if only … it was painful to think it, but she charged forward, determined to follow the cutting truth all the way through. If only Jesus had come when she had sent word. Now, it was too late.

"Martha?" a boy called out as he stepped into the room. Martha quickly rose to her feet, arranged her features, and greeted her neighbor.

"What do you need, Justin?"

"Jesus is coming! He's just outside the village!"

Hope flickered in Martha's heart. Jesus had raised the dead before! Yet, logic quickly added, none of them had been four days in the tomb.

She glanced upstairs to where Mary was lost in her sorrow. She would want to see Jesus too. Martha stepped towards her sister, but then paused. If she brought Mary with her, would Martha get even a moment to speak with Jesus herself?

Martha bit her lip with guilt at her own selfishness, but she needed a calm moment before Mary swept in like a storm. Slipping from the house alone, she hastened to the edge of town. Jesus loved Lazarus like he was family. Martha knew he would bring the sisters comfort simply by his shared grief.

She saw him at last, standing in the shade of a tree with his disciples around him. His face was serious, and she could tell at once that he knew. He knew Lazarus was dead.

He reached out to her. She came and put her hands in his, and as always, she knew he saw her heart.

Her lower lip trembled, but she managed to speak without weeping.

"Lord, if you had been here, my brother would not have died." She looked in his eyes, so full of life and power, and again hope flickered. "But I know that even now, God will give you whatever you ask."

Jesus' face softened. "Your brother will live again."

Martha searched Jesus' face. What was he saying, exactly? She knew Mary would have blurted out her heart, but Martha spoke carefully, not wanting to overstep. "I know that he will rise again in the resurrection at the last day."

Jesus spoke, and authority rang in his voice, "I am the resurrection and the life. The one who believes in me will live, even though they die; and whoever lives by believing in me will never die." He squeezed her hands. "Do you believe this?"

Martha's heart leaped within her. She did believe. Though she did not show it the way her sister did, love for God and belief in Jesus had become part of who she was.

Martha bowed her head reverently. "Yes, Lord. I believe that you are the Messiah, the Son of God, who is come into the world."

There was a moment of hushed silence, and when Martha lifted her head she saw Jesus' eyes shone with pride and brotherly love.

Jesus asked, "Where is Mary?"

Martha glanced guiltily to her feet and said, "I will fetch her right now."

Martha walked briskly home and went upstairs. Mary was staring out the window, her back to the mourners. Martha went to her, and her heart broke at the expression on her sister's face. Tears glimmered on her dark lashes, and her lower lip wavered as she whispered a psalm of David.

"My dear sister," Martha whispered, putting her hand on Mary's back. "The Teacher is here, and he is asking for you. He's by the fig tree on the edge of town."

Mary turned her liquid eyes to her sister at once, gave a little cry of pain and sorrow, and raced from the room in a flutter of rumpled robes.

Eyes followed her. "Poor girl, she's going to the tomb to weep," voices whispered all around the room. They funneled down the stairs after Mary, leaving the calmer, reserved sister behind without a thought. Martha felt a twinge of pain. Sometimes it was so difficult to be the one who kept things together.

Martha came last of all. Jesus was still where she had left him. As she half expected, Mary was on the ground at Jesus' feet, weeping loudly.

The crowd had spread out, hundreds of them, all of them weeping for the young man who had gone too soon. Jesus' eyes brushed over them all.

Jesus rose Mary to her feet. His voice was thick as he asked, "Where have you laid him?"

"Come and see, Lord," Mary said, her voice wavering.

Martha saw Jesus' expression break at her words, and he drew a hand over his face as his shoulders shook. He cried openly with the mourners.

Mary seemed soothed by his shared grief, and she walked beside Jesus. Martha wove her way through the crowd, and she was there with her sister when they arrived at the tomb. She took her sister's arm in her own, worried her pale sister would collapse. Thankfully, Mary looked up at Jesus instead, drawing relief from his tears.

"See how he loved him," Martha heard a woman behind her speak in admiration.

Another voice, lower and grim said, "He opened the eyes of the blind, surely he could have kept this man from dying."

Martha's heart wrenched at the words. She had thought the same thing when she sent word to Jesus. She had been so sure Jesus would come in time, that when Lazarus gasped his last, she had not been able to comprehend until Mary's wail had shattered her belief.

Jesus glanced to some young men nearby. "Take away the stone," he said.

Martha's heart leaped, but caution reined it back. She glanced to Mary with worry, and whispered to Jesus. "But Lord," she said. "He has been in the tomb for four days, there will be a dreadful odor."

Jesus' eyes were full of power. "Did I not tell you that if you believe, you will see the glory of God?"

Martha sucked in a breath and held it. Was Jesus going to raise her brother? Truly? She felt Mary trembling like a leaf by her side.

The young men rolled back the rock, exposing a low doorway that led to the small tomb, dark as night.

Jesus held out his hands, his face serene. He tilted his chin to lift his face to the heavens. "Father, I thank You that You have heard me, as You always do. I say this for the benefit of these people standing here, that they may believe that You sent me." Jesus looked back to the tomb, and he called loudly, "Lazarus, come out!"

Martha stared at the tomb. The crowd was so quiet she could hear a muffled shuffle from within. There was a collective gasp as a figure wrapped in linen appeared at the mouth of the cave.

Women screamed and fainted. Mary sat on the ground and cried out, "Oh!"

Jesus grinned at Martha, who let out her breath at last. "Go, help him take off his grave clothes," he said.

Martha, her heart in her throat, gathered up her skirts and ran to her brother. With trembling fingers she removed the cloth from his face. Her own dear brother, the one she had held as a baby; the one whose scraped knees she had tended; the one she had watched with pride the first time he read from the Torah; her own dear Lazarus looked back to her, his eyes wide with wonder and confusion. Martha swallowed a joyful lump in her throat, nodded once, and went straight to work undoing all the linens she had so carefully applied only days before, her heart singing within her.

Read this story for yourself in John 11:3, 10-44

STORY COMMENTS

Poor Martha! The story most people remember about her is of when Jesus is visiting and she complains that she's saddled with all the chores. Mary gets praised for knowing what is the most important: time with Jesus. No matter how gently Jesus admonished Martha, it still had to sting. (I've yet to meet a woman who enjoys being compared negatively to her sister!)

I think Martha is often presented as what-not-to-be like, and I think that is a tragic misrepresentation. I think John shows there is more to Martha than a fussy housekeeper, she is a woman of faith.

* She believes in Jesus' ability to heal.
* She believes that God hears Jesus.
* She believes in the resurrection.
* She believes Jesus is the Messiah, the Son of God.

That is more than many could say in the days of Jesus!

We could judge Martha's doubts, wonder how she could believe in Jesus' power and yet be worried about a stinky corpse, but we would be condemning ourselves right along with her. How many times have we doubted, after all that Jesus has done for us?

QUESTIONS FOR DISCUSSION

★ Are you more of a Martha, or a Mary?

★ The popular girls in my youth group were the ones "on fire" for Jesus. Which, to us teens, meant they were talented singers, vocal about their faith to strangers, opened up easily in small group, and were not afraid to express their emotions. If you were shy or quiet, it didn't matter how much you loved Jesus, you were never held up by your peers as a role model. What do the "on fire" Christians look like in your group?

★ Does faith look the same in every person?

★ How do you show your faith to the world?

★ How can we support our brothers and sisters in Christ who show their faith in a different way than we do?

Mary Magdalene
The First Witness

Mary jerked away from the nightmare, coming awake with a jolt. Her heart was racing, and her tunic clung to her clammy skin. She took a deep breath, but the close air was stagnant with sweat and sleep. She sat upright, squinting around the crowded, dim room. The men were sprawled along one side, and the women on the other. All of them had stayed up far too late, trying to understand what had gone wrong, and what they were supposed to do now. Now that he was—she swallowed hard—dead.

It was still hard to believe. The whirlwind arrest and trial had left her little time to come to terms with what had happened. Her loving, kind, and powerful rabbi had been betrayed by one of his own disciples and condemned by his own people. She shivered as she remembered in vivid detail the sound of the hammer blows as Jesus was fixed to the cross. She could hear the creak of wood and the straining ropes as the cross was lifted high, holding Jesus up so his accusers could mock and jeer at him. She could remember the taste of dust mingling with her salty tears as the earth quaked at the moment of his death.

Though the horrific images were seared on her mind with excruciating clarity, she would not have abandoned Jesus in his final moments for all the world. Most of the men had fled, fearing they would be arrested and face the same fate. It had been the women disciples who had rallied together and followed Jesus all the way through Jerusalem, keeping vigil with him in his final moments.

The women had watched Jesus' battered body be taken down from the cross by Joseph of Arimathea. Though he was free from earthly pain, Mary had winced for him as the linen cloth was wrapped around the shredded skin of his back. Jesus' own mother had carefully removed the crown of thorns, watering his brow with her tears. The women had washed and bound him in clean linen as the sun dipped towards the horizon, and had torn themselves from his side so the tomb could be sealed.

The sound of the grating rock settling into place had been the moment it all became real. Mary and the other women had fallen to their knees, their keening cries undulating over the Mount of Olives.

Mary felt new tears stinging the back of her eyes and threw back her blanket. The pale light creeping through the shuttered windows told her that dawn was not far off. She would go to the tomb and pray. Scooping up her shawl, she tiptoed around the sleeping forms of her friends and gingerly opened the door to slip outside. She drew a deep breath of the clean, spring air, and paused to put on her sandals.

She was only a few steps from the house when she heard a loud whisper, "Mary? Where are you going?"

Mary turned back and saw with surprise that the other women had followed her outside. Apparently, she was not the only one unable to sleep.

"I'm going to the tomb," Mary said, her voice scratchy with disuse.

"We'll go with you," the other Mary said, and the women nodded their agreement.

The women walked silently down the dusty road until they came to the part of the Mount of Olives that was pocked with tombs. The mountain was thick with olive groves and life, but here it was quiet. Even the birds were silent as the women picked their way down the winding path.

They were nearly to the tomb when another earthquake struck. Her heart turned over, and Mary heard the women behind her cry out in fear. A blinding light burst from the sky, brighter than lightning, and Mary instinctively threw out a hand to shield her face as she stumbled. The grating of rock sliding over rock raised goose pimples on her arms.

At last, everything was still. Mary lowered her hand and crept forward, feeling the other women huddling behind her.

Ahead was the tomb with its small opening. Sprawled in the dust were soldiers, fainted away like dead men. Sitting on the tombstone was a being, something she could only believe was a heavenly messenger from God, for his skin glowed with light, and his clothes were as purely white as freshly fallen snow. Mary's tongue cleaved to the top of her mouth in the presence of the angel.

The angel said, "Do not be afraid; for I know that you are looking for Jesus who has been crucified. He is not here, for he has risen, just as he said. Come, see the place where he was lying."

Mary's heart leaped within her chest like a spring lamb. Risen? Hope tingled in her veins, and despite her fear, she crept towards the yawning doorway of the tomb, fearfully aware of the angel's eyes on her as she approached. She made it to the tomb and was about to go inside when the angel spoke again.

"Go quickly and tell his disciples that he has risen from the dead; and behold, he is going ahead of you into Galilee, and there you will see him."

Mary nodded once, her mind reeling. She ducked into the tomb where the air was cool and dry. Her eyes adjusted and she saw the same small cave where she and the women had prepared Jesus' body. She reached a hand and fingered a pile of empty linen. He was gone! She turned to the other women in joyful fear, and saw their wide eyes and trembling limbs.

"He has risen!" she whispered and felt the truth of it pour into her being and infuse her with bursting joy. She cried it out, declaring it boldly, "He has risen! We have to tell the others!"

Read this story for yourself in Matthew 28:1-7

STORY COMMENTS

Each of the gospels have slightly different versions of this story, though they all have the same message: Jesus rose from the dead, and at least one angel proclaimed the Risen Lord to Mary Magdalene and the other women. Mary Magdalene is one of the first to see Jesus alive. She is told in each account to go and tell the others the good news, making her an apostle to the apostles, for apostle means "one sent".

Matthew's story gives a beautiful picture of how women helped Jesus in his final trial.

We see a woman anoint Jesus with oil in Matthew 26:6-13. This woman is following her womanly heart, while the men are making comments on finances. Matthew leaves her nameless. Is that so each of us can see ourselves in her?

In Matthew 27:55 we see many women are there with Jesus, while the men seem to have disappeared.

In Matthew 27:61, Mary Magdalene and the other Mary go with Joseph of Arimathea to the grave, and they're back again as soon as possible after the Sabbath. Did Jesus show himself to Mary Magdalene first because she was with him to the last?

Many like to point fingers at Eve as being the gender that led mankind to sin, but we can hold up women like Mary Magdalene and the other believing women as examples of how women can hold true to faith and bring hope to the world.

QUESTIONS FOR DISCUSSION

* Why do you think the women stayed with Jesus while the men left?

* What do you imagine the mood was like among the disciples while Jesus was in the tomb? What do you think they talked about?

* Considering the patriarchal society of the first-century world, does it surprise you that a woman was the first one sent to proclaim the gospel?

* Mary Magdalene couldn't have been the first to see the risen Lord if she hadn't tried to be with him. Do you ever long for God to come near to you, and yet you find yourself too busy to draw near to Him?

Peter

Choosing Love

"I can't sit anymore," Peter said, jumping to his feet. Restless energy pulsed through him. "We've talked and we've reasoned, and now we're just going around in circles. I need to do something!"

Six pairs of weary eyes brightened. None of them were scholars. They weren't used to sitting for days on end, hashing over little details.

"He's alive," Peter said, then paused for a moment at the weight of those words. It was still hard to get his mind around it. "But what's going to happen next ... well, only he knows. He'll tell us, but only when he's ready I guess."

"But," Thomas' brow furrowed. "This is the second time he's just disappeared. What if he doesn't come back this time? What if we're supposed to figure this out on our own?" He swiveled his head to look at the others, waiting for their agreement.

Peter didn't wait to hear what the others thought. "Well, talk till dawn if you like, Thomas," Peter said, beginning to bounce on his toes to release some of the energy in his calves. "I'm going fishing." Turning on his heel, he ducked out the low doorway of his Capernaum house and drew a deep breath of the dusky twilight air through his nose.

Home. Everywhere his eyes landed was familiar, yet things didn't look the same as they did before.

Before his rabbi had died.

Before his rabbi had appeared in the closed upper room in Jerusalem where they cowered from the Sanhedrin, fearing they would be next. Yes, the world was different, though he couldn't put his calloused finger on exactly how to define it.

He heard the other men following him out the door and grinned. Without glancing back, he set off to the pier.

"Zebedee!" he raised his hand in greeting as he saw his friend. Zebedee turned from where he was directing his hired men. "Don't hire out my boat today, I will be taking it out."

"It's about time!" Zebedee's voice rolled like thunder across the expanse. His gaze shifted. "I see you've brought my lay-about boys as well!" James and John laughed.

"Only because we feel saddened our father is too old to haul nets!" James bellowed over Peter's shoulder.

"Is that so?" Zebedee put his large fists on his narrow hips, lifting his barrel-sized chest. The forty-year-old man was the picture of mature fitness.

Peter's heart lifted with the familiar banter. Humor sustained the fishermen and softened the hardship, for their trade was a difficult one. Fishing was often done at night when the fish could not see the nets. The boats were cumbersome, the water deep and cold, and the hours long.

Yet, Peter loved it.

He eagerly untied his boat as James and John readied their own. A few quick words and the men divided themselves between the two shallow-keeled ships. The men shrugged off their loose overcoats, freeing their arms. Peter checked over his nets, lowered the square sail, and gave a mighty kick off the dock. The oars were slid into place, and Nathaniel and Thomas began pulling the boat through the water.

Peter felt the rudder fit into his palm like an old friend. The two boats sailed to an open part of the long and deep Sea of Galilee—sometimes called the Sea of Tiberias after Herod Antipas' new city.

The flickering glow of lamps from home grew faint, then disappeared. The moon was their only light.

"Let's try here!" Peter called across the shadowy water to James. Peter and James guided their boats close enough to toss one end of the massive dragnet to the other boat. Then they sailed slowly away from each other, Nathaniel letting the net slide over the edge and into the water. The weighted end sunk out of sight.

Once the net was spread out, Peter and James turned for shore, the net swooping out behind them. He pushed his hat back on his head and felt at home for the first time in weeks. They neared the shore, Peter not feeling any increase of resistance. His buoyant mood sank. They checked the nets. Nothing.

They went back out and tried another place. And another. The men grew frustrated and tired as their nets failed again and again.

The sun began to rise, tinting the graying sky pink.

"Well, that was a waste of time," Andrew yelled crossly. They brought their boats near each other and let them bob gently in place. Peter sat near his rudder. Failure weighed on his heart like an anchor.

Again, he had failed. He shook his head in frustration and whispered, "Lord, can't I do anything right?" The memory of his cowardice still hurt. The crow of a rooster would forever proclaim his failure. His denial of his beloved rabbi was a shame he could never rise from.

He felt a pang of panic. What if Thomas was right? What if Jesus didn't appear again? What if Jesus was disappointed in his disciples and had gone to find better ones?

"Hey there!" a voice broke through his dark thoughts. The fishermen turned to shore where a lone man was standing near a small fire. "I don't suppose you have any fish, do you?"

Peter sighed.

John cupped his hands around his mouth and called back, "No, I'm afraid not."

"Try casting on the right side!" the man yelled back. "You will find a catch."

The men looked at each with raised brows.

"What do you think?" James rubbed the back of his neck, easing his head back and forth.

Peter shrugged and rose to his feet. "What have we got to lose?"

They spread out to the right, the net stretching between them. They turned their boats toward shore.

They were almost back to shore when Peter felt the little boat shudder. They all stumbled forward as the boat jerked. They stopped as suddenly as if they were caught by an anchor. The surface before the net began to froth with a huge catch of fish.

The man had been right!

Peter looked back the shore where the man was watching them, his hands folded behind his back.

One of the disciples laughed aloud. "It is the Lord!"

Jesus!

Peter's heart leaped up into his throat. Without thought, he grabbed his outer coat and threw himself into the sea. Water bubbled over his head, and he kicked to the surface. He swam for shore, the other men laughing at him as they followed behind in the boats, dragging the bulging net.

As soon as he could stand, Peter rose up and sloshed to shore, water weighing down his clothes and cascading in rivulets from his hair.

Jesus was grinning with amusement as Peter stumbled out of the water.

It *was* Jesus, the one who had died and risen again. Peter froze a few feet away, overcome with wonder—and shameful regret. What could he say to the man he had denied knowing?

The fragrance of bread rose to his nose, and his stomach growled.

He flushed. How could he be hungry at a time like this?

Jesus followed his eyes to the fire where flat loaves were baking on the hot coals. He said, "Breakfast would better with fish, don't you think? Go and bring some from your catch."

"Of course!" Peter cried out, glad to have something to do. The boats were nearly to shore. Thomas threw him one end of the net, and Andrew the other. Peter began to haul the in net, his arms straining as he put his weight into it.

The other men jumped out to help, and together they brought the fish to shore. The baskets were laid on the pebbly beach and they gathered up the fish, glancing at Jesus from time to time, as he quietly tended the bread.

"A hundred and fifty-three!" John cried out gleefully, and they all marveled at the catch.

They chose the best of the fish and gutted them, tossing the entrails to some hungry gulls.

As they gathered around the fire, the rough men grew quiet. Jesus accepted the fish and laid them on the coals. They sizzled, and Peter's mouth watered. The damp fishermen hunkered around the warmth silently.

Peter saw the other men pointedly glancing his way, coaxing him to say something. Peter was usually the first to speak, the first to blurt out whatever was on his mind. But what could he say now? Memories of his vehement rejections of Jesus glued his tongue to the roof of his mouth.

Jesus was the one who broke the silence. "Let's have some breakfast!" He used a stick to pull bread and fish from the coals and held it out to Peter. Peter swallowed hard and took it. Jesus served them all and they sat on the pebbly shore and ate breakfast with Jesus.

Peter was licking the crumbs from his fingers when Jesus asked him, "Peter, do you love me more than these?"

Peter swallowed loudly, and tears stung in his eyes. The remembrance of his denial quickened his pulse. His voice was hoarse, "Yes Lord. You know that I love you."

Jesus spoke seriously, "Tend my lambs." He paused for a moment, as the other disciples watched with wide eyes. "Peter, do you love me?"

Peter felt a moment of panic. Did Jesus not believe him? His tone became insistent, "Yes Lord. You know that I love you."

Jesus nodded once. "Shepherd my sheep." He paused only a second before asking again, "Peter, do you love me?" Peter felt sweat break out on his brow. Why was Jesus saying this?

Peter cried out, "You know everything! You know that I love you." Jesus smiled at last. "Tend my sheep."

Peter felt his shoulders sag with sudden relief as if a great burden had been lifted from him. Three times he had denied his Lord. Jesus had given him the chance to replace three denials with three professions of love. He knew in his heart, he was forgiven.

Gratefulness rolled over him, followed quickly by an eagerness to do whatever Jesus asked of him.

Whatever Jesus had planned, Peter was ready.

Read this story for yourself in John 21:1-17

Story Comments

Jesus did something pretty incredible. He was tortured to death, yet three days later he's appearing in a locked room, walking and talking to his disciples, very much alive!

Then he seems to disappear for a while. Why? It doesn't really say. The disciples are left scratching their heads wondering what to do now. I have a feeling that Jesus' rise to glory was not what they were expecting!

The disciples do what I often do when confused, and just go back to life as normal. No matter how crazy life gets, dishes still need to be washed and laundry needs to be folded. I find some encouragement in the fact that these guys met Jesus face-to-face, and still struggled. When I'm not sure where to go with my own ministry, I am in good company!

Jesus shows up, helps them bring in a net full of fish, and true to his usual way of serving others, cooks them breakfast!

John doesn't tell us about Peter being called to be a "fisher of men" (Matthew 4:19) or about the time Jesus told Peter to cast out his net in the beginning of his ministry. (Luke 5:1-11) Both of these stories would tie in really well with this one, making a nice full circle in the story, but neither of them is in John. Most first-century churches did not have all four gospels to read. So what did the original readers hear when they listened to this story?

It seems to me that the highlight of this story isn't just about Peter's calling to shepherd Jesus' people, it's about Jesus giving Peter a chance to make things right. God isn't waiting to trap us or catch us up. He is loving and patient, and gives us many chances for forgiveness and relationship with Him. No matter what you've done or said, Jesus is ready, willing and able to forgive you.

Questions for Discussion

* Why do you think Jesus let them fish all night without catching anything?

* Why does God sometimes make us wait for a good thing?

* When Jesus says, do you love me more than "these", what do you think he was talking about? The breakfast? The disciples? The fishing boats? Or something else?

★ If Jesus was to ask you the same question, what would your "these" be?

Tabitha

A Woman Disciple

Tirzah wrung the cloth and gently dabbed the lifeless fingers, once so strong and nimble. There was a half-healed cut on one thumb that would never have a chance to close over. The pad of the middle finger was calloused from a lifetime of pushing a needle through fabric. These were the hands of a seamstress. She sniffed and a tear dripped off the tip of her nose.

The other widows murmured to each other as they prepared Tabitha's rapidly cooling body for burial. Each one of them had been touched by this kind woman's generosity and warm heart. Tabitha owned a thriving weaving business in the coastal city of Joppa, but since she became a disciple of the teachings of Jesus, she spent the profits on crafting clothing for poor widows and their fatherless children. Tirzah rubbed her nose with the back of her hand and glanced around at the other women. Each was dressed in quality clothing, thanks to Tabitha. Because of Tabitha's goodness, the women could hold up their heads without shame.

"There," one of the older women said, setting down her cloth. Tirzah clenched her linen rag in her fist. It was all happening too fast.

They dressed Tabitha in a soft, creamy white tunic and arranged her hair over her shoulder. The burial shroud would be ready by nightfall, and then the seamstress would be buried in her family's tomb.

"She looks so beautiful," one of the women whispered. "So peaceful."

"I'm glad she's not in pain anymore," another murmured. "At least her illness was mercifully quick."

Tirzah swallowed hard. True, Tabitha hadn't suffered for long, but that was meager comfort under the weight of her grief.

The women filed back downstairs and tossed out the soiled water. Members of the church were gathered below, and Tirzah's ears perked up when she heard eager whispers.

"I'm telling you, Peter is not far from here! He's only in Lydda! Come on, if we bring him here perhaps he can ..."

"Can what?" Brutus' voice was tinged with doubt. "She's dead, my friend."

"If he can cure a man who was paralyzed for eight years, perhaps he can do this! They say the apostles have the same Spirit as Jesus Christ. Didn't Jesus raise people from the dead?"

Tirzah felt her heart turn over and she impulsively cried out, "Do you think he would come?"

The room fell silent as everyone looked her way. The men glanced up in surprise.

"We won't know until we ask him," the first man said.

A dozen voices asked, "Who?"

"Peter the apostle."

A buzz filled the room until, finally, Brutus stood up. "You've all heard about the miracles of the Apostle Peter, and I'm sure you've heard that he's not far away. Our brother here—" he gestured beside himself "—suggests we send for Peter and see if he can help our sister Tabitha." A whisper danced from lip to lip. Tirzah's pulse flew as Brutus asked, "Shall we send men to Peter?"

"Oh, yes!" Tirzah cried out and the other widows chorused their heartfelt agreement. Within minutes, two of the young men were rushing out the door.

"Lord, let them find Peter," Tirzah whispered, folding her hands and pressing her thumbs against her upper lip. "You have seen the good Tabitha has done in Your name. Restore her to us, Lord!" Hopeful expectation swirled into the sorrow that filled her soul.

"Come, Tirzah," one of the older women tugged on her arm. "Sit with us."

Tirzah complied and went with the other women back upstairs to sit with the body. The heat of the day was oppressive, but a soft sea breeze drifted through the open window and brought a breath of relief. This was the time usually reserved for mourning with loud wails and laments, but the women were unnaturally quiet.

Tirzah looked around at their faces and saw their mingled emotions. Their deep sorrow was suspended for the moment, but none of them dared to hope too deeply. What if Peter had already left Lydda? What if he refused to come? What if … ? Tirzah squashed her fears, closed her eyes, and prayed to the one true God.

A little over four hours later, as dusk began to cool the air, there were voices outside the house and Tirzah's eyes flew open. The women rose to their feet and waited expectantly as they heard steady footsteps come up the stairs. Tirzah heard the woman next to her release a tense sob, and she reached out to clutch the woman's arm without taking her eyes off the door. Her heart ached with yearning, and her desire for Tabitha's restoration brought burning tears to her eyes. By the time the footsteps arrived at the upper room, all the women were weeping.

A man Tirzah did not recognize came into the room. At first glance, she was disappointed. He didn't look different than any other Jewish man. She had expected he would look … special. His eyes took in the room and softened with compassion.

Tirzah stepped forward, and said, "Please, come in and see our dear friend. Tabitha was a faithful disciple of Jesus, and she was so kind to us widows. Look! See the garments she made and freely gave to us! She was the kindest person I knew." She wanted to say more, but emotion clogged her burning throat.

One after the other, the widows told Peter about Tabitha's goodness until the air was thick with emotion and tears. At last, Peter held up his hand. His voice was soft but commanding as he said, "All of you, please leave the room."

The women glanced at each other and hastily complied. Tirzah was the last. She shut the door behind herself but didn't go downstairs with the others. Breathlessly, she waited.

She strained her ears, but all she could make out was a low murmur. From the rhythm, it sounded as if the apostle was praying. She heard a floorboard creak. She pressed her hands to her lips when she heard Peter say, "Tabitha, arise" as if he were waking her from a nap.

Tirzah heard a great sigh from the other side of the door, and her heart stopped. She stared wide-eyed as the door swung open before her. Peter nodded at her with a wide grin on his face. At first, Tirzah couldn't look away from him. How had she ever thought he looked commonplace? His eyes shone with the Holy Spirit! Hardly daring to believe, she looked over his shoulder.

"Tabitha!" Tirzah gasped. Her friend was sitting up, looking as fresh as if she had enjoyed a good night's sleep.

Peter laughed and called out, "Come on up, all of you! The Lord has restored our sister Tabitha to us!"

Tirzah rushed past Peter as she heard a great cry of joy rise from the room below. It sounded like a stampede was charging up the stairs, but Tirzah was enveloped in the arms of her friend, tears running freely down her face. She cried out, "Praise the Lord!"

Read this story for yourself in Acts 9:32-42

STORY COMMENTS

Do you want to be loved like Tabitha? (You may know her by her Greek name, Dorcas.) Perhaps you have wondered what will be said about you after you're gone. Tabitha was described as, "abounding with deeds of kindness and charity which she continually did." I would love to have that said about me!

Tabitha was so loved, that when she died, Peter was not only sent for, but asked to hurry. Peter did come, and after he prayed, God brought Tabitha back to life. We don't always see the rewards of our generosity and kindness, but Tabitha's good-nature had won her many friends, and because of their faith and God's will, she lived again.

Tabitha is called a disciple in verse 36. She is the only woman to be called a disciple in the Bible. Of course, she's not the only woman recorded for following Jesus. Luke, the author of Acts, lists some in Luke 8:2-3, and names several other women by name in Acts as well, including Priscilla and Lydia. Yet, Tabitha is the only one given the title of disciple. Why is this?

Was Luke singling her out as a way of showing why she was worthy of this miraculous resurrection? Is Luke giving honor to a woman who stood as a beacon and was loved in the early church? Was she perhaps educated and literate (rare for a woman in those days) and so she was able to study and learn scriptures in a way most women couldn't?

Whatever the reason, we can safely say that the first-century church did accept women as true disciples of Jesus.

As a young woman, I often felt that the Bible was slanted heavily towards men, and thought women were purposefully being shoved back into the kitchen and told to make a sandwich.

While it may be true that women often have the background roles, the more I learn, the more I see how valued women were in Jewish society and to Jesus in particular. I don't need to defend my worth as a woman disciple to the modern world. That is incredibly freeing!

Jesus spoke often on being humble, not putting yourself forward, and being a servant rather than a leader—I think these women of the first century were prime examples of this high ideal.

Jesus showed by his actions that all people are valued. Women of the first century mattered, and women today matter! My sisters in faith, whatever your role is, whether you're teaching in the children's classroom, preparing the communion trays, washing the floor, leading a prayer group, bringing something to potluck, or standing on the stage leading worship, you are a valued and necessary part of the church, and always have been.

Tabitha was loved because she was kind, charitable, and a devoted disciple of Jesus. Let's all try to be like this shining example of a woman disciple!

QUESTIONS FOR DISCUSSION

* What role do you fill in your church? Do you feel that it is valuable?

* Everyone wants to be loved by others. How did Tabitha find love? Do you think she proves the maxim that to have friends you must be a friend?

* Giving kindness is a great way to get friends on earth. Do we need to do anything to earn God's love? (Read

John 3:16, Romans 5:8, 1 John 4:19)

★ If we don't earn God's love by doing good deeds, why should we be good like Tabitha? (Read Romans 6:6-12)

Lydia

FIRST CONVERT IN EUROPE

"I bring you good news!" Paul said. "God has come among us at last! Let me tell you about Jesus Christ."

Tears overflowed from the fullness of Lydia's heart as she listened to the newcomer speak. Paul wore simple clothes and travel-worn sandals. His features were unremarkable, yet from his eyes shone the gleam of inner light and from his mouth flowed truth. Cutting, harsh, beautiful, lovely truth.

Lydia had become a Jewish proselyte years ago, even though the Jews in Philippi were few and the temples to stone gods were many. There were not even enough believing men in the city to have a proper synagogue.

The faithful women met weekly on the day of rest. Without a shared building, they gathered at the river to uplift and encourage each other. It had been that way for years—a small knot of believers in Europe, trying to keep connected to the God of Abraham, Isaac, and Jacob.

This morning was unlike any other. From the pulse hammering in her ears, and the repentance and joy flooding into her heart, Lydia sensed everything was about to change.

Paul casually told them he had been brought to Macedonia by a vision, as if such spiritual movings were normal in his life. He explained how he had traveled a vast distance to Philippi so he could speak to those far from Jerusalem, the believers in Europe.

Paul told them about Jesus of Nazareth—his miracles, his mercy, and his life-changing teachings. Yet, sinful man refused to accept him as the Christ, and instead delivered him up to Rome to be nailed to a cross.

The women cringed and uttered sorrowful cries. How was this good news?

Paul told them how Jesus had been obedient to God all his life, the perfect Israelite, the perfect human. He had given God all the honor He was due. On that cross, the symbol of shame to the world, God declared Jesus of Nazareth as King, and gave him all authority in heaven and on earth! He then raised Jesus from the dead. Death had been defeated, and forgiveness of sins was declared to the world! Lydia's heart leaped within her breast as Paul called out, "Believe in the Lord Jesus, and you will be saved!"

Lydia felt as if she was raised up by strings. She was on her feet before she knew what she was doing. "I believe!" she cried out.

"Then, come and be baptized in the name of the Father, the Son, and the Holy Spirit!" Paul grinned ear to ear and held out his hand to the river.

Lydia heard the other women whispering as she pulled off her head covering and her shawl and removed her shoes. One of the women hastened away, crying out that she was going to call the others. Lydia barely registered her voice. Her breath was quick in her throat and blood rushed in her ears.

The grass was soft beneath her feet as she moved to the water's edge. Paul's friend, Timothy, strode confidently into the river. She stepped into the water, and it was cold. Goose pimples rose up on her arms, but she strode further into the water, up to her waist. She felt her dress tugged by the current, and a shiver ran down her back. She faced the young man, and he beamed.

She let him take her shoulders and lean her back into the water. She pressed her lips together as she was enveloped in the river's embrace. Sound was muffled as the water pressed on her ears. She felt her feet come off the pebbly bottom, and for a moment she was weightless. It felt as if time stood still. Then strong arms heaved her to her feet and she rose back up to the sunlight and happy voices. She gasped in a fresh breath.

The young man clapped her on the shoulder and said, "Welcome to the family, sister."

Lydia laughed aloud, her hair plastered to her head, her pretty clothes bedraggled and limp. She waded to the shore and passed one of her friends eagerly sloshing into the water. She picked up her head covering and shawl and wrapped them around herself for warmth. She watched with a full heart as more and more went into the water to be baptized.

The family is growing fast, she thought happily. Family! What was she doing hanging around here like a freshly dyed ream of cloth? She need to share this good news with those she loved.

She ignored the staring townspeople as she rushed down the streets with droplets of water in her wake. At her joyful insistence, her entire household came down to hear Paul speak. Happy tears overflowed her eyes as her servants, the weavers, the dyers, and their families were all plunged in the waters.

There was quite a crowd at the river now. Rich and poor alike gathered to see what the ruckus was all about. Curious onlookers stood and watched, heads tilted to the side as they tried to puzzle out what was happening. Lydia's heart hammered in her chest. For years they had been a small group of believers in a pagan city. It seemed things were about to change!

Lydia looked over the dripping souls near the river, a laughing, celebratory, shivering bunch. She felt a nudging in her heart. They needed a place to meet. She was surprised when her own house rose up in her mind. She lived in one of the largest houses in Philippi and hired dozens of women to weave and dye the rich purple cloth that was in demand all over the world. She had so much on her shoulders already, yet she felt the pull in her heart to do more.

She walked up to Paul, who was speaking with his companions. They smiled at her, and it gave her courage.

"If you have judged me faithful to the Lord, come to my house to stay," she said.

"We don't wish to impose," Paul said. "We have secured rooms at the inn."

Lydia glanced to Timothy and laughed. "But we are family now! You must come and stay with me. I shall provide for all your needs."

They accepted, and Lydia's heart soared. As she gathered up her household to head for home, in her mind she was eagerly planning.

"Give me guidance, Lord," she prayed. "Let my home be a place of love and teaching for the city. Let my heart be open to serve."

Read this story for yourself in Acts 16

Story Comments

There are many ways to be a woman in the Lord. Lydia was a career woman. She owned a successful, profitable business. She was also the first convert in Europe and opened her home as the first church in Europe too!

Never let someone steal your joy in being a woman, or make you feel inferior to men in the church. There are many ways to serve in the home and out in the world. Any verses about the role of women that seem (in our understanding of a different time and culture) as if we are told to shut up and sit down, must be seen through the lens of the stories and lives of real first-century women.

* Instead of just dropping Jesus in the world, He allowed a woman to carry him in her womb. (Luke 1:26)
* Jesus was anointed by a woman, which gave him comfort in his grief when the twelve apostles did not understand. (Matthew 26:6-13)
* He had women who supported his ministry not only in service, but financially. (Luke 8:2-3)
* Jesus encouraged women to sit at his feet to learn, just like the men disciples. (Luke 10:39)
* The women were with him at his death. (Matthew 27:55)
* He appeared to women first when he rose up, and they were the first to proclaim a risen Lord! (Matthew 28:5-10)

Read through the New Testament and you will hear many women mentioned and greeted as fellow believers and workers for the Lord. Even before the time of Jesus, we read the stories of women like Shiprah, Puah, Deborah, Esther, Rahab, and the five daughters of Zelophehad—women who helped shape the world through faith.

Questions for Discussion

* Lydia believed, was baptized, and turned her faith into blessing others. In what ways, big or small, can you turn your belief into service?

* Could you host a small group Bible Study? Mentor a new believer? Invite someone into your home for a meal? Volunteer in your community?

* How do we give back to God and yet remain humble before Him?

Paul and Silas

LIGHT IN PRISON

Silas stumbled over the threshold, stubbing his toe. He sucked in a breath and wished immediately he hadn't. The stench of unwashed bodies and overflowing chamber pots burned his nose like fire. He gagged, but strong arms pushed him further into the dimness. He could hear jeers and shouts behind the rows of closed cells.

"In there," the jailer's voice was grim. In the light of a feeble torch, Silas could see the room that welcomed them. Barely five feet by five feet, it was a windowless cell with sparse straw tossed over a mud floor. Or perhaps there were stones beneath that mud. Perhaps it wasn't mud at all. He reined that thought in quickly.

"Sit down," the jailer said, snapping his fingers and pointing at the floor. Silas groaned as he bent to sit. His back, seat, and thighs were covered in welts. He was sure he would be every color of the rainbow by morning. Silas looked up as Paul was pushed into the tiny room after him, his movements pained and awkward. The jailer saw the older man's struggle, sighed, and reached out a hand to help lower Paul to the floor. It was a little act of kindness, but enough that Paul looked up and smiled.

"Thank-you," he said.

The jailer grunted gruffly. "Feet in there," he said, pointing to the wall. Silas turned and stiffened when he saw it.

Stocks.

The wooden board was mortared to the wall. It had four holes cut in it, each one ominously stained, and was hinged at the middle. The jailer knelt down and opened the contraption.

"There is no need," Paul said seriously. "We won't escape."

The jailer chuckled. "Is that so?" He reached out and took one of Silas' ankles. Silas didn't pull back, though part of his mind rebelled at willingly accepting the bondage. Within a minute he and Paul were fastened to the wall, firmly pinned in place like a shelf for pottery.

The jailer rose. "No screaming," he said firmly.

Silas wondered at the strange command, but understood better when the torch disappeared and he heard the grating of iron hinges and the clang of the door locking. There was no crack of light. Nothing to distract from the stink that filled his nose, the wood pinching his feet, or the throbbing of the bruises that covered him from neck to knee. Though he couldn't see them, the walls felt very close. Too close. He swallowed hard. The only comfort was the shifting beside him. He was not alone.

"Well this is cozy," Silas said, attempting levity.

"Yes, it is," Paul sighed. "Not even enough room to stretch out. If you wanted to." The floor was not inviting. "Just wait till they hear we are Roman citizens." He sniffed angrily.

"How long do you think we'll be in here?" Silas dared to ask. He heard a rustle of fabric and guessed Paul had just shrugged.

"I don't know."

The men were silent for a time. The only sounds Silas could hear were angry voices cursing, weeping, and occasionally a scream that chilled a man to his marrow.

Silas was beginning to despair himself. He felt his pulse quicken. He couldn't quite draw a full breath. The walls and roof seemed to move towards him. He tried to smother the feeling, but the more he suppressed it, the stronger it became. He was on the urge of crying out when he heard a new sound, one close to his ear. A soft whisper.

Paul was praying.

Silas trembled. How had he forgotten to pray? He began at once, whispering his pleas to God. He prayed for courage. He prayed for fortitude. He even found himself praying for the jailer. After a while the men took turns praying aloud to encourage each other. As the hours slowly stretched, they switched to singing.

"I will lift up my eyes to the mountains," they sang. "From where shall my help come? My help comes from the Lord, who made heaven and earth. He will not allow your foot to slip; He who keeps you will not slumber. Behold He who keeps Israel will neither slumber nor sleep.

"The Lord is your keeper; The Lord is your shade on your right hand. The sun will not smite you by day, nor the moon by night. The Lord will protect you from all evil; He will keep your soul. The Lord will guard your going out and your coming in, from this time forth, and forever."

The last note seemed to hover in the air, and Silas sighed, but it was a peaceful sigh. They were kept in jail, but God was their true keeper. They were under guard, but One greater than all else was guarding them too.

He realized that it was utterly quiet. No angry oaths. Not a moan nor a scream disturbed the air. Either the late hour had put the other prisoners to sleep, or they were listening. Silas felt that they were listening.

"God, You are good," Silas chuckled lowly. "Even here, You give us the opportunity to preach of Your lovingkindness."

They sang another song, and then another. They were halfway through a fourth song when a sharp jolt jarred them and cut through the notes. The whole building began to shake and shift. Men cried out in alarm. Silas cringed in the darkness, wondering if the roof would break and crush them. The stocks around his ankles rattled, rubbing painfully.

He heard rocks splitting and tasted dust on his tongue. The stocks burst open, and the earthquake stopped. Silas lifted his feet out and struggled to stand. His soreness was worsened by cramps in his legs.

"The door!" Paul's voice came in the pitch black. "It's open!"

Silas moved towards Paul's voice, his fingers outstretched. He felt the heavy wood of a door and ran his fingers to the edge. Paul was right. He slipped out into the hallway, and in the blackness, he could hear other men milling around.

"What happened?" a voice wobbled in the chilly air.

"It was those men singing to their God!" another voice exclaimed. Murmurs of fear reverberated through the building.

"No, it can't be!" the jailer shouted from down the hall, back towards the entrance. "They've escaped!"

Silas heard the unmistakable sound of a sword being unsheathed.

"Stop!" Paul's voice cried out in the darkness. "Do not harm yourself. We are all still here!"

There was a moment of silence, then a call. "Bring a light! I need a light at the prison!"

Within a moment there was bright flame thrust into the prison, and Silas raised a hand to shield his eyes.

The jailer came forward with his torch high, and Silas could see a dozen men standing in the darkness, every door unlocked. Every chain was broken. It was far beyond a natural occurrence. It was a miracle.

"It was them that did it," a voice said, almost accusingly. "Praying and singing to their God."

The jailer turned his wide eyes on Peter and Silas, shaking from head to toe. He dropped to the ground at their feet.

"Sirs, what must I do to be saved?"

Silas' heart felt full to bursting. God, You work in strange ways! Paul pulled the jailer to his feet. "Believe in the Lord Jesus," he said.

Silas put a hand on the jailer's shoulder. He saw that tell-tale light in his eyes. The light of a man who believed. He spoke with confidence, "Believe and you and your household will be saved."

Read this story for yourself in Acts 16:22-33 and Psalm 121

STORY COMMENTS

The early Christians had to live with a strange tension. Here we see that God did not stop the magistrates from beating Paul and Silas with rods, yet He freed them from prison. I've always thought this story was about how God rescues Paul and Silas, but then I discovered a different angle. One worth exploring.

Over and over we see God does not shield believers from all harm. In fact, sometimes it seems as if they are thrown in harm's way on purpose! Who's to say that God didn't intend to use this beating and jailing simply to save one man? Who's to say that Silas and Paul weren't locked up so that a prison full of men could hear songs to God?

I don't think this is simply a story about rescue for the faithful. The men would have been set free in the morning, even without an earthquake! (Acts 16:35). I think this is a story about continuing in faith when things are at their bleakest. Two wrongfully imprisoned men continue to do what God asks of them, and the result is that they shine bright for those who are seeking a light.

It's a strange tension you and I still live with today. The world is running amuck and Christians are swept up in the suffering like everyone else. We wish God would put a hedge around His children and protect them from disease, disaster, and cruelty, but He keeps us right out in the thick of it with everyone else. He keeps us out in the darkness where our response should be to shine bright with God's love to the world. Even if we have nothing happy to sing about. Even if we're not sure if we're doing any good. He might use your suffering to bring another one home.

QUESTIONS FOR DISCUSSION

★ Do you think God can use suffering to bring about His glory?

★ Do you think Paul and Silas would willingly have been beaten and jailed if they knew it would save the souls of a man and his household?

★ Have you ever sat with a chronically ill or dying Christian and felt their love for the Lord, despite their pain and their looming death? How can they have faith and joy despite their suffering?

★ Can you think of a way that you might shine bright for God, even when you're struggling, sick, grieving, or badly treated?

Priscilla and Aquila

PARTNERS IN FAITH

Priscilla shifted around the queue surrounding the covered booth. Men and women examined the silver statues of the goddess and dropped good coin for a souvenir of their visit to the world-famous temple in Ephesus. Priscilla glanced up to the gleaming, white marble temple. The enormous roof was supported by a hundred and twenty columns, each sixty-feet high. She knew within the temple was a massive wooden statue of the goddess Artemis, darkened with age. Vast quantities of coins, jewelry and other treasures passed through that great doorway as supplication and homage to the deity.

She shook her head at the patrons of the temple, feeling her thick braid bounce between her shoulder blades. The Ephesians were so fiercely proud of their moon goddess, and they boasted of their city's wealth as proof of her blessing. If only they knew they worshiped a dead god.

She turned and walked away, breathing a prayer of gratitude that she had found the Way. She wished she could say that she had never been as blind, but as a girl, she had knelt with her mother before the house idols. She had lit candles and gave offerings for the goddess of hearth and home, Vesta. Yet God had seen her, even then.

She was in her early teens when her father converted to a new faith.

The entire family became proselytes of Judaism, renouncing the old gods. It had been a struggle for Priscilla to take on the purity traditions and strange laws. Yet, blessings had come too.

In the synagogue in Pontus, she met Aquila the tent-maker. Priscilla fell head over heels in love, and the happiest moment in her life was when she learned he felt the same. She and Aquila were wed, and in their first year of marriage he had taken her on pilgrimage to Jerusalem.

The visit to Israel had not been as she had expected.

At first, she was swept away with the excitement of the journey. She marveled in the magnificent temple to the one true God and shared Aquila's pleasure in being in his homeland for the first time.

One morning, when she and Aquila were out seeing the sights, a procession interrupted their stroll. With all the wailing women, she assumed it was the funeral procession of some great man. Then she and Aquila saw a prisoner flanked by Roman guards. His clothes were soaked in blood, a crown of thorns pierced his head, and he bore a heavy cross. She had stared, unable to look away.

The newlyweds returned to their guestroom and wondered, who was that man?

Their hosts were too polite to discuss the crucifixion, but when Aquila pressed, they admitted that the man was not a typical revolutionary, but a traveling rabbi, and some said he was a prophet with healing powers. If you believe such things.

Aquila and Priscilla remained in Jerusalem until the feast of Pentecost. It was then that everything changed, and her life was never the same.

A group of men and women had stood in the open and proclaimed God's mighty works in dozens of languages. A man stepped forward, backed by eleven other men, and told the gathered crowd about a man named Jesus. Priscilla and Aquila were stunned to realize that they themselves had witnessed Jesus' death during Passover. This man preached that Jesus had not stayed in the grave, but had been raised to new life!

Then he had implored them to turn to God, to repent, and be baptized in the name of Jesus Christ for their sins, and promised them the Holy Spirit.

She and Aquila had been among three thousand who had believed and were baptized that first day. They stayed in Jerusalem long enough to learn the whole truth and history of Jesus, and then they had gone back home to share this wondrous news with their synagogue, friends, and family.

It seemed life kept changing after that. When the Jews were expelled from Rome, she and Aquila fled to Corinth and opened their home as a church. They met an apostle named Paul there, and he had partnered with them in their tent-making business. Paul became a dear friend, and they worked with him to spread the good news of Jesus throughout Corinth.

When, after a few years, Paul had decided to move on, they had come with him as far as Ephesus. The couple hoped to help the Ephesian church grow while Paul continued his travels.

Now, looking around at bustling Ephesus, she shook her head as she recalled the Lord's lament, "The harvest is plentiful, but the workers are few." She and Aquila had been praying hard for the Lord to raise up more men and women to help teach the Way.

Priscilla passed the meeting place and heard a man speaking to a crowd. She paused to listen, caught by his rich tones and good elocution. She realized with a jolt that he was preaching about John the Baptist and Jesus! Her heart gave a leap. Was this the answer to their prayers?

She ran the rest of the way home. She ducked through the doorway and Aquila looked up from his work table.

"Come on, you need to hear this man!" she said.

They went back to the meeting place where a crowd had grown. Aquila listened for a while and grinned at his wife. She squeezed his arm in excitement.

Priscilla noted how many were captured by his powerful voice and passionate expression. She felt a tingle go up her spine. This man had surely been sent by God.

When the man finished, it felt like a song half-sung. Something was missing. Her eyes widened.

Aquila looked at her, and at the same time they said, "He doesn't know!"

They wove through the people until they caught up to the man, and without hesitation, they introduced themselves and drew him aside. The man smiled at them. "I'm Apollos. I've just arrived from Alexandria."

"You have a real gift," Aquila clapped the man on the shoulder.

Apollos looked pleased.

Aquila said, "You spoke the truth, but you're missing the end of your story."

Apollos eyes clouded with uncertainty, and Priscilla held out her hands in peace. "We'd love to share the full story of the good news of Jesus Christ, as taught to us by the apostles. I promise you'll be blown away!"

Aquilla nodded and gestured towards their home, "Please, come stay as our guest. We would love to hear your story, and teach you the Way. And, if you are willing, I will baptize you in the name of Jesus so you may receive the gift of the Holy Spirit."

"The Holy Spirit?" Apollos looked intrigued.

"Oh, just you wait," Priscilla looked at her husband and grinned. "Just. You. Wait."

Read this story for yourself in Acts 18:1-4,18-21, 24-28

STORY COMMENTS

Priscilla and Aquila go together like peanut butter and jam. They are always mentioned together (1 Corinthians 16:19, Romans 16:3-4) and they seem to be true partners in faith. They are not merely an example of a wife dutifully following her husband, but a couple fully united in purpose. Both are equal servants of the faith.

My little story is fiction, but based on the Bible. It mentions Aquila as a Jew, but not Priscilla. Aquila is born in Pontus, so he was one of the diaspora, Jews who lived away from their homeland. While the Jews were commanded in the scriptures to come back to temple for Passover, the Jewish people accepted that for those who lived far from Jerusalem, this was just not practical. However, at least once in a person's life, they would journey back "home" and celebrate Passover. Jerusalem would swell with pilgrims, filling every available room.

In the book of Acts, it is during the festival of Pentecost (the Jewish spring harvest festival that falls seven weeks after Passover) that Peter gets up to speak to the people. There are pilgrims from Pontus present for this momentous speech, which was Aquila's birthplace. (Acts 2:8)

When exactly Aquila and Priscilla met, married, and became

Christians isn't explained, but it's clear that they were journeying through life as one. They left their home when the Jews were kicked out of Rome, and together they went to Corinth, and then Ephesus. They both risked their lives for Paul, and together they taught Apollos. They are a powerful example of a godly couple.

What is a tent-maker? There were still people who lived primarily in tents in the first century. Their tents were woven of black goats hair. Goats hair was chosen because when it is dry, the weave contracts to allow air to filter through, which would help keep the tent cool. When it is wet, however, the goat's hair cloth swells up and becomes watertight.

The process of weaving goat's hair is similar to sheep's wool. It is gathered from live animals by combing or trimming, then is washed, combed smooth, and spun into strands used for weaving on a loom. Long, narrow strips of cloth would be sewn together to form a tent.

A big part of tent-making was repairing tents or expanding them for a growing family. Tents were also used as temporary shelters for travelers. When people traveled to watch the athletic games, like the Isthmian games near Corinth, huge tent cities would pop up nearby.

A tent-maker might have also woven linen for awnings, shade shelters, and sails. They also might have worked in leather.

Priscilla and Aquila worked in their trade together, like most working-class families of the time.

Men raised their sons in their trade, and there were many trades that required the women to help as well. The whole family depended on the income of the family trade, and wives, daughters, and daughters-in-law pulled their weight.

There are women in the fields in the Bible. (Ruth 2:8-9) There is evidence women could also work as bakers, perfumers, and cooks. (1 Samuel 8:13) A Proverbs 31 woman is a shrewd and prosperous businesswoman, and it brings praise to her family. There was a distinction between men and women's roles, but don't confuse a Bible-era woman with a Victorian woman or a 1950's housewife.

The important part of Priscilla and Aquila's story is not that they worked together as tent-makers, but how they worked together in faith. They opened their home and hearts to host a church within their home, and they taught the truth.

Questions for Discussion

★ How important is it that Christians marry believing spouses?

★ How can couples grow and work together in faith?

★ It says in Acts 18:26 that "they" took Apollos aside and explained the way of God. Do you think this is an example of a woman teaching a man?

★ Is Priscilla helping instruct Apollos in line with or against your idea of roles a woman can fill?

And Now For Your Turn

As I writer, I look at the book of Acts and I say, "It's not finished! Where is the final scene?" We are left with a cliffhanger. We've been eagerly turning the pages through the New Testament, soaking in the excitement of the fledgling church and all its miracles and danger. We've become emotionally involved with these bold men and women. Then it suddenly stops. We flip the page of our Bible and find a series of letters. We never learn what happened to the remaining apostles, or Paul, or any of the others.

The final line of Acts reads:

> "And he stayed two full years in his own rented quarters and was welcoming all who came to him, preaching the kingdom of God and teaching concerning the Lord Jesus Christ with all openness, unhindered."

I read this and I hear an invitation. A call to pick up the banner and run with it. We too can preach the kingdom of God and teach about Jesus. There is no concluding scene because the story is not finished. We can't slide the Bible onto the shelf like we do a novel and feel like we have reached the end of something powerful and then move on with our lives. Instead, the story leaps from the pages of the Bible and into our daily lives. God is still working. He's not done yet, neither is the church, and your story isn't finished either.

So this is your chapter now. Put your name at the top. Describe the moment you came to know the Lord. Tell us how your belief changed your life. Tell us the things you have done in faith, whether gently like Tabitha or boldly like Gideon. Who did you tell about Jesus? What hardships did you endure? When did you lose heart and stumble? What made you rise up and find courage again? If you find yourself staring at a blank page with nothing to write, it's time to rise to the call. Give yourself to God, and see what amazing things He does with your life.

If You Enjoyed These Short Stories,
take a peek at Katrina D. Hamel's full length novel, available now!

DIVIDING SWORD

IN A TIME WHEN ROME RULES THE WORLD, A
CONTROVERSIAL RABBI DIVIDES FAMILIES AND
FAITH. EXPLORE THE STRUGGLES OF
ENCOUNTERING CHRIST THROUGH THE EYES
OF A WOMAN AND A PHARISEE.

1

Veil of Innocence

The air rippled under his feathers as the raven mounted the wind and soared high over his domain. In the heights, he could not see the borders that broke the once whole land into three territories, governed by puppets held over unwilling subjects by the iron fists of Rome.

Suspended beneath the clouds, the raven did not discern between Jew and Gentile, nor did he understand the vast separation in culture, customs, and belief that split the little country into jagged bits that pricked and cut each other without mercy.

All the raven saw were the lands that in ancient times had been promised to the descendants of Abraham—craggy mountains and grassy slopes, harsh wilderness and fertile fields of sprouting vines and grains, trees and wildflowers nudged to new life by the spring sun.

With a glittering eye, the raven saw a long road. The road went through valleys, hugged canyons, rose to the heights, and then sunk once more, sometimes even and cobbled, more often rough and almost impossible to trace. The road was traveled by a steady flow of people. Their journey had been long, and sometimes dangerous. Where the people were going, the raven didn't know, nor did he care.

He was more interested in filling his belly.

The circling ravens overhead should have been a warning, but Beth and

Reuben were innocent to the dark omen. The cousins broke away from their traveling group and raced ahead, each determined to be the first to set eyes on the city walls.

Their friends and family fell behind them; old and young moved steadily by foot or on donkeys, some with rugged carts. They were but one group in a massive country-wide pilgrimage headed to the festival. They were near the end of their three-day journey from the north.

The children were eager for their very first view of the city where the mighty King David had ruled in the distant past, in the glorious years of their forefathers.

A shepherd with his long staff drove a flock of sacrificial lambs ahead of him on the grassy plain beside the road. Beth could hear the bleating over Reuben's laughter. Disappearing around a bend in the road, a merchant caravan of camels plodded, their loads swaying. Only a small hill stood between them and their first view of the city of Jerusalem. Deaf to calls behind, the children dashed far ahead, fueled by the fresh spring day.

They stumbled to a stop.

Reuben flung out an arm and caught Beth's sleeve. Unable to tear their eyes away, they fumbled and found each other's hand.

Gaping and frozen in place with horror, they stared up at a contorted face. Flies buzzed over sunburned limbs that were spiked to a splintered cross. Crusted blood ran down his forearms and dripped from his feet to the packed dirt below. The man's chest rose and fell sporadically. He was unable to pull a full breath through his swollen lips. Fresh blood oozed from his wounds as he strained, trying to raise himself to take a breath. His glazed eyes rolled, unfocused. The smell of the man made Beth's stomach roil. Her nose burned with the coppery scent of blood and the sour stink of urine.

Nailed to the cross were letters on papyrus, but Beth couldn't read. In this case, she didn't need to. The message was clear. This man had been an enemy of omnipresent Rome.

An inky raven came and perched over the man's shoulder, turning its glinting eye this way and that, deciding if it was time to begin his feast.

A shifting movement startled Beth as she noticed a trio of Roman soldiers keeping guard. Two were sprawled on the ground, but the third stood with a wide stance and his muscled arms crossed over a dull metal breastplate. He watched the two children with mild curiosity on his scarred face.

"Run back to your family," he said. His voice rang with authority.

Beth wanted nothing more than to obey and escape from this horror. She tugged on Reuben, whose wide-eyed gaze was still fixed upon the cross. He didn't move. She bit her lip to keep from crying as she yanked his arm once more, hard.

"Come on!" she hissed at her cousin. Reuben tore his eyes away. Together they fled back around the turn in the road.

They collided with Zebedee, who was coming to find them. Their uncle was broad of chest, with unusually long, thick, and curly hair tied back at the nape of his neck with a leather thong. Panting, the children flung their arms around the kindly man's waist, and Beth took comfort as his large hand rested on her back.

"What is it?" he asked in his deep voice.

Reuben looked up at his uncle, his expression full of bitterness. "There's a cross, with a rebel." It was the first cross the cousins had ever seen with their own eyes, though every child had heard whispers of the horrible fate that awaited a traitor to Rome.

Zebedee's eyes hardened as he gazed at the road ahead, and his voice rumbled like thunder. "What? They should have been emptied before Passover!"

Beth's mother, Tamar, bustled towards them. She wore a frown on her face and Beth's baby brother on her generous hip. The rest of the travelers from Capernaum were not far behind.

"There's a cross up ahead," Zebedee grunted to Tamar, sparks in his eyes. Tamar looked at her daughter with concern, and Beth tried to swallow the ache in her throat. "It's right by the road. We'll have to pass by it."

Tamar pressed her lips together until they formed a thin line, then puffed out her breath. "Well, there's no helping it. Even at Passover, they can't let us forget." She clicked her tongue and turned around to warn the others so they could shield their children.

"Come, Beth!" her mother called over her shoulder.

Beth obeyed at once, Reuben hastening with her as they wove their way through friends and neighbors to find their families.

Reuben came up to his parents and two younger brothers first, and the cousins shared a look before Beth pushed deeper into the moving throng. Tamar came up to her husband, Benjamin, and spoke to him in clipped tones as he led the soft-eyed donkey beside him. Spread over the donkey was a harness that held two large baskets on either side, baskets that still smelled of fish. One held their traveling supplies, and the other basket held Beth's two-year-old sister, Hannah.

Tamar passed little David to her eldest daughter. Beth held her baby brother close. She drew in the sweet scent of his downy head greedily, trying to wash away the stink of human waste and the tang of blood. Tamar took Hannah into her arms, and drew her mantle round her little daughter, shielding her from witnessing the grisly scene.

The crowd pushed ever forward. Like a wave, silence rolled back from the front until the only noise was the shuffle of footsteps and the rattling of wheels. Beth felt her heart pound as she came around the bend once more and heard the piercing cry of the ravens.

She tried to avert her gaze. She lifted her chin, and with narrowed eyes she fixed her gaze down the dusty road to where it led right through the large gates of Jerusalem—the city she had longed to see with her own eyes for as long as she could remember.

The enormous Northern Gates were thrown wide, and from this distance, she could see a blurry mass of people funneling into the city. She forced herself to notice the bulky, yellowish stone walls. She looked over the walls and saw towers that rose into the sky—the overbearing feature of the Roman garrison. That blight on the most Holy City was called simply the Antonia. She shuddered. She didn't want to think of Romans just then. A glint caught her eye, and her gaze shifted so she could see the top of a gleaming, white and gold structure, a building so dazzlingly beautiful it could only be the Temple.

The pilgrims pushed forward in their unnatural hush. Beth clutched her brother to her chest and tried to ignore the agony beside her. Her gaze wavered, and then, almost against her will, her eyes stole up and looked at the dying man just as they passed.

His breathing was even more ragged now. His muscles trembled. How much longer could he endure? Beth realized she was holding her breath, and let it slip out.

The soldiers glared as the pilgrims passed. Beth wondered if they expected trouble with the Passover festival so near. It was a festival of freedom after all. With her heart in her throat and her stomach knotted, she did not feel free.

At last they were past the torturous scene. Little by little, conversations resumed and her pulse slowed.

Beth's extended family left their traveling companions a little before the city and walked the rough road to Bethany.

Beth's father, Benjamin, her Uncle Zebedee, and Reuben's father, Ebenezer, were brothers, fishermen all. Zebedee was eldest. He had inherited his wealth and his valuable boat from their prosperous father. Her father and Ebenezer had also inherited a boat each, but Ebenezer, for reasons not clear to Beth, had lost his boat and was obliged to rent from the guild.

Their cousin, Simon, was a Pharisee and shopkeeper. He had a good-sized house in the town of Bethany, just two miles from Jerusalem. Simon's home would be full of relatives now, all come for the yearly Passover and Week of Unleavened Bread. As they ducked under the doorway, Tamar and Benjamin greeted their distant relations joyfully. Beth followed them inside and found the house was packed full of noisy bustle. Unnerved still, Beth huddled near her mother.

Tamar found a seat with the other mothers. All the women talked at once, their daughters clustered around them. Beth wondered how anyone could understand anything, but heads bobbed all around. Her mother took David from Beth to nurse him while Beth minded Hannah. As usual, the determined toddler kept trying to wander off. Benjamin went to the courtyard with the other men. Their voices carried into the house as they shared the news from their respective areas.

Beth's mind was full, but she knew her mother wouldn't wish to discuss the horror she had seen. Beth chewed her lower lip and wished she could speak to Reuben away from the others.

A little while later, Beth discerned a shift in the mood and conversation. Families began filing back outside, and Beth wondered where they were going. Reuben left with his family. He gave her a small wave as he passed. With a swoop in the pit of her stomach, Beth realized it was nearly time for the evening sacrifice in the Temple. She was used to stopping to pray at the time of the evening sacrifice in her hometown far to the north, but perhaps from here, she might be able to hear the shofar blow.

She looked up as her father came over, smiling. "Would you like to go and see the Temple, my girl?"

Beth felt her heart skip a beat, and nodded. "Yes, Papa!"

They left Tamar with the two little ones in the house, busy in happy conversation. Beth followed her father out the door and over the mountainous ridge. Her heart pounded, and it had little to do with the sharply ascending road.

They paused atop the Mount of Olives and looked down over the city. "Stop here for a moment, my girl," Benjamin said. He wrapped his arm around her shoulders, and she leaned against him. Standing together, the father and daughter could see over the low Eastern Wall and into the Temple Courts. The Courts were an enormous raised platform lifted above the rest of the city.

Her father said, "From here, you can see everything. If your eyes are good, you can see over the Golden Gate, over the gates to the outer and inner courtyards, and perhaps even through the Temple doors. If you had the sight of an eagle, you could perhaps see to the curtain of the Holy of Holies itself."

Beth felt a surge of ancestral pride and awe. She wrapped her arms around her father in a sideways hug.

"It's so beautiful!" she breathed.

"It's the most beautiful Temple in the world!" her father exclaimed, tipping back his chin and raising a hand to the heavens. "As it should be."

Beth had heard the Temple described to her again and again by her father. He had detailed the rooms and their purposes and told her all about the careful way the priests performed the rites and sacrifices. As she saw it with her own eyes, she thought it was more wondrous, and more enormous in scale than she had ever imagined. Her entire town could fit upon the Temple Mount, with room to spare. The vast number of tiny people that milled in the courts staggered her mind.

They could have stayed and gazed in wonder for hours, but the Temple sacrifices were precise, so they hurried on. They descended the Mount of Olives and crossed the valley. Fearful she would be separated from her father, Beth kept her hand within his as they joined the great crush outside the Eastern Golden Gate.

Beth looked upwards in amazement as they passed through the thick city walls. The gateway alone was far larger than her house.

When they emerged on the other side, they were under a colonnade that wrapped around the entire complex—a roofed area supported by double columns. She looked up once more and saw the underside was elaborately engraved wood. The area sheltered many merchants and noisy animals. The din was overwhelming.

People streamed into the vast Court of Gentiles from the many large gates. Two gates were to her left, below the Royal Stoa where her father had told her the client king liked to entertain overlooking the spectacular Temple. Four more gates stood opposite her, and to her right was the infamous Antonia fortress, with a little gate allowing easy access for soldiers. The entire courtyard was paved in multi-hued, intricate stonework. In the Temple even the floor was beautiful.

She caught all that in a moment, then her gaze was fixed upon the dominating feature before her—the Temple itself. It was a marvel to behold, gleaming with gold trim and dazzling white marble. This was the place where God met with His chosen people.

Her heart soared with eagerness. She was about to speak to her father, but then her gaze was caught. Pushed out of the way was an old man dressed in rags. His milky eyes were almost hidden in deep wrinkles, and he held a beggar's bowl in his shaky hands. Near him was a middle-aged woman sitting on the intricate tiles, her legs twisted and deformed. Beth's joy drained away and her stomach wrenched. Here, so close to the one true God's Temple, how could there be the poor and the sick?

Beth tugged on her father's hand until he looked down. She tried to voice her questions, but tears rose and the words stuck in her throat. She gestured to the beggars. Benjamin glanced at them, then at his daughter. Her father smiled at her. He wove his way to the beggars and dropped a hard-earned coin into each bowl.

"Peace be on you," the old man whispered, and the woman bobbed her head with a small smile. Beth felt a little better, and she smiled again.

Benjamin led his daughter over to where people waited to pass through a narrow opening in a low balustrade. This was where the Court of Gentiles ended.

"What does that say, Papa?" Beth pointed to an engraved sign.

"No man of another nation is to enter into the barrier and the enclosure around the Temple. Whoever is caught will have himself to blame for his death which follows." Benjamin rested a hand on her hair. "The Temple's only for the Jews, my dear. We are the Lord's chosen people."

They made it through the narrow gate and climbed the steps that led to the Temple's inner courts. They crossed through another gateway into the first court, the Court of Women. It was full of people in preparation for the evening sacrifice and prayers. On the western side was a large, ornate gateway that led to the next courtyard, and men climbed more steps and went up to the Court of Israel. The gate between the Court of Women and the Court of Israel was thrown wide to reveal the Temple building on the highest platform with the large stone altar before it. The area directly around the Temple was the third courtyard, the Court of Priests. Beyond that courtyard, only the priests went into the Temple itself, and only the High Priest ever entered into the Holy of Holies, the most sacred place in the entire world.

Standing in awe of her surroundings, her inner turmoil melted away as she stood in the courts of the one true God. The pagans had their own temples, with figures of men or beasts that they sacrificed to. But none of those gods were real; they were not like Israel's God.

"We can go no further." Benjamin lowered his head to speak to her. "But we will listen to the prayers and the songs here, won't we?"

Beth saw that her father was happy. He beamed and nodded at the others around him, and they smiled at him too. Beth was in the midst of more people than ever before in her whole life. Young and old, men and women, all were gathered for worship. Commoners stood side by side with the wealthy. She stared at the man in front of her. She had rarely seen such fine clothes. His garments were embroidered in the Greek style, and he wore thick rings on his smooth hands.

"Beth!" a voice called, and Beth glanced back as Reuben pushed through the crowd with his father and two younger brothers scrambling to catch up. "I'm glad you came. Isn't it more glorious than we ever imagined?" Beth smiled to see her favorite cousin. Reuben's eyes widened, and he pointed over her shoulder. "Look," he said. "That must be a rabbi with his disciples."

Beth turned and saw a man with a faded beard and a striped shawl over his shoulders. Several young men clustered close before him, and he appeared to be instructing them as he pointed at one of the enclosed, smaller side courts.

Beth saw Reuben's face grow wistful as he said, "They're so lucky."

A long, rich shofar blast rose and filled the Temple Mount, echoing from a corner tower and rippling over the entire city. A hush fell. It was time for the evening sacrifice. Beth knew that on the enormous altar the priests were ritually sacrificing a lamb, as they did every morning and evening.

A priest, dressed in his spotless white robes and turban, appeared and stood before them in the gateway. Men of the priestly tribe of Levi came and lined the steps. The priest led the people in prayer. In one voice the crowd chanted the prayers by memory. The shofar blew again and they all knelt on the ground and pressed their foreheads to the beautiful stone floor before standing to their feet again. Beth had never prayed among so many people at once, and the vibration of the multitude of voices pulsed through her like an extra heartbeat. The Levites began their songs, and Beth soaked in the lilting melody with a hand pressed to her chest. A man jostled her as he passed. A glint caught her attention, something silvery. Even with the loud music, she heard the splatter of thick drops of blood hitting the stone. Her eyes widened as she stared at the wealthy man in front of her.

"Papa!" she cried out, wanting to flee but paralyzed with fear.

The wounded man turned towards her with glassy eyes, blood bubbling between his lips. He fell sideways, blood blooming on his embroidered robe. He convulsed, clutching his chest with twitching, jeweled fingers. Beth tasted bile.

Benjamin gripped her shoulder so hard it hurt. He tried to pull her away, but the crowd was too close. A woman screamed, interrupting the prayers, and the music broke jaggedly. People turned to look, crying out and pulling back. Within seconds the whole courtyard was in turmoil, people pushing past each other in their haste to flee.

Beth felt like the world spun around her. She was hoisted up and carried away by her father.

"What's happening, Papa?" she cried out, wrapping her arms around his neck.

"I don't know, my girl, I don't know." His voice was grim, and his head swiveled back and forth.

They were held back by people in front and pressed forward by people behind, all squeezing towards the nearest gate. Everywhere Beth looked were white, fearful eyes. She was relieved to see Reuben and his family manage to escape the courtyard ahead of them.

"If the man with the knife was here in the courts, then he's a Jew, isn't he?" Beth whispered.

Her father's eyes flicked to her face, but he didn't answer. Beth buried her face in his shoulder, feeling that the world was a violent, bloody place. When she lifted her head, they were through the gate. Temple guards appeared, holding their long spears upright. Roman soldiers were also marching from their garrison, hands on their sword hilts.

"You there!" a Roman demanded, drawing his sword and pointing it right at Beth and her father. "Are you armed?"

"Of course not," Benjamin answered, setting Beth down and putting an arm around her. Beth clung to him as the fleeing crowds buffeted her. "I am here with my daughter."

The soldier's cold eyes flicked to her, and Beth flinched beneath the hatred. She hid behind her father. The man swung his sword to another Jew and repeated the question.

Beth's father clutched her arm, and they rushed out of the Court of Gentiles and back through the Golden Gate. They ran until Beth was panting with a stitch in her side.

They paused to catch their breath at the top of the mount. Her uncles and cousins were there, waiting for them. She was surprised to her cousins James and John were excited rather than scared.

"You're safe!" Reuben came and grasped her hand as the adults spoke to each other in low voices.

She realized she was trembling and squeezed his fingers. His face was ashen, his eyes wide, and she wondered if she looked just as fearful. Her first visit to the Holy City had not been as she expected.

She peered down upon the magnificence of the Temple, still glinting in the setting sun. It was empty now. Everyone had fled except the Temple staff. The emptiness was haunting. As she gazed at the gleaming white marble and the dazzling gold, almost too bright to look at, she knew something more than worshipers was missing.

Every Jew knew it.

In Moses' day, the Shekinah—the presence of the Lord--descended and filled the Tabernacle. Why didn't the Lord come down to be with them anymore? Why was He so far away? He had promised to be their God and they were to be His chosen people, like a bride joined to a good husband. Why had her ancestors been unfaithful to Him? Was that why there was so much pain and suffering in the world? It was more than her child's mind could understand.

That night, curled up in the crowded upper room with her aunts and cousins, Beth listened to the layered sounds of breathing and tried to find her bearings. Her safe childhood world had tilted, and the veil of innocence had slipped to reveal a bloody side to the world she had thought safe and beautiful.

She felt the need to make water, so she rose from beside her sleeping mother. She tiptoed through the crowded room and went down the stairs.

On her way back to bed, she saw a lamp was lit in the lower room of the house. She paused to peek inside. The men were sitting in a circle and speaking in hushed tones.

Beth listened for a moment and realized with a lurch in her stomach that the men were discussing what had happened in the Temple.

"The courtyard is being purified. What a disaster," Reuben's father, Ebenezer, said with a shake of his head. "I think they must have chosen the inner courtyard purposefully, to send a message. Perhaps the assassin was from the Essenes. They are still not pleased that a foreign ruler rebuilt our Temple."

"Perhaps," another man replied, drawing his hand down his long beard. "But that does not seem quite their way. The Essenes have withdrawn to their hidden places in the wilderness, waiting for the Lord to send their Teacher of Righteousness."

"It's the bold teachings of that Judas the Galilean, mark my words," another man cried out. "I heard him once, preaching against the sin of paying taxes to Rome. He called it allegiance to their false reign, selling ourselves in slavery."

Benjamin shook his head. "I just hope we don't have another failed uprising like we did when King Herod died. They are still rebuilding Sepphoris after the disaster with Judah ben Hezekiah." Heads bobbed all around the room. Benjamin's face was grim, and he clutched his hands together in his lap. "My wife was born near there, and her family was either killed or sent away into slavery when the uprising was crushed. Her grandparent's quick-thinking saved her life."

Beth pressed her hand over her mouth. She hadn't known that. To discover that her mother had a past of suffering felt strange. Her mother was like all the other mothers. She cooked, sewed, taught, and cared for them. Beth couldn't imagine her as a little girl running for her life.

"That was a dark time, truly." Zebedee reached out to put a hand on Benjamin's shoulder. "Rebels were crucified all over this country. I heard the total was two thousand men hung up to die."

Beth swallowed hard. A single victim had been torturous for her to behold. She tried to imagine two thousand dying men. That many crosses would be a stark forest of death.

She trembled and fled from the conversation, creeping up the steep stairs into the upper room. She wound around prone forms. How could they sleep so peacefully, knowing all the cruelty that existed in the world?

Long into the night she tossed and turned. The memory of the hungry raven at the cross pecked at her, and she wondered if she would ever be able to forget.

Acknowledgements

Thanks be to God who gave me a love of words! I pray that my writing will bring glory and honor to You. Thank you, Lord, for giving us the Bible and making it a book full of inspiration and life-giving truth.

I would be remiss if I didn't thank the authors of the Bible for their dedication to recording truth and wisdom with cramped, ink-stained hands as they were inspired by God.

A great big thank-you to my dad, Lee Patmore, who inspired me to write my first short story.

Thanks to my readers and book-loving friends who read my words and offered their support and encouragement as I was compiling these short stories into a book.

My long suffering husband, who puts up with my insecurities and weird working hours, deserves a huge thank-you. Love you, honey!

About the Author

Katrina lives in Alberta, Canada with her husband, Chase, her four children, and their two cats. She considers herself blessed to have grown up hearing the gospel in her home with believing parents. Because of their examples in faith and teaching, she was baptized at the age of twelve and is proud to call herself a Christian.

Katrina welcomes comments and questions at her website: www.katrinadhamel.com